PATRICIA ILICH

Red Curls

First published by Editions Dedicaces in 2017

Copyright © Patricia Ilich, 2017

ISBN: 978-1-77076-674-7

This book was professionally typeset on Reedsy.
Find out more at reedsy.com

Contents

ACKNOWLEDGEMENTS

I would like to thank my daughter Alexis for her help with proofreading and amendments and my husband Michael for his patience and assistance with my many computer problems.

DEDICATION

I would like to dedicate this book to my four beautiful grand-daughters, Jessica, Regan, Olivia and Gabriella.

1

THE GIRL WITH THE RED CURLS

Shopping for groceries, in fact shopping for anything was not something that twenty four year old, quiet, reserved Jim Emery was comfortable or happy doing. On the few occasions that he had actually accompanied his mother and grandmother to the shops he had been acutely embarrassed by their insistence on haggling unashamedly with the greengrocer, the butcher or whoever. Both women had been brought up in a small village in Sicily where haggling was expected, in fact it was almost a national pastime. However since his mother and grandmother had both passed away Jim had been forced to do his own, everything; cooking, cleaning, shopping, laundry; everything. Whilst his mother had been alive there was no problem, but things were different now, his life had changed significantly.

Jim had never been lonely before but was now starting to feel he needed something,

some-one in his life, something more than his weekly games of soccer and his judo, in short his hormones were jangling and he felt the natural desire of his species for female companionship, and even more for some close female physical contact. The girls he'd dated previously had all been girls he'd met at the office.

There were plenty of girls there but it was always difficult and his mother had never approved of him dating girls at work. "You know Jim," she used to admonish him, "you should be very careful dating girls from work, or anywhere that might cause a problem; don't mix work and play, its why dogs don't poo in their own kennels, you can't make a mess where you have to live or work. Do you know what I'm trying to say? It's maybe alright at first but it can get very messy and inconvenient when the play comes to an end and you still have to meet and interact with the girl where you work.

No, you should keep your private life with girls completely separate from your work life." Jim knew his mother was right and the few times that he had dated girls from work the other guys had teased and tormented him about it. No, he wanted a girl in his life but realised he would have to look elsewhere.

A few days later he was in the centre aisle of the supermarket at the shopping mall when he felt a tap on his back and turned to see the most beautiful girl he had ever seen. She had striking long red curly hair and a generous wide smile with the whitest almost dazzling teeth. "Excuse me." She asked, "You are quite tall and I can't reach that jar of pickles, could you pass it down to me please?" Jim faltered for a moment, stunned by her beauty, in fact his breathing had temporarily stopped. He swallowed hard as he answered, "Not a problem, there you are." The girl thanked him and moved further on down the aisle. Jim was smitten, he wanted to do something but he didn't know what. He was basically quite a shy young man and really wanted to talk to the girl but he just didn't know how. In his mind he was telling himself, "talk to her, ask her something, but what? What can I say? Maybe she's married with six children, maybe she's a famous film star. For goodness sake, just talk to her."

At some distance he followed the girl, up and down the aisles, watching and hoping she wouldn't be noticing him. When the girl had finished her shopping she fell into line to pay for her groceries. Jim very much wanted to be the next in line and maybe pluck up enough courage to start up a conversation but unfortunately an elderly lady beat him to the queue and Jim had no option but to line up behind the old woman. He considered just abandoning his trolley and following the girl but thought the security cameras and anyone watching might think he was stalking the girl, which is basically what he wanted to do. However, he stayed in the queue and when the girl had paid for her groceries she moved off in the direction of the chemist shop. The old lady moved up and started to off load her trolley and Jim watched in frustration as the old lady took her time fumbling with her purse and chatting to the cashier. Jim wanted to get his groceries paid for and dash off to the chemist to pretend he was shopping there, but in essence to follow the girl.

He was hopping from one leg to the other losing his patience, willing the old woman to hurry up. Eventually after querying the price of two items the old woman moved off. Jim bagged up his groceries as quickly as he could and paid for them before trying to look casual as he entered the chemist shop. It was a large chemist shop with many aisles and three different counters. He hurriedly checked out each aisle looking for the girl but was dismayed and disappointed as he failed to find her. He checked all the aisles for a second time and when he was completely sure she was not there he hurried out of the mall hoping to see her in the car park or at least walking down the road. His hopes were dashed, the girl was no-where to be seen. His ineffectual search brought tears to his eyes. "Oh, I'm such an idiot." He told himself, "Why didn't I talk to the girl? She's gone and I doubt if

I'll ever see a girl as gorgeous as that ever again."

For the next two weeks Jim shopped at that same mall hoping to see the girl again but fate was against him and each fruitless visit left him feeling angry with himself, his inadequacies, his shyness, he felt thwarted and impotent.

Two dogs a cat and a budgie were now the only companions for Jim. He was basically a quiet young man and he loved his Saturday amateur games of soccer at his local club. His parents had divorced when he was very young and so he never really knew his father at all. Jim's grandmother sadly passed away in January with bowel cancer and now only six months later his mother had also passed away with the same terrible disease.

The cat was a rover; an unscrupulous uninvited guest who regularly meowed piteously outside various neighbour's front or back doors begging for a scrounged meal and a sleepover. He was well fed at home but obviously enjoyed variety if he could get away with it. Jim also thought the cat may have a girl friend or two somewhere in the vicinity. The cat came home most nights, like the Prodigal Son, expecting to be forgiven for staying away so long, but occasionally stayed away six or seven nights on the trot. It didn't worry Jim, he was fond of the cat but realised, like most cats, Monty was quite independent; sort of snooty and aloof. So long as he was being well fed and had a warm bed to snuggle into he was happy.

The dogs were a pair of enthusiastic walkers who bounded and bounced around barking enthusiastically whenever they heard the rustle of their leads, which announced Jim's intention for taking them for a walk. Both were neutered and one, Stan, was a nervous tall spaniel with floppy ears and a pleasant nature. He had the softest hair which felt more like fur than dog hair. The second dog, Tex, was an aggressive bully of an overweight terrier cross, only half the size of the larger dog. He was overweight due to the fact that he quite often stole most of the first dog's dinner before the tall spaniel could get to it. Tex was only twelve inches high but would annoyingly try to hump anything and everything; the coffee table leg, the kitchen stool, the bed post and any unfortunate visitor. A quick whack on his oversexed rump with a rolled up newspaper usually stopped him in his tracks. The budgie didn't have much to say for itself, it was a beautiful blue but remained a silent witness to all that happened in that cosy household.

2

THE NIGHT CLUB

Jim worked for the Government at the Department of Immigration and at work he was efficient and methodical. Following his normal office practise he decided to make a list of his possibilities for finding a girl, not just any girl really, but one as beautiful as the girl in the supermarket, the one with the red curls. He addressed the dogs who sat at his feet, "Right you guys, what do you think of this then?" Stan the tallest of the dogs cocked his head to one side looking as if he understood but Tex the terrier showed a distinct lack of interest and closed his eyes trying to get an afternoon nap after his energetic playing in the garden most of the morning. "This is a list; a plan of action really. I'm going to get myself a girlfriend." Stan put his head across Jim's knees and gave a little sigh, as if he really understood. "So, first on the list is a nightclub. Lots of guys meet girls at a nightclub, I don't see why I shouldn't do the same, and you never know, she might be there. Second, I know people meet on the internet, I'm going to give that a go, see what that turns up. Thirdly I'm just going to go out to the cafes and lunch bars and see if I can see some girl that takes my fancy, and maybe chat her up. What do you reckon Stan?" Stan just gave an answering whimper which showed some sympathy but not much practical help.

When Saturday night came around Jim showered and changed into his best shirt and cargo pants. He knew there was a nightclub in the centre of town but had never ventured into such a place before. As he walked along the footpath he could hear the music from the club well before he could actually see the entrance. Actually he couldn't make out any real music only a mind numbing thump, thump, thump from the excessively loud base. Undaunted though, after a short time queuing he paid his money and entered the melee. He made his way to the crowded bar and ordered a beer before having a good look at all that was going on. There were so many people on the dance floor that it was impossible to see exactly what kind of dance they were doing, it just appeared to be individuals gyrating furiously alone, some with their eyes closed and some with a drink of whatever in their hands. The lights were almost non-existent except for neon strobe lights which blasted into the dark, lighting up the crowd only every two or three seconds. Jim had heard that strobe lights can give someone an epileptic fit and he could readily understand how that could happen, he was trying to focus his eyes on the girls around him but found the flickering lights were starting to give him a headache.

An effeminate young man standing at the bar sidled up to Jim and whilst shouting above the noise asked subversively, "Do you want to get out of here man, go somewhere where we can be quiet and do our own thing man, if you know what I mean?"

"Err, no thanks." Shouted back Jim.

"Okay, suit yourself." With that the young man turned and tried to chat up the barman. Jim moved away to one side and tried to peer through the gloom to see if any of the girls on the floor were of interest, and especially to see if the girl with the red curls might just be there.

Another man, much older this time sidled up to Jim and shouted into his ear, "Hey Dude, do you want a couple of 'mother's little helpers?' Good shit, honest." Jim had absolutely no idea what the man was referring to but noticed the man had a tiny plastic envelope in his closed fist. Jim shook his head negatively as he assumed the man was selling some sort of pills or drugs. "Are you sure mate?" Jim turned his back on the stranger and moved out away from the bar.

There must have been over a hundred people in the hot, steamy room which smelled of a mixture of cheap perfume and body odour, and it seemed to Jim that they were mostly young females, in a state of high intoxication and wearing the most skimpy and daring outfits that he had ever seen. The skirts were so high and the cleavages so low, it appeared to Jim that many girls were in danger of popping out of their tops. He watched in fascination as two girls twisted and contorted their nubile young bodies threatening to lose their tops completely, but he concluded they must have glued their tops to their bodies, there was no other way the tops could have remained in place.

Eventually the two girls noticed Jim and, still gyrating, came off the dance floor and shouted at Jim. "Hi, I'm Sally and this is Heather, we've not seen you here before. Come and dance with us."

"Oh no thanks, I'm just having a beer." The girl who had introduced herself as Sally brazenly took Jim's beer out of his hand and pulled him onto the dance floor. Heather the other girl took his other hand and together they wiggled and squirmed their bodies up against him, doing what he supposed must be the current fashion in dancing. Both girls had incredible hair and makeup. Sally had the longest false eyelashes and bright green hair swept up into a sort of pyramid on top of her head. Heather had black kohl rimmed eyes which reminded Jim of a Chinese giant panda.

There didn't seem to be any stopping and starting of the music, one piece just melted into the next with no discernible break. There was no band or disc jockey and Jim couldn't work out where the loud music was actually coming from.

Jim couldn't shake the girls off, each time he tried to leave the dance floor Sally and Heather would drag him back but after a while both girls declared themselves exhausted and begged Jim to buy them a drink.

Ever the gentleman Jim made his way to the bar with the girls in tow and as he tried to make his way to the front he shouted to make himself heard and asked the girls what they wanted to drink, "What's it to be girls?" Sally giggled as Heather rubbed her body up against Jim and shouted in his ear, "We only drink Champagne." Jim was not unduly perturbed and ordered Champagne for the two girls. As soon as the girls had their drinks in hand they took off into the crowd. Jim turned to pay the barman and was shocked to be told how much he was expected to pay. "What? Are you kidding me mate? I only ordered two Champagnes, not a whole crate load, I didn't actually want to buy the whole frigging vineyard you know."

The barman was large and had beefy bulging muscles. He folded his arms across his huge chest and threateningly asked, "Are you going to pay mate or am I going to have to get my guys to shake it out of you?" Jim took a step backwards whilst shaking his hands in front of him, "No, no, I don't want any trouble. I'll pay, but hells bells it's a bit steep."

The two girls came back after a few minutes and having devoured their drinks tried to pull Jim back onto the dance floor. "No, no, I'm no dancer. I'll just watch." The girls wouldn't take "no" for an answer and pulled furiously at poor Jim who refused again and again until he was so exasperated that he just pushed the girls away and strode out of the club and into the fresh air. He walked home swearing to himself that he would never venture into a night club ever again.

When he got home he pushed Tex off the settee and asked both dogs, "Where do the nice girls hang out guys? That's what I want to know."

3

ONLINE DATING

The next day dawned with a light pink hue over the park and all the buildings. Jim took the dogs for a walk and spent a pleasant hour throwing a ball for the dogs to catch and retrieve. He had been thinking all night about going online and joining a dating site. He had no idea how complicated the exercise would turn out to be. He was asked so many questions as he put in his profile. Not only the expected height, weight, age, occupation, marital status, sports, hobbies and other normal questions but he had to fill out the questionnaire giving details of his aspirations, opinions on all manner of topic as well as favourite food and drink, holiday destinations, favourite sporting identities, film stars, television programmes and so many questions he thought his mind was going to explode.

Once he had completed the questionnaire about himself he was then requested to nominate what kind of woman he was looking for, age, height, weight, occupation, education and so on. He really had difficulty pinpointing what he was actually looking for. He considered putting in a request for girls with red curls only, but decided that might not be a good idea and anyway would cut down on his opportunities. In truth though the girl he had seen in the supermarket was all he wanted, was all he dreamed about, fantasized about. He wanted to put down "just a woman," but thought that might be misconstrued and so gave vague answers covering a range for each question. It took two days for the computer to come up with suggestions, photos and profiles of three women that were considered "good matches," and who had been given Jim's profile and were willing to meet up with him.

The first woman's profile stated that she was twenty four the same age as Jim and looked like a spectacularly beautiful brunette in the photograph. She had reported that she was a retail manager and was "looking for love." Jim arranged to meet the woman, Susanne for a coffee in town on Saturday morning. He told her on the phone that he would be wearing a blue jacket in case she didn't recognise him. Jim had studied her photo and was sure he would recognise Susanne in the café. When he arrived at the café he could see no-one looking at all like the photo and so sat at a corner table to wait for the woman. After a moment a woman with long dyed blonde hair and far too much makeup approached him, "Hello, are you Jim? I'm Susanne." Jim was flustered, the woman didn't look anything like the photo he'd seen posted on the internet. This was a much older woman and blonde instead of brunette. "Oh, hello, I'm sorry I didn't recognise you, you've changed the colour of your hair."

"Yes, do you like it?" Jim motioned for the woman to sit down and when the waitress came he ordered coffee for them both. The woman talked nonstop as she kept running her fingers through her long blonde hair and pushing it back from her face. Jim didn't know what to say, he knew he had been cheated, "This woman must be at least forty," he thought. In order to get over his embarrassment he asked the woman about her work and was surprised to find that rather than being a retail manager the woman was a part time checkout assistant at the local supermarket. She was coarse, loud and vulgar telling smutty joke after joke with a loud raucous laugh that grated on his nerves and caused other clients in the café to turn and give the two some disapproving looks. Jim liked a good joke and heard many bad taste jokes told by the guys at the pub or in the soccer change rooms but coming from a woman it just didn't seem right, and especially from a woman he didn't even know. Jim couldn't wait for a decent time to elapse before he could make his apologies and say goodbye. "This is definitely not the woman for me," he thought to himself, "Oh where are you red curls?"

Undaunted Jim agreed to meet up with the second woman on the list of possible candidates. This time he arranged to meet the woman at the city art gallery. He thought it might be a good idea if he could scrutinise the woman first, before actually introducing himself, and this way he could see if she lived up to her description in the photograph. He told her he would be carrying a book and would meet her in the lobby. From the photograph the woman looked slightly younger than the twenty five years she professed she was. In fact she looked very young, to Jim's mind, probably only eighteen or nineteen. From her profile Jim found out that the girl was called Sophie and was a librarian who collected dolls. She looked attractive and professed herself to be outgoing and a fun person to be with.

Jim recognised the girl as soon as he entered the lobby of the art gallery. She was indeed quite attractive, a good figure and well presented. He walked up to her and asked "Hi, I'm Jim are you Sophie?" The girl blushed a deep pink which travelled visibly from her throat to her forehead. The girl put her hand out to shake Jim's but at the same time put her head down, as if she was focussing on his shoes or the square tile that he was standing on. There was a small café adjacent to the gallery and Jim invited the girl to go with him to have a coffee. Once the coffee was ordered the pair sat down and Jim tried to find out what he could about the girl. He asked her, "Did you have any trouble getting into tow today, it's quite busy isn't it?" The girl just shook her head not meeting Jim's eyes. Jim tried again with a different question, "So you're Sophie, do you have any brothers or sisters?" Again the girl just shook her head, presumably meaning that she didn't have any siblings.

Jim realised the girl must either be very shy or slightly embarrassed by the meeting. He decided it might be easier if he filled her in on his own background, maybe talking about himself might encourage her to talk about herself. "Well I don't have any siblings, I don't even have any parents. Well, I suppose I have a father somewhere but he and my mother split up when I was very young and I've never seen him since then. My mother died only a few weeks back, so apart from my pets I am on my own. Well I do have an aunt and a cousin but that's all really. Do you have any pets?"

The waitress brought them their coffees and the girl mumbled a polite "thanks." Jim tried again, "So Sophie, do you have any pets? I have two dogs a cat and a budgie."

Sophie again shook her head stirring her coffee but not looking at Jim at all. Jim was starting to get a little exasperated and decided to ask a question that couldn't be answered with just a yes or a no or even just a shake of her pretty head. "So tell me something about yourself Sophie, I mean tell me about your work or your hobbies, you're a librarian aren't you? What do you like best about being a librarian?" Again no response. "Look Sophie if we're going to get to know each other you have to talk to me. Can you tell me a little about yourself?" The girl had a sip of her coffee and without looking up spoke quite softly, "There's nothing to tell." Jim thought he heard a slight Scottish accent and so offered, "Do I detect a slight Scottish accent? Where were you born Sophie?"

The pair sat in the coffee shop for half an hour with Jim trying to get Sophie to talk to him but he it was like getting blood out of a stone. He invited Sophie to walk around the art gallery and tried his best to get the girl to chat to him, to show some interest in the paintings, but the girl was almost completely uncommunicative. In the end Jim said goodbye at the large glass exit doors and walked home in a deep depression.

4

THE DANCE CLASS

T he only person Jim felt he could confide in was his Aunt Bridget. He called in to see her on his way home and asked for her advice. Bridget was a kindly woman and sympathised with Jim but could only offer, "I don't know Jim, it's years since I was out there on the dating scene. You shouldn't worry, you're a good looking fellow and have a decent job. Just let nature take its course, you'll meet someone one day."

"Actually I have seen someone, a girl, a gorgeous girl, with red hair."

"Well there you are. Who is she, what's her name, where did you meet her?"

"Well I didn't really meet her, I just saw her at the supermarket."

"Well did you talk to her?"

"Not really."

"So you let her slip through your fingers. Is that you're trying to tell me?"

"Sort of. I was going to talk to her, I meant to talk to her, but then I lost her in the mall."

"Oh, I see. Well, as I say, don't worry, you'll meet someone one day. Stop fretting about it."

Jim did worry though, he was becoming obsessed, he couldn't

get the girl with the long red curls out of his mind, her dark red ringlets, a beautiful smile with a sprinkling of the most adorable tiny freckles, like glitter across her cheeks and nose. However the thing he couldn't get out of his mind were her big dark honey coloured eyes, just quite beautiful. As for his pets, well, as companionship went, his cat and dogs were great, but they were not enough, not now.

Jim now understood for the first time, how people who tried one hit of a strong drug could get hooked their first time; he felt like that had happened to him. This girl, he had met her just the one time and now he felt like he might die if he never saw her again. In a matter of a couple of minutes, he had become well and truly hooked.

Two days after seeing his Aunt Bridget Jim got a phone call from her. "Listen Jim, I've just had a great idea. Can you dance?"

"Actually no, why do you ask?"

"Well in my local paper there's an advertisement for a dance class, you could kill two birds with one stone; one, learn to dance and two, there's bound to be lots of girls in the class so you could meet someone that way."

"Aunt Bridget if you think I'm going to get dressed up in a tutu and pirouette around the place you're greatly mistaken."

"No, you Nellie, not ballet dancing, it's ballroom dancing, you know, face to face, holding onto a woman, looking into her eyes and all that romantic stuff."

"Oh, I don't know, I don't think I'd be very good at that."

"No, you don't have to be a Gene Kelly, just go along to meet some girls."

Jim took all the details from his Aunt and arranged to join an afternoon class the following Saturday. To say that he was nervous would be an understatement, he was terrified, but the instructor was reassuring and stood Jim at the back of the class which was just starting. Jim had a good look around the class and was disappointed to see that there was no girl or woman there that would have been suitable girlfriend material, and definitely not the girl with the red curls. In fact most of the people seemed to be middle aged couples, two elderly ladies and three teenagers. No-one his own age.

Everyone was introduced and the instructor showed the class how to hold a partner, or in the case of the females how to be held. Jim was paired with a matronly fifty something year old woman called Elsie who was a very large curvy lady who had an enormous chest, a large rear, but a surprisingly small waist, proportionally speaking. She had on a long gold necklace that disappeared down into her ample cleavage. Jim felt a little ashamed that he noticed such a thing, but tried to focus on what he was being taught. Elsie turned out to be quite amiable, and she also proved to be nimble and light on her feet. The instructor demonstrated the basic steps for a waltz and the class attempted to follow. No-one had any problems except Jim who just couldn't feel any rhythm in the music and insisted on trying to look down at his feet to check if they were moving as instructed but unfortunately Elsie's enormous chest prevented Jim from seeing his feet, Jim wondered what was wrong with him, his mind and body just didn't seem to be connected.

The instructor took Jim aside and attempted to show him the pattern his feet were supposed to be making. "Just follow the music Jim, now; one two three, one two three, one two three, like that."

"I'm trying, really I am." It became obvious very quickly that Jim had no sense of rhythm, no sense of timing and no connection between his brain and his feet. Poor Elsie struggled through the class trying to "lead" but it was no use, Jim, she realised was never going to be a dancer.

Jim was embarrassed and disappointed. He drove home and when he was met with the loving eyes and wagging tails of his dogs, Jim addressed them both "What are you two looking at? I can't dance, so what? I'm just a useless twit." Jim's Aunt Bridget rang later that afternoon. "How did it go Jim? Did you meet any nice girls at the class?"

"No I friggin' well didn't, what a waste of time. To start with there were no decent girls there and secondly the teacher tried showing me some complicated steps that everyone else managed to learn but my feet must be too big or something. I just couldn't get the hang of it. I can do the twist and just jigging around, but actual dancing is just not for me."

"Ah well, you gave it a go. Sorry it didn't work out." Jim thanked his Aunt Bridget for the suggestion of dance classes and agreed to go to dinner as usual later that week.

After the phone call, Jim sat dejected on the settee and resolved to, as Aunt Bridget had said before, "Just let nature take its course. You'll either meet someone or you won't."

5

AUNT BRIDGET TO THE DOCTOR

A few months later while Jim was at his Aunt Bridget's for dinner and during the meal she lamented, "We're going to miss your Mum Jim, she was not only my sister-in-law but she was also my best friend. How are you managing now on your own?"

"Oh, I'm fine. The last few months have been difficult but I'm coming to terms with being on my own. I'm managing to feed myself and keep the house clean. As you know Mum did everything for me but it's not rocket science. I've mastered the cantankerous noisy washing machine and the dishwasher. I don't bother ironing anything since I put all my clothes through the dryer as I can't be bothered hanging them out on the line, and as for cooking, well I've started buying ready-made meals that only need zapping in the microwave. Actually I mostly eat out or get take-away." Bridget shook her head as she was clearing the table and put her arms around her nephew. "Well Jim I know the dance class didn't go down too well but how's the dating scene now, have you met anyone yet? Did you ever see your red- headed girl again?" Jim truly loved his Aunt, he was glad he had someone like her in his life. Jim breathed in his aunt's scent which was a comforting combination of her favourite perfume, her brand of shampoo and the laundry softener she used on her clothes. With a large disappointed exhale, Jim disentangled himself from his aunt's embrace, faced her and replied, "No, I'm sorry to say I never saw the red-headed girl again. I like girls, I've had girlfriends before but there has been no-one special. I'm in no rush, as you said once before, it'll happen when it happens."

Bridget walked back to the kitchen, and over to the freezer where she took out a handful of ice, and with a little tinkle dropped the ice into two small glasses, then went to her drinks cabinet and poured them both a Bailies, she handed Jim the glass, which he accepted with a shudder, "I'd rather a beer."

"Try it, it's really good." Jim winced at the sweet milky fluid. Bridget took an appreciative sip and put her hand on his shoulder and asked carefully, "How about if I invite you over for dinner one night, and maybe I'll invite one of the girls over from my Pilates class?"

Jim choked on the drink he just swallowed and sputtered, "Oh no, please don't. Don't go setting me up with anyone, I'll find my own girls, thank you, but no."

"Well I just think you are such a nice young man any girl would be lucky to have you. I know your Mum would say the same thing." Just the mention of his Mum caught Jim off guard, and tears welled up in his eyes. It was at moments like this that he really felt the loss of his Mum. Jim whispered sadly, "I really miss her you know." Bridget nodded solemnly in agreement and answered gravely, "I do too sweety."

Taking another sip and mentally giving herself a shake, Bridget declared in a practical tone, "Okay, listen Jim, both your Grandmother and your Mum were hale and hearty before this cancer thing. They always looked after themselves but I think the cancer might be in your genes. Bowel cancer is probably hereditary, have you thought about getting yourself checked out?"

"Do you really think I should? I mean, I swim and play league soccer every week, I'm fit and healthy. I'm only twenty four, surely I'm too young for this to be a problem for me?"

"No, you're not too young, it can affect anyone."

"Well I'm feeling fine; I'm mean I'm sad with Mum not being around but I'm fine and healthy, really. I'm fine."

"Yes but are you really fine? I mean how would you know if you're not fine?"

"Please Aunt Bridget, leave me alone, I'm fine, really."

"Well I think you should check with your doctor, you know they can do tests these days, and it would be better if you caught it in its early stages."

"Caught what in its early stages? I haven't got anything, I tell you I'm fine. Please, can we drop the subject, how many times do I have to tell you, I'm fine."

"Well, promise me you'll go and see your doctor. You never know. Promise me."

"Good grief, okay, okay, I'll go and see my doctor."

"Promise?"

"Yes I promise." Jim's eyes rolled heavenwards as he heaved a great sigh of resignation.

"Anyway, listen who's talking, I remember Mum going on and on at you to see the doctor about getting your annual woman's exam done, you know what I mean. Did you ever actually do it? I remember you promised Mum you would."

An expression of guilt and shame washed over Bridget's face as she remembered the conversation between Jane, her daughter, and Jim's Mum. "Well your Mum got sick and things just got put on the back burner. I know I should get one done, but like you, I'm fine, I really don't want to get one done."

"You promised Mum, and you know women of your age should really have one done every year. I can't believe you've never even had one, not even one."

"Yes I know, and I will, one of these days. Jane is always going on at me about it. I just don't want my old doctor, especially a man of his age looking at my lady parts."

"For goodness sake Aunt Bridget any doctor will see women's bits every day of their lives, it's nothing to them, you've nothing to be embarrassed about, it's an everyday procedure for a doctor, don't be so silly. It's really important that you get it all checked out. Now promise me you'll do it?"

"Oh, for goodness sake, okay, honestly what with you and Jane getting on at me, there'll be no peace in this town until it's done. You're terrible bullies the pair of you."

Bridget's daughter Jane was nineteen now and "plain Jane" she definitely was not. When Jane turned eighteen she decided she wanted to make a statement and declare her individuality. On her eighteenth birthday, very much against her mother's advice, she'd paid for three tattoos to be put onto her arm, her chest and her buttocks. Since then she'd progressed to body piercings, which involved six or seven piercings along the length of her ears, a ring in her navel and one in her nose and eyebrow. She was also in the process of stretching her earlobes and each month put in the hole something that resembled a cotton reel. She had to keep putting in larger and larger ones to stretch the hole making it wider and wider. It looked dreadful to everyone in the family but there was no talking her out of it.

She often wore black lipstick and painted her long nails all different colours and applied a white make up which made her face look almost ghoulish. She had the most beautiful blonde hair but continued to corrupt her natural beauty by changing the colour of her hair on a weekly basis using various assorted colour hair sprays. Last week it was red with silver bits through it and this week it was electric blue glitter. Bridget had given up trying to talk any sense into her daughter. Jane was a wilful, wild nineteen year old, not like steady conservative Jim. Bridget wished Jane was more like Jim, but reasoned that although Jane might be wilful and wild, she was also a very smart girl who had a good job in I.T. Jane was not a bad girl, she kept herself clean, always smelled really nice and helped her mother around the house and loved her mother very much.

Bridget was a typical middle aged mother, slightly overweight but never really worried about her own health. She had joined a Pilates class to try and get fit but only attended sporadically and when she did, it was only with a half-hearted effort. She had however certainly promised her sister-in-law that she would get a Pap smear done and so, very much in fear and trepidation rang her doctor to make an appointment.

Bridget had been seeing her family doctor, an old man now of about sixty five, for fifteen years and really didn't like the idea of him seeing her lower regions. Other than when she was having a baby, no-one had ever seen her nether regions, not even her husband who had died many years earlier. Theirs had been an "old school, old fashioned," personal, intimate relationship only carried out in the dark, under the sheets and never talked about. She had never even seen him naked and he had never seen her naked either. When she needed to get dressed or change her clothes she had always done so in the privacy of her bathroom, never in front of her husband. She couldn't imagine ever flaunting her body, she never had and she didn't want to start now. The appointment with the doctor was made for the following day and Bridget was terrified at the thought of the ordeal. She was scared and embarrassed but had promised her late sister-in-law, her daughter and Jim and so was going to go through with it.

On the morning of the appointment she showered, washed her hair and made herself as presentable as she could. She changed her knickers three times, not knowing exactly what to wear and not knowing just how much of her underwear the doctor would actually see. She didn't want to wear her navy knee-to-navel knickers; "passion killers" as Jane called them, and she didn't want to wear her colourful slim line bikini knickers, which she had never actually worn, that Jane had bought for her at Christmas either, as she thought the old doctor might think she was trying to look like "mutton dressed as lamb" and so in the end opted for simple white cotton briefs that were not too showy and were quite conservative. She dabbed on a spot of "lily of the valley" perfume behind her ears and was ready to go. She felt a little like a Christian being thrown to the lions, but was determined to be stoic and brave about the whole thing.

Time was running out and she was rushed but at the last minute decided that she might need to smell nice in her lower regions and so dashed into Jane's bathroom to borrow a quick spray of her "Fem Fresh," a feminine spray for the female undercarriage.

When the receptionist announced, "The doctor will see you now." Bridget thought she would faint she was so nervous. The doctor chatted for five minutes like an old friend but Bridget was not listening to him, she just wanted the whole thing over and done with as quickly as possible. The doctor asked her to undress from the waist downwards and then lie down on the bed. He put a sheet across her midriff and closed the curtain, even though there was no-one else in the room. Bridget closed her eyes and tried not to think about what was happening. As the doctor carried out the procedure he kept up a barrage of questions, "How is Jane these days? Where did you go for your holidays?" Bridget couldn't concentrate on what he was saying, she just wanted to get out as soon as she could. All she could think of was "get on with it, shut up gabbing and get on with it." She didn't say that out loud but that's what she was thinking.

As he finished and took off his rubber gloves he was still chatting. He remarked, "Well thanks for coming in, I'm glad you finally decided to get a Pap smear done, the results will be available in a few days and if there's anything we need to discuss I'll give you a call, and it was nice to see that you took so much trouble coming here today." Bridget wasn't really listening and just mumbled a goodbye and left as quickly as she could. She was acutely embarrassed and swore to herself that she'd never go through with that again.

Relieved that she'd been brave and finally fulfilled her promise she drove home. While driving home something the doctor said came back to her, "What did he mean?" she mumbled to herself, "It was nice to see that you took so much trouble coming here today. What had he meant by that?" She was perplexed and couldn't understand what he had meant but shrugged and put it out of her mind. Shortly after returning home, Bridget answered nature's call and went to the bathroom. Mindlessly she pulled her knickers down and proceeded to use the loo. Absently she looked down and was immediately confused with what she saw. The inside lining of her stark white pants was blue. Bridget swore aloud, "What the hell?" and then it dawned on her what it was. Almost screaming she let out a loud wail, "Oh no! Oh no! Oh no!" She looked down at her private parts and wanted instantly to just die. To her acute embarrassment and absolute horror all she could see without her reading glasses was a blur of electric blue sparkles.

6

THE HOSPITAL

Jim had never been in a proper relationship, he'd dated a couple of girls from his office but nothing serious. His dreams at night now were nearly always about the girl with the red curls, she had even invaded his daydreaming too. It was as if her features were burned into his brain, every line and curve remembered in obsessive detail.

Jim had really loved his over protective Mum, she'd spoilt him and cosseted him and he missed her dreadfully. Even though Jim had his cat and dogs the house seemed so empty, so lifeless. He was managing on his own but had no idea really how to do the weekly grocery shopping or cook a proper meal; his mum and grandmother had always competed for space in the kitchen and he'd always been happy to let them bicker as to who was cooking the evening meal and how it was to be done. His mother had been an excellent cook. Now he was existing on simple food; baked beans, frozen pies smothered in tomato sauce, in fact anything that could be microwaved, or bought, ready prepared in the local supermarket. He knew he was perfectly healthy, but also knew his diet was not the best. In the back of his mind he had the nagging worry about what his Aunt had told him. He thought to himself, "Maybe there is something hereditary in this cancer thing, maybe I should go and get it all checked out. I don't suppose it could hurt."

Remembering his Aunt's advice and concerns, Jim, true to his word arranged for an appointment with his doctor the next week to discuss the possibility that he might be prone to the same cancer that his mother and grandmother had succumbed to. His doctor was quite sympathetic to Jim's loss and agreed with Aunt Bridget that it wouldn't hurt to have a simple test done, just as a check to make sure all was well. The doctor explained that the best test would be a simple colonoscopy which can reveal if there are any problems in that area.

Jim had no idea what a colonoscopy was, or what it involved, however agreed for the doctor to make an appointment for Jim to see a specialist who would do the procedure. Jim's doctor explained that it was an extremely simple procedure whereby the specialist would examine the colon making sure that it all looked healthy. No problem. Jim happened to mention it to a couple of his team mates on the next Saturday as he was changing for his usual soccer game. The other young men all got a fit of the giggles. Jim got quite angry and reminded those who were laughing that both his mum and grandmother died from colon cancer. "What's so funny?" He questioned them. "It's just a simple procedure. The doctor says it's all over and done with in an hour." No-one enlightened him as to the details of such a procedure and he just dismissed them as being silly overgrown teenagers.

Jim attended the consultant's suite attached to the city hospital and saw the specialist, a gastroenterologist who explained the procedure in far more detail. Now Jim didn't think the man was actually a ghoul, but he did seem to get exquisite pleasure from seeing poor Jim squirm as he explained the procedure. The doctor showed Jim an artist's impression of what the colon looks like and explained how long it is and what function it plays in the digestive system. Jim looked at the complicated diagram and nodded his head trying to look as if he was highly intelligent and understood all that was being explained. That is, until the specialist explained what exactly would happen. "You're going to put a what, in where? No, no, no, I don't think so." No-one had ever seen his nether regions since his mother had changed his nappies, some twenty years earlier, and he had no intention of letting anyone stick anything into his rear end, especially anything that was going to explore the miles and miles of his convoluted internal plumbing. "Well, I'm sorry young man, but I'm afraid this is the only way; the best way we can assess if you have a problem, major or minor. And, in view of the fact that your mother and grandmother had bowel cancer, I do truly feel we should give you this simple procedure." Jim felt mortified.

"Simple! Simple? It doesn't sound simple to me."

Jim felt faint with just the thought of the procedure and asked carefully, "How long will it take and will it hurt much?"

"No, it won't hurt at all, you'll be fast asleep and won't feel a thing, honest. It's only a day surgery procedure so you'll be allowed to go home in the late afternoon."

The specialist booked Jim into the city hospital for the following week and gave him some written instructions which included a prescription for two packets of powder which were to be his pre procedure preparation. Jim didn't like the look the white uniformed chemist gave him as she handed over the two packets. She seemed to have a look of sympathy whilst at the same time trying not to laugh. He had no idea why.

The packets were much larger than he thought they would be and Jim wondered how he was going to take the contents. It was obviously a powder of some sort and as he read that he was only supposed to take the powder the day before the procedure he put the packets into his kitchen cupboard and tried to put the whole matter out of his mind.

Jim was quite nervous about the formidable procedure and wished he could talk to someone about it, but was too embarrassed and had no-one close enough that he felt he could confide in. He had plenty of friends, the blokes at the pub, the guys at work but he suspected they would all have a good laugh at his expense if he told them what he was booked in for, just like the guys at the soccer club. He did however answer his Aunt Bridget's telephone call and confess to her that he had been to see the doctor and a gastroenterologist and he was booked in for a colonoscopy the following week. Bridget was delighted by his confession and simply said, "I'm proud of you, well done, it will give you peace of mind." It didn't give him peace of mind though, his mind for the next week was anything but peaceful. He could barely sleep for worrying about what was going to happen. He told his boss at work that he needed a few days off work to sort out his mother's estate, although, being an only son there was nothing really to sort out.

On the day before the procedure Jim took out the two packets and read carefully the written instructions. He was not to eat any solid food that day but was allowed water and clear chicken broth. He didn't have chicken broth or even soup in the pantry but he could remember his mother making some chicken soup once, and he hadn't liked it, so that was no great loss. He drank copious amounts of beer instead as his stomach started rumbling with emptiness. He wasn't duly upset and thought a diet of beer only was actually not too bad. The instructions on the packets had told him to drink water or clear broth, it didn't say anything about beer but Jim reasoned that beer was a clear liquid and wasn't a solid food, therefore he was sure it would be okay.

In the evening he did as instructed and mixed the two packets of powder together in a large plastic jug which was a one litre container as specified, and he was instructed to fill the jug with lukewarm water and eventually pour into two further containers with more water making two litres in all. He only had one large jug and so utilised an empty lemonade bottle as a substitute for a jug. Jim had been drinking beer all day and looked in fear and trepidation at the two litres of liquid he was now supposed to drink. He didn't think his stomach could take so much liquid and realised, too late, that he maybe shouldn't have drunk so much beer in the day. However, the instructions didn't specify how long it would take to drink that much and so undaunted he started in on the first litre.

Jim was unprepared for this experience and nothing in his vocabulary could realistically describe the taste that met Jim's palette. The first mouthful was spat out with such force it covered the kitchen work top. "Bloody Hell!" was the best he could do at that moment. He took the two empty packets and inspected the wording carefully. He thought he must have missed something, surely they couldn't really expect anyone to drink this stuff, could they? Not only was it the most vile thing Jim had ever tasted, but he had two litres of it to get down. He sat down at the kitchen bench and a slow sweat started on his forehead and travelled down to his upper lip. "No, I can't do this, I just can't," he decided he needed to vent some anger or at the very least complain bitterly. He picked up the phone and rang his Aunt Bridget.

"Aunt Bridget, it's Jim. Listen I'm booked in for this colon thingy tomorrow and I've got to drink this vile stuff they've given me. Two bloody litres of it. I can't do it. I really can't."

"Oh, for Goodness sake Jim, stop being such a baby. Drink the stuff. Hold your nose if you must. Actually I think you can put some lemon juice into it if you want, that might make it a bit better."

"No Aunt Bridget, I can't do it."

"Yes you can. Stop being a big baby, think of your Mum and Nan, I know you can do this. Ring me after your procedure and let me know how it went."

Poor Jim was desperate he really didn't think he could drink the vile stuff. He looked to the two dogs and appealed to them, "What am I going to do?" They both cocked their heads to one side and tried to look sympathetic. He went to the pantry to see if there was any lemon juice and was relieved to see there was, not exactly lemon juice but a bottle of diet lemonade. "Close enough." He told the air around him. He poured himself three quarters of a glass of the vile preparation and then topped it up with lemonade. He took one taste and spit it out. "Bloody Hell that's worse than before. It tastes like cat's wee mixed with dog's vomit." The dogs did their best to look sympathetic but failed miserably. The cat ignored them all and curled up on the settee for a short nap. The budgie as usual had nothing to say.

Jim pushed the cat off the settee and sat for an hour dejectedly looking at the two litres that he knew he had to get down him. Eventually, with tears in his eyes he poured himself a glass of the vile brew. He held his nose just as his Aunt had advised and drank, slowly over the next three hours. It was so awful, he had three times retched with tears in his eyes but struggled manfully and actually got the whole two litres down.

In disbelief Jim kept reading the long list of instructions on the pack to see if there was some way he had been mistaken, but no, he couldn't find any apology or reason for the awful taste, or any way it could be made any more palatable.

The instructions did however give the warning that "*a loose, bowel movement can be expected following these instructions.*"

This warning Jim considered later, was the understatement of the year and must have been written by a professional comedian. As he drained the last dregs of the liquid torture he found that his problems had been nothing compared to what was now happening to his traumatised body. He made a violent dash to the bathroom and only just made it in time before his whole bowel seemed to explode and turn itself basically inside out. He felt almost like a jet propelled Concorde blasting off down the runway to hell. He was terrified of leaving the sanctuary of the bathroom and sat there for hours eliminating his body of every vestige of fluid that he had ever consumed. Mount Vesuvius came to mind and even Niagara Falls. There seemed to be no end to it. It just kept on and on.

He was tired and wanted to go to bed, but he didn't dare leave the safety of the bathroom. He sat there in solitary, total abject misery for hours, cursing his Aunt Bridget, his doctor and the world in general. Eventually the elimination ceased and Jim, too exhausted to leave, pulled some towels onto himself for blankets and fell asleep on the bathroom mat; he hadn't been willing to risk an accident in the bedroom, or in his bed. Mum was no longer there to do his laundry and it would not be a pleasant laundry that he would be faced with, to do himself, so sleeping on the bathroom floor seemed a safe bet, if somewhat uncomfortable.

The next morning Jim, in his drowsy state made the mistake of causally popping off a fart, and was initially confused, not only by his location, but by a feeling of wetness in his pants, it was then that he became instantly and fully awake, appalled by the horrid realization that he'd had a small accident in his pants. With butt cheeks clenched and as fast has he could waddle, not wanting to risk any further abuse to his underpants, he pulled himself up from the tiled floor and groped his way to the toilet, further cursing this whole affair. After showering and getting ready to go to the hospital, and by way of a security blanket, Jim packed his pants with toilet paper, just in case, and made a mental note to himself, "DO NOT FART." He drove himself to the hospital and hoped that the other patients in the waiting room would not misunderstand the unnatural bulge in his pants. As he had arrived early he was surprised to see at least a dozen other uncomfortable, exhausted and embarrassed patients sitting in the cheery reception area. The cheery reception area only seemed to mock his mood. He felt anything but cheery.

In spite of feeling conspicuous and embarrassed Jim was shocked and surprised to see that the hospital receptionist who greeted him with a reassuring smile was no other than the goddess of his dreams; the girl with the red curls. If it were possible she was even more gorgeous than he had remembered. Her luxuriously long red hair and expressive eyes were just as he remembered. She had a sprinkle of freckles across her turned up nose and high cheekbones. She had naturally arched eyebrows, and in Jim's mind a perfectly beautiful face. Jim thought with extreme exasperation as he mentally looked heavenward, "Why now? Why here?" Why did she have to be seeing him, at what Jim felt was his worst. He was more than a little flustered and tried desperately to put the girl out of his mind and concentrate on why he was there.

The girl presented Jim with a large folder holding an incredible amount of forms which he was instructed to complete. He shook his head at what seemed to him to be so many stupid questions; was he allergic to this and that, what childhood ailments had he suffered, what religion was he, what ethnic background was he, what were his parent's medical history and their parents too. He resisted the urge to put down some silly answers and dutifully signed his consent to whatever hell they were going to put him through. He handed the folder back to the girl and was dazzled by her smile as she told him to take a seat in the waiting room.

Jim had resigned himself to the utter degradation of the whole embarrassing procedure but he had never been admitted to hospital before and was totally unprepared for the undignified attire he was assigned to wear. It took him so long to work out how to put the hospital gown on that eventually a nurse came to his rescue and showed him that, "Yes, you have to put it on backwards."

"But my backside is hanging out."

"No-one is bothered about looking at your backside. Come along they're ready for you."

"Whatever kind of sadistic pervert designed these gowns?"

"Come along, everyone's the same. No-one else is making such a fuss."

Once in the theatre holding area, a cap and gowned different nurse came to check if Jim was really Jim. She checked his wrist band, took his blood pressure and went through a host of the same questions that he had answered on the forms only a short while ago. "Are you Jim Emery? What's your date of birth? Are you allergic to anything? Did your parents suffer from high blood pressure? What medication are you currently on? Are you on any blood thinners?"

"I've just answered all those questions on the forms they gave me in reception."

"Yes, but you have to answer them again."

In an exasperated tone, Jim acceded, "Good God, fine. Well, yes, no, no, no, and no."

With that the efficient but no-nonsense nurse placed a paper cap over his hair and produced a horse sized needle and syringe, at least it looked like a horse needle to Jim. She searched and rubbed the back of his hand, looking for a vein, and none too gently inserted the needle. Jim involuntarily gasped at the sharp pain. The nurse shook her head and muttered something under her breath about him being a girlie girl. He wasn't too sure exactly what she said so let it pass but was too nervous about what was going to happen to him to care about her.

As he was being wheeled into the theatre he looked around and saw equipment, lights, machines, tubes and apparatus that he felt should really be in a torture chamber; it all looked very scary. The enormous overhead lights were blinding him and he could hear a couple of doctors discussing the local cricket scores. He wanted to shout at them to concentrate but discretion he decided was the better part of valour. He was putting his life in their hands and he thought it was probably not a good idea to be rude to them, not until afterwards anyway.

Another nurse came and inspected the needle in the back of Jim's hand and he tried to call her back to explain that she had forgotten to take it out but at that moment the anaesthetist hooked another three tubes into the needle, Jim had no idea why. The anaesthetist asked Jim again what his name was and his date of birth. "For the love of God I've just answered those questions." When the anaesthetist got the right answer he placed a soft plastic breathing mask over Jim's nose and mouth, the anaesthetist was still speaking, but Jim didn't hear what was being said anymore. It was at that point that Jim panicked and decided that he had changed his mind. He tried to tell the doctor, "Listen I think I've made a mistake. I've changed my mind. Can we do this another d............"

Jim woke up in another room and wondered if he had died and gone to heaven. Everything was antiseptic white, the bed he was on was all draped in white, the walls of the room were white and there was soft music playing somewhere far off. He could distinguish the music and recognised it as the Moonlight Sonata. He felt utterly relaxed and quite sleepy and so closed his eyes and just gave in to the soft, warm ambience of the room. In only a short while an angel appeared and asked him how he was feeling. As his eyes gradually focussed he realised the beautiful woman at his bedside was a nurse not an angel, she had no halo or wings. As his mind came into focus he realised he was being asked a question. "How are you feeling Mr. Emery?" He wanted to say awful, suddenly remembering why he was there, but in actual fact he felt wonderful, totally relaxed. A doctor appeared and announced that Jim's colon was as clean as a whistle, "One of the nicest colons I've ever seen, and as far as I can tell you are in perfect health."

The hospital orderly wheeled Jim's gurney back to his assigned recovery room, which was not actually a proper ward room. As Jim looked around him he was surprised to see a filing cabinet, a desk with pigeon holes above and a second bed. "What's all this then? This is not a proper hospital room." The orderly explained, "Yeah, sorry about this but there's been a terrible multi-car freeway accident and suddenly we've go over 30 seriously injured patients. We've simply run out of room. You'll be okay here though, I know it's just an office but the nurses will look after you, no problem." Jim was not unduly worried, he knew he was just a day patient and in a short while he would be going home. At that moment an empty gurney arrived, and was parked next to his. Jim heard a man groaning and moaning in the hall outside his room. Jim watched as the orderly helped the groaning man onto the second bed and left promising to have the doctors examine the man in a short while

Jim was concerned and asked the man if he needed any help, or anything. The man introduced himself as Johan Metters and explained to Jim that he had come to the hospital complaining of headaches, sore throat, stomach ache and pain in his joints and muscles. He told Jim the triage nurse had admitted him for further examination. Johan looked around the room and asked Jim where the toilet was, he needed to go urgently. Jim had no idea but helped Johan down from his bed and supported him as the two went looking for the bathroom. Half way down the corridor Johan had a coughing fit and to the surprise of both of them a small splattering of blood landed across the lower half of Jim's hospital gown. A nurse who had been walking towards them saw Johan coughing up blood and calmly ushered the two to the bathroom. The nurse asked Jim to step into the shower cubicle and helped him to take off the soiled hospital gown which she took away explaining that she would return with a fresh gown shortly. She asked him to take a shower in case any blood had touched him. Johan meanwhile explained that he simply had to use the toilet straight away and the nurse offered him assistance but he assured her that he could manage on his own. The nurse explained to Jim that the road accident had been horrific and all the doctors and available staff were attending to the large number of severe casualties.

Once Jim and the nurse got Johan back into his bed Jim asked if he could be released and go home. The nurse explained that he couldn't be released until the doctor had made sure all was well and that Jim was not having any undue reactions to the anaesthetics or the procedure he had just had. Finally after two hours Johan was attended to by a young doctor who took a blood sample. The doctor sent the sample off to the pathologist with the nurse and once that was underway proceeded to ask Johan a series of questions about his health. He asked Johan if he had recently been on holiday to Asia or Africa and Johan explained that he was working for the American Peace Corps and had returned a week ago from a holiday in the Bas-Uele region of the Congo. The doctor raised his eyebrows.

Both Johan and Jim waited for their respective doctors to either release them or in Johan's case to find out what was wrong. After an hour, with Jim pacing the floor two gowned and masked doctors came into the room and announced that Johan's blood sample showed that he had contracted Ebola, a very deadly disease. "My God," declared Jim, "Let me get out of here." He made for the door but the tallest of the doctors barred his way. "I'm sorry young man but I have to ask, have you touched Mr. Metters at all?"

"No" lied Jim.

"Well that's not what Nurse Jenkins told me. She told me how she saw you assisting Mr.Metters to the bathroom when he had a coughing fit and coughed up blood onto your gown, so I'm sorry young man but you've been potentially exposed to the deadly virus Ebola and as such you can't be allowed to leave. You are hereby quarantined until we can be sure you are not contaminated."

"What, are you serious? So what now? Do I have to stay here? Am I going to die?"

"I'm really sorry. We'll give you every assistance with letting your folks and work know, but you'll be here for a few days, or even weeks until we know for sure you're not contaminated."

"Oh my God, this can't be happening to me, and we're not even in a proper hospital room. Look, there's no toilet, no shower, they're all down the corridor."

"Don't worry about this room, we're going to move both of you to our special isolation rooms in another part of the hospital."

"This is awful, what about my pets? I have responsibilities, I can't just stay here indefinitely."

"Don't you have anyone, a relative or a friend who can take care of your pets?"

"Well, I guess so, but bloody hell, this is not what you expect when you come into hospital for a simple procedure."

Aunt Bridget was contacted and agreed to look after the pets and Jim's boss was notified also. It was two weeks before Jim was released. The whole time he complained of the terrible hospital food, the constant noise making sleep almost impossible and the lack of any creature comforts; no television, no radio, no visitors. Johan was taken to a separate room and Jim was isolated. He suspected Johan had died but he wasn't sure and the hospital staff wouldn't tell him anything. He was bored out of his brains. He desperately wanted to get out of his prison cell, as he called it, and make his way to the reception area to talk to the red-headed girl but he was simply not allowed out of his room. He had read and reread the only reading material he was given, one book he'd read a year earlier and two women's magazines. He was at his wit's end but there was nothing he could do about it. Eventually he was given the "all clear" and allowed to go home. Luckily he had not contacted the disease.

He passed the reception desk and as the red-headed girl was not there he asked the girl on the desk where the previous receptionist was and what was her name. The girl on the desk told Jim, "Sorry but I'm new here. I think the previous receptionist just left, she got a job somewhere else, I don't know where."

"Well does anyone else know where she went?"

"Hang on a moment, I'll ask."

"No, I'm sorry, we don't know where she went, we only know she's not working here any longer." Jim was stymied, and frustrated, but had no alternative but to just accept the situation.

As soon as Jim got home he rang and complained to his Aunt Bridget for putting him through that awful experience, "I'm back Aunt Bridget. Thanks for looking after the dogs and cat and budgie, I'll be over shortly to pick them up and I'll be giving you a piece of my mind, making me go through all that awful experience."

"Now, now young Jim, it couldn't have been as bad as all that."

"Worse, you've no idea."

"Well come on round and we'll have lunch." Once Jim arrived at his Aunt's house she settled him into her most comfortable chair and questioned him, "So how was everything?" Jim tried to explain, "Well, the colonoscopy was not too bad actually. They put me to sleep and when I woke up it was all over." Giving an involuntary shudder Jim outlined his terrible experience with the pre-operation powder preparation. "Honestly Aunt Bridget, taking that stuff was a complete and terrible experience, you've no idea." He told her about his night on the bathroom floor, "And after all that hassle, like I told you, turns out I am completely fine. There's nothing wrong with me. Me and my colon are just fine."

"Well I'm glad young Jim, at least we have peace of mind now."

"I had peace of mind before. You know I was never worried, I told you I was fine."

"Well I'm truly glad you're fine."

"Yes, thanks, I'm fine. But wait, that's not all, not only was the lead up to the colonoscopy bloody awful but I very nearly contracted Ebola; I could have died."

"Come, come Jim, you're being a bit dramatic aren't you? It couldn't have been that bad, after all you were in hospital and being waited on hand and foot. All your creature comforts were being met and not costing you a cent."

"Are you mad Aunt Bridget, it was just about the worst experience ever, I think I've been traumatised for life. I had no-one to talk to, the chap who actually caught the Ebola was really sick and I think he died. I had no television, no radio, hardly anything to read and nothing to do. I was isolated, bored and fed up.

"Oh dear, you poor thing, but was the food good?"

"Are you crazy? Breakfast every day was simply a small box of cornflakes and milk. Lunch every day was exactly the same; I had curried sawdust and cardboard cheese sandwiches. At least that's what it tasted like."

"Don't exaggerate Jim."

"I swear I'm not exaggerating, I'd have been given better food if I'd been locked up in jail."

"Well what about dinner, it must have been better for dinner?"

Dripping with sarcasm Jim replied, "Oh yes, that was the best ever! NOT! Every evening I was given a thin slice of some meat, I have no idea what kind, it was totally tasteless and unrecognisable. It was always covered in a watery gravy and served with overcooked vegetables, obviously frozen vegetables, I don't think they ever served vegetables that were fresh. It was disgusting, honestly. The only good thing that came out of the whole terrible experience was that I saw the red-headed girl again."

"Oh, that's brilliant, I'm glad to hear it. Did you talk to her? Tell me all about it?"

"No Aunt Bridget. She was the receptionist at the hospital and had left by the time I'd served my prison sentence,"

"That's a bit strong Jim."

"Well, maybe but by the time I was let out of ebola quarantine she'd moved on and left the hospital. She got a job somewhere else. I'd missed my opportunity again. Anyway I don't want to talk about it anymore. I'm really cross with you for making me go through all that. So what about you? Did you go and get a Pap smear done, as you promised?"

Bridget remembering her embarrassing event with the doctor blushed and squirmed in her seat as she answered, "Yes I did, and like you I'm just fine." There was no way she was ever going to tell him or anyone else about her unfortunate blunder, and no way she was ever going to return to that doctor. She didn't care how far she would have to travel but resolved never to return to her old doctor and would find a new surgery somewhere far away.

"Great, so we're both fine."

"Yes, we're fine."

"fine."

7

THE BLOOD BANK

J im went back to work and settled into the routine of
everyday living. Although he lived alone he was not really
lonely, he had the dogs and the cat to keep him company
and each week he played soccer and attended a judo class and
occasionally entered competitions. Jim's home was a modest
single storey, three bedroom house not too far from the centre
of Perth, Western Australia. He loved the beach and especially
fishing from one of the many wooden jetties along the coast. He
was not the best sailor and usually felt a little sea sick if he was
in any kind of small boat, so fishing from a jetty was ideal for
him. He didn't really care if he caught anything or not, he just
enjoyed the anticipation of a catch and the peace and calm of
fishing. If he did however catch anything he would take it home,
clean it and simply fry it for his dinner. The cat usually enjoyed
the left over head and tail of any fish. The budgie also enjoyed
those visits to the beach as Jim usually brought back a cuttlefish
bone which the budgie gnawed upon and used to keep his beak
from growing too long.

Jim usually took the dogs with him when he went fishing and
one day as he was making his way to the jetty he noticed walking
in front of him a fellow dog walker pulling along an unwilling

little poodle. The figure in front of him, obviously a girl, wore tight jeans on a slim body and had long blond wavy hair that hung down to her waist. Jim had a soft spot for poodles and an even softer spot for girls with long hair.

He was always daydreaming about the red-headed girl but realised he might never actually see her again. He'd missed his opportunity and that was that.

Instead of taking the turn off to the jetty he followed the girl with the long hair along the coastal path for about a kilometre wondering how he could strike up a conversation with her. At last the chance arose when her little poodle absolutely refused to go any further and just sat down stubbornly refusing to get up again. Jim had a chivalrous streak in him and strode up behind the girl asking gallantly, "The little chap doesn't seem to want to walk any further, can I carry him for you?" The blonde wavy hair was pushed to one side as the poodle owner turned around and frowned ferociously at Jim. A blonde moustache and beard covered an aggressive masculine scowl as the poodle owner growled, "Are you trying to be funny mate? Bugger off!"

It was two weeks later that Jim was walking through the busy centre of town in his lunch hour when his attention was taken by a female just in front of him who had long red curly hair. His heart skipped a beat or two and he could barely breathe. "Please God, please God, let it be her." He wasn't too sure if this was the same girl, but she certainly had the same kind of hair and reasoned, curly red hair was pretty unusual. Jim forgot where he had intended to go for lunch and just desperately followed the girl, with no intent or idea of what he was actually doing. He was following her trying to think of what he could possibly say to her, what opening gambit would be best, what would sound reasonable and not too trite. After about two blocks the girl turned into the parking lot of the local recreation centre. To one side of the parking area there was a mobile blood bank in a long caravan and the girl mounted the stairs and disappeared inside. Jim wanted to follow but wasn't even sure it was the same girl, as he had only seen this one from the back. Nevertheless he just felt compelled to follow and so mounted the narrow stairs with no plan in his amorous young mind.

Once inside the airy caravan Jim watched as the girl made her way around the counter with her back to him. The anticipation was killing him, was it her, or not? Mentally Jim was repeating over and over, "Turn around, turn around." To his profound joy as she turned he was thrilled to see that the girl was his red headed goddess. His heart was pounding. She was obviously now the receptionist at the blood bank and asked him if he was there to give blood. Her question abruptly brought him back to reality. He answered with a hesitant, "um,Errr, um yes?," To himself he thought "Oh what the hell, if I have to give blood to get to know the girl, well, why not?" He tried to smile at the girl through his nervousness and spoke with a slight wobble to his voice. "I understand you people are always looking to recruit new donors. I'm young and healthy if you want some blood."

"Yes, thank you for coming. Is this your first time donating?"

"Yes, I've given a sample of blood when the doctor sent me to a pathologist to check out my cholesterol, but not actually a blood donation as such."

"Well this is a little different, but you'll see it's no big problem. Now if you'll just take this file and fill out the forms we'll get you started."

Jim took a seat and started in on the file she had given him. He filled out basically the same forms that he had signed at the hospital when he was there for his colonoscopy. They wanted to know everything, childhood illnesses, sexual practises, religion, lifestyle choices, on and on they went. Jim barely read the questions and ticked each box as he found it difficult to concentrate; he was distracted by her beauty. He kept looking at the girl hoping she was looking at him too, but she was busy with other clients and took little notice of him. Apart from questions there were also instructions which Jim basically ignored. One of the instructions expressed the inadvisability of donating unless one had eaten within the last few hours. Jim was in his lunch hour and hadn't eaten a thing since a slice of dry toast at breakfast but didn't take much notice and didn't put much importance on the suggestion.

Eventually he completed the long list of formalities and returned the forms to the smiling girl. He saw she had a name badge and took note of the name "Samantha." Oh, his mind was in a whirl now, he could put a name to his vision of loveliness. "Samantha, Samantha," he let the name roll around in his empty head and liked the sound of it.

A nurse or doctor, he didn't know which eventually took him into the inner sanctum of the long caravan and asked him to roll up his shirt sleeve and lay down on the waist high gurney. Now Jim couldn't see Samantha and started to hone in on the reality of what he had unthinkingly let himself in for. His only experience with blood was the small vial that he had given up when he'd had his cholesterol checked. "So how long will this take?" he asked the doctor, "and how much blood are you going to extract?"

"Oh we usually take a pint, that's normal." Jim sat bolt upright with shock.

"What do you mean a pint? That's an awful lot isn't it? I expected it to be the same as the pathologist took when I had my cholesterol checked. I mean a pint would be equivalent to a full arm or leg of blood. I can't walk around with no blood in my legs. I mean an empty leg of blood would be no use at all."

"You'll be fine, a normal person has about eight pints of blood in their system and you make up that one pint very quickly."

"Oh, I don't think I can spare a whole pint. Can't you just take out a little bit?"

"No, you'll be okay, now just lay back and relax."

Jim couldn't relax though; he hadn't enjoyed the procedure when the pathologist took out just a little, now the thought of a whole pint being extracted was terrifying him. He watched in mute terror as he saw the doctor approach with a hypodermic needle the size of a knitting needle, or so it appeared to him. A nurse assisted the doctor and put a rubber sleeve around the top of his arm. Jim protested strongly "You're putting that thing on too tight, it's paralysing my arm. Look it's making my veins stand out."

"Yes, that's precisely what it's supposed to do. Now make your hand into a fist please."

"Why? Am I supposed to hit someone?"

"No, it helps to make your veins stand out." With that the doctor rubbed Jim's arm and then deftly placed the needle into the vein. "Now that didn't hurt did it?"

"Yes it bloody well did. Well is that it, can I go home now?"

"Oh my goodness, we've only just started, it will take quite a while to get as much as we need. You can't go anywhere for at least an hour." Jim groaned and felt quite sick as he watched the hanging plastic bag of his neighbouring donor slowly fill and realised his would be filling equally slowly. He actually couldn't see his own plastic blood bag as it was suspended below his gurney. He remembered that he was in his lunch hour and hadn't made any provision for this diversion. What would his boss make of his absence for so long? He realised how stupid he was not thinking this whole thing through. Then his thoughts turned to Samantha and he closed his eyes and wondered if she considered him a hero for donating so bravely.

Jim drifted off to sleep and had no notion that this was not normal. He dreamt that he was saving Samantha from a burning aeroplane as he deployed his parachute and held on to her. She was enthusiastically kissing him all the way down to a soft landing in his back garden. His mother was there and gave them both a sandwich as they landed at her feet.

Eventually the doctor came, woke him up and detached the tube and needle from Jim's arm. "Come on along young fellow, thank you very much for your kind donation. Come and have a cup of tea and a biscuit or two." Jim sat up quickly and just as quickly passed out. Cold.

The concerned doctor had never seen anyone react so violently to a donation and called an elderly nurse over to watch over Jim as he massaged Jim's outer cold extremities. After a moment a startled Jim came to and asked what had happened. The doctor questioned Jim about how much food he had consumed that morning. "Oh, I just had a small piece of toast at about seven, and I skipped my coffee as I was running late." The doctor groaned. "Didn't you read the instructions you were given saying that it was inadvisable to donate blood unless you had eaten a hearty breakfast and drunk plenty of fluids?"

"Err, I don't remember that bit."

"Well this is what happens if you give blood and you haven't eaten enough and drunk enough to counter the loss of blood. You should have told us you hadn't really eaten or drunk anything." Jim tried to sit up but found each time he did he felt that he was going to faint and so had to gently lie down again.

This went on for two hours. As he lay there worrying about not being at work he could hear the angry doctor and nurse discussing the situation and complaining about the fact that it was time to close the centre, but they couldn't close up until Jim was stabilised. He realised they were quite furious with him for not obeying the instructions and causing them to stay open longer than they had intended.

Eventually the elderly nurse helped Jim to sit up and gingerly walk across the small room to be handed a warm sweet cup of tea and three biscuits.

The doctor and nurse were keen to close the centre but were reluctant to leave Jim on the busy street alone and still quite vulnerable. Much to Jim's surprise and ecstatic happiness Samantha suggested she watch over Jim and escort him back to his work or his home. The doctor was only too pleased to hand his charge over to Samantha as he had an urgent appointment elsewhere and really had to go as soon as he could.

Jim didn't want to appear to be a weakling or a softie and so tried to put on a brave show. He didn't want to lose face and so after covering only a few metres decided that he should hail a passing taxi to take him back to work. He thanked Samantha profusely for offering to look after him but assured her that he was just fine now and she shouldn't worry about him. He was about to ask the girl for a date but he was too slow, she had turned her back on him and was walking away quite briskly.

The impatient taxi driver leaned across the front seat and yelled at Jim, "Are you getting in mate or not?" Jim wanted to run after the girl but faltered and decided against it.

Jim returned to the office and had to explain to his boss that he had come over "all faint" and thought he was coming down with something. It was obvious from his white ashen face that Jim really wasn't feeling too well and his boss readily agreed that Jim should go home immediately.

Once Jim arrived back home he berated himself for not having taken advantage of the situation and hadn't made any advances towards the beautiful Samantha. He couldn't get the vision of loveliness out of his mind and had his usual erotic dreams of her for the next few nights. Jim wasn't the most romantic or experienced of lovers and wondered how he could possibly meet up with Samantha and maybe ask her out, for a coffee, dinner, or whatever. He knew nothing about her except that she worked as a receptionist at the blood bank. Even though he hated the idea of going back and donating blood again, he resolved to return to the blood bank, on the excuse of giving blood and see if he couldn't pluck up enough courage to ask her out.

The next day, remembering the doctor's admonishments, he ate a hearty breakfast of three eggs on toast washed down with two cups of coffee and made his way, like a gallant soldier marching into battle, to the blood bank. Unfortunately when he got to the recreation centre the mobile caravan simply wasn't there. He went into the centre and asked the duty manager there if the blood bank was due to return. The busy manager looked up from the file he was reading and informed Jim that the blood bank only set up operations in their car park in the first week of each month. That meant that Jim had to wait for three long interminable weeks before returning to see if he could meet up with Samantha.

On the day he knew the blood bank would be at the recreation centre Jim again ate a hearty breakfast washed down with lots of coffee and proceeded to the centre. He had taken a day off work and was quite excited at the thought of meeting up with the beautiful Samantha again. He had dressed carefully putting on his best shirt and trousers and had a haircut at the barbers straight after breakfast. He was keen to make a good impression. At the top of the stairs and through the heavy door Jim was met with a different receptionist who gave him some forms to fill in again and after checking over the answers took him straight into the donation's room and had him lay down on the waiting gurney ready for the doctor.

The doctor happened to be the same one that had taken blood from Jim the first time and as soon as he saw Jim he asked about Jim's food and drink intake for that morning. Once satisfied with the answers started with the simple procedure. Jim gasped once again as the giant sized needle (to his mind) was viciously (to his mind) stabbed into his arm. He hoped Samantha was somewhere around admiring his brave and stoic, if not heroic donation. He tried to sound casual as he asked the nurse at the end of the procedure as she was pouring him a sweet cup of tea, "So where's Samantha today, I didn't see her as I came in?"

"Oh, Samantha left us a week ago, she didn't like the work here, you know, moving from place to place all the time."

'What! You mean I've gone through all this again, for nothing? You could have told me she wasn't here before you stole all my blood."

"Well you didn't ask did you, and if that's why you came then you should be ashamed of yourself. You're supposed to give blood for altruistic reasons, not as a platform for chasing all the girls. Shame on you."

A very aggrieved Jim and walked out slamming the door behind him. He stomped around the block frustrated and stymied wondering what to do about the situation and decided he had no other option if he wanted to meet up with Samantha again, but to return to the blood bank and ask if they knew how he could contact the girl. The same haughty nurse met him at the entrance door and asked none too gently, "Well it's Romeo back again, what do you want now?"

"I'm sorry for being rude to you but could you tell me how I can contact Samantha, I really must see her again?"

"And why should I tell you anything? You slammed the door as you left."

"Yes I know, I was wrong; it was rude of me but I was frustrated and I really like the girl, please can you help me?"

"You really don't deserve my help, but all I can tell you is that Samantha applied to the A.I.D. Centre for a job. I don't even know if she got the job, anyway that's all I know and I have other patients here now, goodbye." With that the impatient nurse threw back her head and turning her back on Jim disappeared into the inner recesses of the caravan. Jim had no idea what the A.I.D. Centre was and went home to lick his wounds and to look it up in the telephone directory or go online.

8

THE FERTILITY CENTRE

J im found out that A.I.D. stood for Artificial Insemination Department, attached to the local hospital's fertility clinic, and there was a branch in the next suburb to him. He basically knew that unfortunate couples who couldn't conceive naturally sometimes resorted to an egg donor for the women or a sperm donor for the men. The thought wasn't repulsive to him and if Samantha worked there, well maybe it was a way for him to get to know her and maybe ask her for a date. He rang the centre the following day and was told to get certification from his doctor as to his current health and past medical history. He was to take this along with him the following week.

Jim felt somewhat of a hypocrite when his doctor congratulated him on his altruistic reasons for such a donation, not knowing of course the real reason, and readily supplied all the necessary references as to his health. Armed with certification of good health and medical history Jim approached the A.I.D. Centre. He had dressed for the occasion, a clean shirt and new trousers, hoping again to impress the beautiful Samantha. He vaguely knew that he would be required to supply a sample but was really only thinking about an opening gambit with the girl of his dreams. He had a vision of himself as a sort of Knights

Templar bravely going off on a crusade to fight the Saracens, the ungodly, or whoever. He felt brave and courageous and fervently hoped that he would be impressing the gorgeous Samantha.

On entering the large old ornate building he was directed to the clinic for donations and was thrilled to see the golden/red curly haired Samantha at the reception desk. She recognised him immediately and asked how he was as she handed him yet again a file, asking him to complete the required questionnaire. Jim handed her the information he had been asked to obtain from his doctor, before sitting down to complete the involved questionnaire she had given him.

When all was completed Samantha directed Jim to a sterile waiting room prior to a private interview with a professional councillor. The councillor asked Jim many personal questions especially with regard to his understanding of the contract he was making and with regard to his willingness or otherwise for contact details to be registered and used at some time in the future. None of it was important for Jim; his mind simply wasn't on the questions he was being asked nor on his answers. He was only daydreaming about the good impression that he hoped he was making on Samantha. He kept looking around hoping she might be watching him; again he was daydreaming as to how she might be viewing him and his acts of chivalry making altruistic donations. His mind started wandering and he vaguely thought he could offer to give one of his kidneys away or a liver or something, she'd have to consider him a hero then.

For her part Samantha was beginning to feel that it was probably a bit more than a coincidence that this young man kept turning up in her life. She liked the look of him, even though he seemed a little shy and reserved, but that was not a bad thing, in fact it quite appealed to her. She knew she was attractive and many, many men tried to flirt with her, most with little success. Those that were openly "forward" and "flashy" just didn't appeal to her; she liked the quiet ones. She had already read through Jim's file when he turned up at the blood bank and was quite familiar with his background, address, medical history and occupation.

Having passed the councillor's interrogation Jim was led to a small room and given a small clear container with his name and a registration number written on the side. The councillor pointed out that there were magazines if he needed them on the coffee table and when he had finished he was to take the sample out to the receptionist.

Up until this moment Jim hadn't really thought out the process, his only concern was to be near to the gorgeous Samantha and to try and ask her for a date. The moment of truth was here though, he now had to produce a sample and take it out to the receptionist. That would be Samantha. He looked at the small container and realised that any sample he produced would be seen by the girl of his dreams. He went cold and sweaty as he suddenly realised how embarrassing it was going to be to hand over his "handy work." The more he thought about it the more he simply couldn't do it. He thought if he could disguise the jar; maybe wrap it in his hanky he could do it, but he didn't have a hanky on him; nothing.

He quickly looked through the stack of magazines, some ordinary women with no clothes on; some bizarre photo shoots that sent his mind reeling; some men's magazines that were 'X' rated and some with every ethnic depiction of pornography that a mind could conjure up. Still he couldn't do it. He felt trapped by his own inadequacy, by his own stupidity. Now a dreadful thought occurred to him. What if he just couldn't do it at all? How could he face the lady of his dreams and tell her he had nothing to show for his efforts; no donation. He would be mortified.

He paced up and down the tiny room; sat on the hard plastic chair; paced up and down the room again, all to no avail. He was in that room for two hours sweating profusely; too embarrassed to admit defeat and return an empty jar, and too embarrassed to be able to supply a donation. He didn't know what to do. He swore and cursed himself for being such an idiot. Eventually there was a knock on the door and a strange voice asked solicitously, "Are you alright in there Mr. Emery?"

"Yes, I'm fine."

"Well no rush, just take your time."

"Thank you. I will."

Jim thumbed through the magazines to no avail. In the end he just closed his eyes and gave in to his erotic thoughts of Samantha. He forced himself to think of what a relationship with her might entail. Eventually he was able to produce a specimen and only then did he start to have further worries and doubts about what he had done. What if I have a low sperm count? What if I'd be firing blanks? What if my wrigglers aren't wriggling? What if, what if, so many what ifs. He knew Samantha would find out if there was any deficiency in his donation. He cursed himself for being so stupid coming to such a place. Now he had more worries than ever. He would be eternally embarrassed if there was anything wrong with his donation. How could he face the woman of his dreams? He knew he couldn't stay in that little room any longer, he was almost in tears with his predicament; that beautiful woman was about to take his sample from him and would see what he had produced. Too embarrassing for words, but he had to do it.

He took the jar and in a red faced panic just plopped it on Samantha's desk; he didn't dare look at her, and left the office without a word. He caught the bus home soaked in sweat and swore to himself that he would never, ever do anything so stupid again. "So Samantha is the most beautiful woman I have ever seen, so what? Too bad. All too embarrassing. Why couldn't she have been a legal receptionist, or a shop assistant, it all would have been so much easier. I could never face her again now, not ever."

He berated himself over and over for his inability to face the girl. He confided to the dogs and the cat and the budgie, "I'm just a pathetic creature, no back bone, no guts. I don't even know why you lot hang around, I'm a miserable excuse for a man, she deserves better than me." The dogs whimpered in sympathy and with their heads to one side looked as if they understood his pain. The cat miowed piteously, but then he always did just before he was due to be fed. As usual the budgie was a silent witness to Jim's rantings and had nothing to say.

9

FLORENCE

Four days after his ordeal at the Fertility Clinic Jim got a phone call from his Aunt Bridget. "Hi there Jim, how are you?"

"Fine thanks Aunt Bridget, how are you?"

"Good, good. Listen I was wondering if you'd like to come over for dinner tomorrow night, I'm doing a lamb roast, Jane's just informed me that she is going to the theatre with a friend and it seems a shame to cook a lamb roast just for one."

"Oh, okay, sounds great. What time do you want me over there?"

"How about seven? We'll have a drink first and we can eat about seven thirty."

"Okay, I'll bring some wine. See you then. Cheers."

Jim was five minutes late when he arrived at his Aunt's house and was surprised to see a strange car in the driveway. Aunt Bridget opened the door and took Jim through to the dining room where there was a young lady already seated at the table. "Florence, this is my nephew Jim, Jim this is Florence."

"Oh, please call me Flo, everyone does." Jim shook hands amiably with the girl but looked daggers at his aunt. He realised straight away that he had been "set up" and was furious with her.

There was nothing to do but to accept the situation and get on with the evening. Jim was angry but not angry enough to walk out or embarrass the poor girl.

As the meal progressed Bridget kept asking questions of Flo hoping that Jim would be interested in the girl and hoped that he would appreciate the effort she was making for him to meet her. For his part Jim was mortified and not at all happy, presuming that the girl knew that they both had been "set up" by Bridget. He took note of the girl and whilst she was not repellent or repulsive he did consider her unshapely, homely, dumpy even and really quite awkward. He wondered how on earth could his Aunt think that he would be attracted to this girl, but even if he had been attracted to her he was so angry at being tricked into a meeting that he wouldn't have taken the initiative and ask the girl out anyway.

Flo for her part had agreed to attend the dinner knowing exactly why she was there. Bridget had boasted of her nephew's good looks and availability. She had told Flo of his good position in the Department of Immigration and how she thought he was probably lonely and needing a woman in his life. Bridget had been extolling Jim's virtues prior to the dinner and told Flo that she considered Jim a "good catch." As Flo looked across the table she could only agree with Bridget's prior boasting as she too considered Jim quite good looking and probably quite a "good catch."

As soon as it was decent Jim made his excuses and informed his Aunt and Flo that he had an early morning meeting the next day and so should be getting home. He said his farewells and drove home fuming, resolving to ring his Aunt the next day and give her a piece of his mind.

Later Jim tried to recall all the answers that Flo had given to

Bridget's questioning. He couldn't remember anything; he could only remember that he was angry and bored. Flo had nothing interesting to relate, he couldn't remember what occupation she had or what her interests were. He simply wasn't interested and had been consumed with anger and embarrassment. He rang Bridget the next day and berated her for putting him through that trauma. "How could you do that to me Aunt Bridget? I told you before I'll find my own girlfriends, if, as and when I want to. I don't need you to do it for me, I'm not a child. Don't ever do that to me again."

"Oh, I'm sorry Jim, I thought I was doing you favour. Flo is a really nice girl, you should give her a chance." Jim was exasperated and holding the phone in one hand with the other ran his fingers through his hair, trying not to raise his voice, "Look, I know you mean well but please, please let me lead my own life, I don't need any help, and if I do you'll be the first to know. I have to go now but promise me you'll never do that again?" Bridget hesitated and really wanted to help Jim but realised the sense of what he was saying. "Okay, I'll not try and set you up again. I think you're being stubborn and missing out on a really nice young lady, but as you say, it's your life and you should be able to do things your own way."

"Okay, thanks Aunt Bridget, I'll talk to you later. By the way the dinner was really good and the lamb, just brilliant."

10

SAMANTHA

Samantha smiled to herself as she saw Jim bolt out of the door. Many "first timers" at the Fertility Clinic had the same reaction; good first intentions followed by acute embarrassment. It sort of endeared her to him. She decided she liked the look of Jim, he was sort of shy but not critically so, and sort of tall and good looking, but not devastatingly so. She had a good look at his completed file and in particular checked out his "character profile." She discovered that he enjoyed gardening, fishing and was a member of a local judo club and played soccer.

She realised he was not likely to come back to the fertility clinic and thought if she wanted to see him again, and she was interested, then if, as they say, "Mohammed won't go to the mountain, then maybe the mountain must go to Mohammed." Samantha looked up the list of judo clubs in the town and as there were three clubs listed she decided to have a look at each one until she hit upon the one that Jim attended.

Samantha was not particularly athletic but thought she could go along to a judo club and have a look and see what it was all about, maybe it would be something she could have a go at, and meet up with Jim at the same time. It was a good excuse anyway.

After ringing the club secretaries Samantha discovered that

two of the clubs met on a Thursday evening and one on a Monday, all at different venues. The first one she chose to have a look at was on a Monday and she spent half an hour deciding what to wear. She wanted to make a good impression but realised it would be stupid to turn up in a short skirt or tight jeans. Judo was obviously a very energetic, rough and tumble kind of sport and she decided it was probably a good idea to wear a tee shirt on top and some loose trousers on her lower half. Nothing too sexy or provocative, but a close fitting top that would show she was all female.

Samantha turned heads as she walked into the gymnasium asking to see the head coach. There appeared to be about twenty males, ranging from prepubescent teenagers to grey haired elderly veterans. Samantha was relieved to see that there were some females, if only three. She couldn't see Jim there at all. She was welcomed and introduced all round. Everyone was friendly and the class began with gentle exercises. Samantha found she could join in, standing at the back of the class following what the others were doing. The teacher gave Samantha a club jacket and the exercises progressed to tumbling and learning how to land on the ground. Nothing too difficult but quite exhausting as she wasn't used to such exercise.

Eventually Samantha was paired with one of the other girls and so began a series of instructions in techniques for holding down an opponent. Samantha found that she was quite enjoying the lesson, but reminded herself that this was not what she was there for. Jim wasn't there and so decided that the next Thursday she would attend one of the other classes to see if she could see him. However her body was resisting any more exercises for a few days. She had been using muscles that she didn't know she had. For the next three days she could barely move; her body was aching from top to bottom. She felt about ninety years old and realised that she should have taken the class a little easier. It was a full week before she felt she could face another class, but was sensible enough to start doing some gentle stretching and exercising at home in preparation.

Meanwhile Jim was having a minor problem. Two days after the dinner at his Aunt's house he was met as he came out of his office building by the young woman who had been at the dinner, Flo. At first Jim barely recognised her, she had changed her hairstyle from a severe bun to a short bob. She greeted him quite cordially with "Hi there Jim, remember me?" Jim frowned aggressively hoping this meeting was a coincidence and not deliberate. "Hello Flo, yes of course I remember you, but you look quite different."

"Yes I had a haircut, do you like it?" Jim tried to walk past the girl but she fell in step with him as he walked down the steps from his building. "Look Flo, it doesn't matter whether I like your haircut or not. What are you doing here? Are you just passing or did you actually mean to bump into me?" He carried on walking as the girl kept pace. "Well I remember Bridget told me where you work and so I thought I'd just come and give you a gift. I remember Bridget told me that your mother had passed away recently and that you are no great cook so I baked you a cake, here." Flo had in her hand a colourful cake tin with a lid and tried to hand it over to Jim. "No, you shouldn't have done that. I don't want a cake, and I don't want you meeting me at my office." Flo's face sort of crumpled as two tears dribbled down her chubby cheeks. "I'm sorry, I didn't mean to offend you, I was only trying to be friendly." Jim stopped walking and turned to face the girl. "Look, I'm sorry if I appear rude and I do appreciate your offer, you're obviously a kind and caring person but I don't eat cake and I don't want you, or any girl for that matter meeting me outside my office."

"Well maybe we can go somewhere for a coffee or something?"

"No, I'm sorry Flo, I'm really busy and can't do this."

Jim strode off quickly down the road leaving Flo still holding onto her cake tin. He was confused and angry and vowed to ring his Aunt Bridget as soon as he got home. He didn't want this girl pestering him and thought she was crossing a line bringing him a cake, even though it may have been well intentioned.

On the following Thursday Samantha was fully prepared and attended this new class with a certain confidence and a little knowledge. As soon as she entered the hall she saw Jim and he saw her too. His mouth went dry and he could hardly believe his eyes; she, the girl of his dreams was there, at his club. "Was it a coincidence or was she there to see him?" He asked himself.

The coach met Samantha at the door and welcomed her into the club. As he introduced her to the other members it became obvious that she and Jim knew each other. "Oh, that's good you two know each other. Jim can you keep an eye on this young lady then and make sure she is well looked after?" Jim found a spare jacket for Samantha and the class started. It began with a series of warming up exercises and progressed to tumbling and practising how to fall and land after being thrown. Samantha noted with some concern that she was the only girl in the class but it didn't seem to matter and she was treated as an equal with the other enthusiastic pupils who ranged in age from eleven or twelve to a couple of over sixties.

When there was a break for drinks Jim managed to talk to Samantha. "Gosh I never thought I'd see you again. How are you? I didn't know you were interested in judo?"

"Well I have to work late some nights and I was worried about walking home on my own and so I thought it would be good to learn some basic self defence." This excuse seemed to satisfy Jim who really didn't think that Samantha was there just to meet him. He really thought it was just a great coincidence.

The class progressed from exercises to learning some hold down techniques. As they were obviously acquainted the instructor allowed Samantha and Jim to stay together to learn the moves. Jim had always enjoyed his judo and was a competent brown belt, but he had never enjoyed the classes as much as he did on Samantha's first night. At the same time he had never been so nervous and embarrassed.

The hold downs involved quite a fair amount of physical contact and it was impossible for Jim to ignore the fact that he was holding and touching this beautiful woman, and it was legal. Samantha was perfectly aware of the effect that she was having on Jim and realised what discomfort he was feeling at such close quarters holding on to her. As the holding down became more concentrated Jim began to realise that his body was reacting most uncomfortably to her presence. He could smell the subtle perfume from her body and as he needed to put his head close to hers he could smell her hair also. It smelled like apple blossom and his mind was reeling with unfamiliar emotions that he was finding difficult to control. He tried to tell his lower region to behave itself, but his body had a mind of its own and he became acutely aware of a really embarrassing situation. Whilst they were on the ground, going through the hold down techniques it wasn't too bad but he knew it was only a matter of time before the whole group would be instructed to stand up and commence the next part of the class. It would become obvious then how much Samantha was affecting his mind and body. He needed to excuse himself from the class and go to the bathroom and do something about the situation. It was just impossible for him to continue in his present condition.

He released Samantha from the hold down they were learning and getting up from the tatami mat keeping his back to her, excused himself, telling the instructor that he needed a bathroom break. The instructor shook his head and continued with the class unaware of the tension between Samantha and Jim. Samantha smiled to herself and with a woman's intuition thought she knew where and why Jim had suddenly disappeared. Jim resumed his place back in the class, somewhat flushed in the face but much more comfortable.

At the end of the evening, the ever gallant Jim offered to take Samantha home and as she was within walking distance of her house they sauntered along the paths leading to her house, chatting and getting to know each other. Samantha liked Jim; she liked his quiet nature and his good manners. Jim on the other hand was smitten. He was head over heels in love and his next few nights were spent dreaming of how he could progress the courtship and turn it into a real relationship.

Two days passed before a box arrived on Jim's doorstep. It had not been posted and had *"this way up"* written across the top. When Jim took the parcel into his kitchen he was surprised to find that it contained a ceramic casserole with a lid. There was a note inside the parcel which read: *"Dear Jim, I'm sorry if I did the wrong thing by meeting you outside your office, I realise now it was inappropriate, however I'd like to make amends and hope you'll accept this chicken casserole. I know now that you don't like cakes but everyone likes chicken casserole. Anyway I'll pop over to your house tomorrow and collect my dish if that's alright with you. Regards Flo."* Jim was in a quandary.

He was angry at being compromised but actually quite grateful for the casserole. He decided that it would be churlish if he didn't actually eat the casserole, but on the other hand he didn't want to encourage the girl. He had no interest in her whatsoever and so decided that he would eat the casserole, wash the dish and leave it on his doorstep the following day with a note asking the girl not to bring him any more gifts. His note was quite succinct and read, *"Flo. Thank you for the chicken but please do NOT bring me any more gifts, food or anything else. I am not looking for a relationship. Jim."*

The next day was Thursday and so "late night shopping" in Perth. Jim deliberately went shopping for nothing in particular and had a meal at a small restaurant in town. He didn't want to bump into Flo and decided not to actually go home until after ten o'clock.

He had left the clean, washed casserole with the note on his doorstep and hoped that the girl would get the message and leave him alone. When he arrived home he was shocked to find the casserole dish in pieces, shattered on his doorstep. The note was nowhere to be seen and he could only surmise that Flo had deliberately smashed the dish. He went inside and rang his Aunt Bridget. He paced the floor as he waited for his aunt to answer. He was angry, confused and perplexed. When Bridget answered the phone Jim poured out his problem to her, "Aunt Bridget, do you know what you've started? Flo is becoming a real pain, a problem actually."

"Oh come come Jim, what's wrong now, are you exaggerating? What's happened?" Jim related all that had happened and asked, exasperated, "What am I supposed to do Aunt Bridget? I'm not interested in the girl, I just want her to leave me alone."

"Okay, calm down. I have a Pilates class tomorrow, I'll talk to

Flo if she's there. I know I started this, I'm sorry if it's got a bit out of hand but you have to admit the girl is a sweet thing with a heart of gold, she's only trying to be nice to you."

"Well she's becoming a pest. Tell her to leave me alone."

"Okay, okay. Leave it with me."

11

FELIX

The following week Jim was not partnered with Samantha at the judo club and he was beside himself with jealousy when the instructor partnered Samantha with Felix. He could see Felix touching and holding down his beloved Samantha and whilst there was a fiery rage in his heart there was little he could do about it. There was really nothing to it; Felix was only participating in the sport, appropriately, with no ulterior motive and he was not particularly interested in Samantha as he was a happily married man with two children. However jealousy was a green monster residing in Jim's bosom and he felt he would explode if something didn't give.

At the end of the class, as usual the instructor would call up two of the most experienced players and pit them against each other for a short match. On this particular night he called out Jim and Felix. It was just what Jim wanted. He was desperate to punish Felix for laying his hands on Samantha and at the same time his masculinity was on the line and he felt he had to show his beloved just how good a man and an athlete he was. In short, he was going to show off and hopefully impress the woman of his dreams.

Jim felt like a gladiator entering the coliseum about to wrestle the hungry lions and save the fair maiden from being torn apart.

The two were evenly matched, both being brown belts and started the match by the traditional method of bowing to each other and to the instructor who was to act as referee. The rest of the class sat back off the tatami mat and watched, hoping to learn some advanced techniques. The two combatants circled each other before grabbing the lapels of their opponent's gi, the traditional jacket. Each tried to throw the other knowing that a single throw would give them the ultimate ippon, or single point for a direct win. Whilst neither could get the upper hand they pulled and pushed to no avail; eventually Jim tripped and went down on his back. This was not a winning point for Felix and the bout continued with both men on the floor wrestling to get the upper hand. After a while, with both men rolling over and over trying to get a "hold down" Felix managed to grab Jim from behind. Felix crossed his wrists under Jim's chin and held onto Jim's jacket. His knee was in Jim's back and he was basically strangling poor Jim. In the rules of Judo Felix would win the bout if Jim tapped out. That is the sign given that indicates a submission and ultimately the bout is over. Normally Jim would acknowledge defeat by tapping out but now he was being watched by the beautiful Samantha; he wanted to be her champion and there was no way he was going to tap out. His face started to go red and then slightly purple. The watching students started shouting advice to Jim, "Tap out, tap out!" Jim didn't want to tap out he wanted very much to impress Samantha. He struggled and twisted every way he could but Felix had him in a vice like grip and wasn't going to let go.

The instructor jumped in and tapped Felix saying, "Okay Felix, it's over, let go, you win."

Jim was furious, "Coach, you shouldn't have stopped us, I could have got out of that."

"No you couldn't Jim. You must understand like a card player, "know when to hold 'em and know when to fold 'em."

Jim walked Samantha home and complained bitterly all the way. "I could have got out of that hold. Coach shouldn't have stopped us." Samantha just smiled and understood why Jim was so upset. She knew he had wanted to show off and how mortally wounded his pride was and that she should see him defeated. She understood completely.

Up to that point Jim had only met Samantha at the judo club but now he wanted to ask her for a date and really didn't think she would want to see him again after failing to win his match with Felix. He stopped at the gate of her house and decided it was now or never. If she refused him he reasoned it would be because he had lost his match with Felix. He had no idea if Samantha actually liked him or not or was just being friendly. Samantha for her part had a feeling he would be asking her for a date and was looking forward to seeing more of him. He was a strange, quiet, gawky sort of man but she liked him and could see herself in a long term relationship with him, but he wasn't the man to be rushed and she waited patiently for him to ask her out. She knew he had no idea that she had joined the judo club just to meet up with him, and she wasn't ever going to tell him either.

"Err, Samantha, would you like to have dinner with me one night, I know of a nice little restaurant overlooking the river? They do a crispy skinned Atlantic salmon that just melts in your mouth."

"Sure, that sounds great, how about Saturday?"

"Okay, I'll pick you up at seven. I do have a car but I only use it at weekends. I catch the bus to work; the rush hour traffic is just too awful and there's never enough parking. So I'll see you here at seven on Saturday."

When Jim arrived home he checked his mail box and was surprised to find amongst other things an invitation from Flo to a party at the weekend. Apart from arranging to see Samantha on Saturday he really didn't want anything further to do with Flo. The invitation was from her and asked for a R.S.V.P. The invitation gave a phone number and he called it immediately. Flo answered the phone with a cheery "Hello. This is Flo, can I help you?"

"Hi Flo, this is Jim, Bridget's nephew. I got your invitation and I'm sorry to say I can't make your party. Actually I have a girl friend now and I have other commitments. It's probably better that you don't contact me anymore, but thanks for the invite anyway. Must fly, cheers, Jim." Without waiting for an answer Jim put the phone down. He was beginning to feel that Flo's attention to him was somewhat a little over the top and he was decidedly uncomfortable with it all. For her part Flo was not one to be easily put off. She had seen what she wanted, i.e. Jim, a future man in her life, and she was not one to take rejection lightly. She was angry at being dismissed so conclusively. She had hoped that the smashing of the casserole dish on his doorstep had shown that she was not someone to be messed about with. She had to find another way. As Jim had called her on his mobile she knew, with a sly smile that she now had his phone number.

12

ROTTNEST ISLAND

Over dinner Samantha told Jim all about her family and how they had emigrated to Australia from England only a year ago. She was new to Australia and loved it already. She explained that she had been trained as a medical receptionist and was on her third job. She hadn't liked the hospital job and she hadn't enjoyed the blood bank job either, but she was settled now at the fertility clinic and really enjoyed her work there. Her boss and co-workers were all pleasant and friendly people who welcomed her into their fold.

Jim told Samantha all about his work at the Department of Immigration and realised he had probably processed her family's application many months earlier. The two chatted amiably and enjoyed the ambiance of the restaurant overlooking the river and praised the chef on the wonderful salmon that he cooked for them. The chef surprised Jim by telling how he had actually caught the salmon himself, just off the coast. As Jim was a keen fisherman himself the two exchanged ideas about bait and lures.

Towards the end of the meal Jim's mobile phone rang and he apologised to Samantha as he started to turn the phone off. "Sorry about that, I should have turned the phone off earlier." Samantha smiled across the table and answered, "Oh, that's okay, I'm always forgetting to turn my phone off, but maybe you should keep it on, you never know, it might be important." Jim took the phone out of his pocket and asked Samantha, "Well, is it okay if I just check who it was, in case it was my Aunt, she's getting on a bit now and, well, you never know." When Jim checked the number he realised it had been Flo calling him. He certainly didn't want to talk to her but thought it might be a good idea to tell Samantha about the girl and how she was starting to become a nuisance. "Listen Samantha, I need to tell you something. I have a small problem, well, I think it's starting to be a large problem really." Samantha noted Jim's worried look and asked, "What kind of problem, anything I can help with?" Jim took a deep breath and related the problem of Flo from the beginning when he attended the dinner at his aunt's house.

Samantha looked worried and chewed her bottom lip as she tried to think what the woman, Flo was all about. "Well Jim, it's obvious that she has the "hots" for you, it's really a case of what are you going to do about it if she continues to bother you. I mean, did you give her any encouragement, is there any real reason why she should be pursuing you?" Jim shook his head. "No, in fact quite the contrary. I wrote on the note that I left her that I didn't want a relationship. I was even, I'm sorry to say, quite rude to her when she met me with the cake. I even told her I don't eat cake, which is absolutely not true. Honestly I haven't given her any reason to think that I am interested in her, and believe me I'm not."

"Well I believe you but you have to get it across to her if she continues to bother you."

"Okay, can we change the subject now I don't want our evening spoiled by thinking about her." Samantha agreed and nodded thoughtfully as she took a sip of wine.

Jim told Samantha about the social club at work and how they were organising a "firm's outing" the following weekend, and would she like to go with him. The social club had organised for a day trip to Rottnest, or Rotto as everyone calls it, the small island just eighteen kilometres off the coast of Western Australia. Samantha readily agreed to accompany Jim on the day trip to Rottnest. He told her all about the tiny friendly marsupials that live on Rottnest called quokkas and explained how there are no public cars on the island and usually people hire a bicycle to get around the incredibly beautiful bays. He told her all about the crystal clear water and the colourful corals that one could swim around in the shallows. He explained how he would take snorkel and masks for them both so that they could swim amongst the thousands of small fish that inhabit the warm waters. Samantha was excited about the trip and asked all sorts of questions about the island, including how would they get there.

Jim explained that they would meet the rest of the company staff at the ferry station at nine in the morning and the journey across the water would take about an hour. He would pack a picnic lunch and they could take the return ferry at five in the afternoon. He advised Samantha to take her bathers and wear a hat and shorts or trousers as they would hire a bicycle to get around.

Samantha was quite used to riding a bicycle back in England and had no compunction about riding around an island for a day, however Jim hadn't really thought through the exercise. It was actually one of his failings in life; he just didn't completely think through whatever he was planning to do, he took life as it came to him, met it head on and resolved any issues as they arose. He had learned to ride a bike when he was ten years old and assumed that, as they say, "one never forgets how to ride a bike," however the truth of the matter was that after that initial learning phase Jim had never actually ridden a bicycle. He'd always caught a bus and once he got his driving license, driven his car. Bicycles were just something that he'd never had much to do with, but the thought didn't bother him, he was comfortable in his ignorance.

The day of the outing should have been sunny and calm, but unfortunately there had been a tropical cyclone a week before, some way up north, and now the dying effects of that cyclone were being felt in Perth. It was cloudy and windy but not sufficient to cancel the outing.

Most of Jim's work colleagues met at the ferry terminal and there was much banter and good natured laughing as they all looked at the foaming water that the wind had whipped up and considered the rough crossing that they were all about to undertake. Jim had never been good on water, he wasn't comfortable with the motion of a small boat and always kept his fishing activities to the town jetty. He'd been on the water before but only on large ships, car ferries and such. He had once taken an ocean cruise on an enormous ship around the islands of New Zealand, even though the waters were calm he still was not happy with the slight motion of the sea.

However he thought the ferry across to Rottnest would be over in an hour and as it was a fair sized boat it shouldn't rock with the motion of the sea too much. He was sure he would be alright.

As they boarded the ferry Jim could feel the boat heaving from side to side, even tied up alongside the harbour wall. He tried to put his misgivings to one side and concentrated on chatting to Samantha. For her part Samantha loved being on the water. She had emigrated to Australia with her parents only a year earlier and they had travelled by boat. The journey had taken eight weeks calling at various ports around the Mediterranean on the way. It had been a fabulous luxury cruise and a great start to their new life in a new wonderful country.

The ferry left the centre of Perth and made its way down stream to the mouth of the Swan River at Fremantle. Fremantle is a busy port and there were ships and boats of every kind on the river, from small two-man "tinnies" to the large dirty container ships and even two cruise liners. It was a fascinating ride past all the river traffic and most people on the ferry were out on deck admiring the scenery. The boat was gently rocking on the wind whipped small waves. As the ferry came into more open water the sun went behind a cloud and it became quite cool. Jim and Samantha decided it would be more comfortable to find seats inside the large deck cabin, however as soon as the ferry left Fremantle harbour the boat began to roll ominously on the much larger waves. Jim felt his mouth go dry and his head felt light, whilst his face turned a sickly shade of green. He didn't like the pitching of the boat as it proceeded out to sea. The further it got out the more violent the rocking became.

Jim knew he was in trouble. His stomach started doing cartwheels. He needed fresh air and made a dash for the outer deck. As he looked at the mountainous waves crashing into the side of the ferry he knew he was about to lose every vestige of composure, dignity, and his breakfast.

There was nothing he could do about it. Samantha just stood by patting him gently on his back as he heaved and threw up his whole stomach. He was beyond embarrassment; beyond any chance of trying to save his dignity. He just wanted to die, both of shame and of the awful sickness that his wracked body was going through.

An hour can go so slowly when one is in pain, is ill, is wanting to curl up into a ball and just die. He could only repeat, "Sorry, Oh God this is awful, I'm sorry," to Samantha. She had been trained as a medical receptionist and so was not unduly worried about Jim's seasickness; she knew it would pass, and she knew how embarrassing it was for him.

During the course of the journey the friendly captain gave a running commentary informing his passengers about his boat and extolling the virtues of Rotto. He explained that the island was just composed of nineteen square kilometres and was known as Wadjemup by the local Aboriginal people. Samantha listened to the commentary and was quite interested in all the captain was explaining, but Jim was in a world of his own, his misery was all encompassing. As they approached the island the captain outlined some of the history of the island, especially referring to the World War Two defences, and pointed out the various land marks that could be seen. He also showed his passengers a few of the locals that he had noticed frolicking in the shallows, being one or two sea lions and fur seals. Jim could not have cared less if the ferry had actually sunk, he was beside himself with self pity and embarrassment, and of course the journey did come to an end.

Once the ferry had tied up alongside the harbour wall at Rottnest the rocking of the boat ceased. Samantha persuaded the now frail looking, pale faced Jim to walk gingerly and slightly wobbly down to the hotel at the end of the jetty where they ordered a cup of tea. Jim's face started to take on a healthier looking hue and roses reappeared in his cheeks. After a second cup of tea Jim declared himself very much recovered and just kept apologising for his mal de mer. Samantha was supportive and sympathetic; Jim's indisposition had not bothered her at all, in her line of work she had witnessed many patients who were ill and unable to keep food down.

The wind dropped down and the sun came out. It looked as if, after all it was going to be a beautiful day. Samantha asked if Jim felt up to the bicycle ride that he had promised her. She had seen the sign on the wall advertising the hire centre and was keen to get away from the busy hotel and see the much lauded beautiful island. Jim agreed and was looking forward to showing Samantha the cute little quokkas that inhabited the island. They'd just seen one in the distance and were keen to take a closer look.

The man in the hire store fitted the pair out with the right size bikes and helmets and gave them a small map of the island to follow. There was really only one road around the perimeter of the island and so they couldn't really get lost. Jim put his backpack with the picnic into a large basket on the front of his bike and they set off in high spirits.

Samantha had no problem with her riding and took off some metres ahead of Jim, the vanguard trailblazing the way. Jim on the other hand was having some difficulty with his balance; the bike seemed to have a mind of its own. A few metres from the bike store however, the road went down a small hill. Gravity took Jim down this road with no problem and he could feel the gentle breeze wafting through his hair. It was a pleasant feeling and he relaxed as he heard Samantha starting to sing some old-fashioned song about cycling, he'd heard the song before and recognised the tune but couldn't recall the words.

At the end of the small hill the road veered sharply to the left and so began a gently climb. Now Jim had to exert some pressure on the pedals and found cycling wasn't as easy going uphill as it was going down. There appeared in front of him a rut in the road and he swerved violently to avoid it. With his bike top heavy with the back pack, combined with his lack of experience Jim felt himself losing his balance. He put one foot down on the ground and an arm out to cushion his fall but still he couldn't stop himself from falling ignominiously down into the dusty, gravelly side of the road. He yelled from the pain as his upper arm dislocated from his shoulder and the skin was ripped from his elbow and forearm.

It was not Jim's day. As Samantha tried to attend to Jim they both were surprised to see two inquisitive little quokkas hop out of the bush to see what all the fuss was about. In his pain Jim couldn't appreciate the moment, but Samantha did and was delighted to reach out and pat the two little marsupials It was a moment she would never forget.

Two other tourists and three members of Jim's social club at work, who happened to be passing helped Samantha to get the bikes back to the hire shop and to get Jim to the medical centre. There was a two hour wait for attention as some elderly gentleman was having a heart attack and his wife was having hysterics. Many people had been seasick and were also needing medical attention. Eventually Jim had his arm painfully put back into place and was stitched up, bandaged and strapped. He'd tried to be brave but the pain of the relocation of his arm was too much and he gave way to an embarrassing scream as the doctor pulled and pushed on his upper arm. The cleaning out of the gash on his arm and stitching of his torn flesh was no better as he unsuccessfully tried to appear calm and brave. The sight of the needle going into his gash was more that he could stand and unfortunately poor Jim's body let him down again as he fell unmanfully into a short faint. When Jim came to all he could see was his angel of mercy, Samantha, calmly wiping his sweating, fevered brow with a damp cloth.

The day's hell was not over as Jim realised he had to face the return ferry ride over the sea back to Perth. He didn't think things could get any worse, but they did.

It was quite warm for the return journey and so Samantha suggested they stay on the top deck, enjoying the noisy seagulls and the fresh breeze. Jim hadn't eaten any lunch and so thought that it would be impossible to be seasick as he had nothing inside him to throw up. Wrong! The sight of the waves and the motion of the boat churned Jim's poor stomach and he started heaving from the moment they left Rottnest. The retching was worse than any actual being sick. Jim had no idea how he could still throw up food that couldn't possibly still be in his stomach, but he did. He was sick for the first ten minutes of the journey and then spent the remainder of the time dry retching, moaning and groaning. Gone was all thought of romance and trying to impress Samantha. Gone was any vestige of dignity, he was humiliated and mortified. In his shame he daren't even look at Samantha. For her part Samantha sympathised and her mothering instinct took over. She cradled Jim in her arms, trying not to hurt his shoulder and bound elbow. If anything she was not offended or disgusted at Jim's frailty, on the contrary, it endeared him even more to her. He was a big strapping healthy young man, but was human and had flaws like everyone else. A big baby really.

13

BRIDGET AND SAMANTHA MEET

Samantha realised that Jim was so embarrassed by the Rottnest trip that he may not feel that she would want to see him again, but she did, and so rang him the next day and the next to enquire how he was. Jim assured her that he had recovered from the seasickness and his arm was healing. Jim was careful to check his phone each time it rang. He was being pestered three or four times a day by Flo but refused to answer her calls, he didn't know how he was going to stop her calling him and thought that maybe the only solution would be for him to change his phone number. He didn't want to but was considering it as an option.

On Samantha's third phone call he realised that she had not been put off by his unfortunate accident and frailty on the boat, and that his chances with her had not been dashed. He thought he would have one more go at dating her and accepted an offer from one of the guys at work. Jim's workmate Jack had obtained tickets for a show in town but at the last minute had come down with the flu and so offered the tickets to Jim. When Jim rang Samantha to ask if she would like to go to the show she readily accepted. Jim was really surprised that she would want to see him again after the debacle that was the Rottnest trip but she had agreed and so he arranged to pick her up at seven.

As Jim was leaving the house he was confronted by the unwelcome presence of Flo on his doorstep. "Flo, whatever are you doing here? Didn't I make it clear to you before that I'm not interested in a relationship with you and I really want you to leave me alone, and stop calling me on the phone." Flo had in her arms a parcel and held it out in front of her. "Yes, I know you did Jim but I saw this in a shop and I thought you would really like it, so I got it for you," Jim tried to walk past the girl but she stood in front of him with tears in her eyes. "Please take it, I know you'll like it."

"For God's sake Flo, how many times do I have to tell you, I don't want you to give me any gifts, don't buy me anything, don't cook me anything. Don't call me and don't come to my house ever again, I can't say it any clearer. I don't want you in my life. Leave me alone." Flo started crying with tears washing her mascara making tramlines down her face. "Please Jim, just give me a chance."

"No, leave me alone. If you approach me again I'll go to the Police and take out a Restraining Order. I'm serious. Now leave me alone." With that last threat Jim pushed past the girl, got into his car and drove away. He was upset by the encounter and realised if Flo persisted in bothering him he would really have to go to the Police. He didn't want to but felt he had no choice. He tried to put the incident behind him and enjoy the evening. He felt he really should discuss the encounter with Samantha but decided against it as he didn't want to spoil their evening by involving Samantha and then both of them worrying about Flo and her obsession with him.

The show was the stage production of "The Lion King." Neither of them had seen the original film and had heard little about the stage show. Jim vaguely thought it might be a bit childish but was absolutely amazed and fascinated at the production. Samantha for her part marvelled at the costumes, and was astounded and dazzled by the story and the music. At the interval they had a glass of champagne and Samantha's bright eyes were shining with pleasure, excitement and anticipation for the second half. During the second half Jim felt brave enough to take Samantha's hand and was encouraged when she didn't pull back. He was in heaven. He barely paid any attention to the show, he was concentrating only on the tiny hand that he felt in his, on the utter perfection that he knew beyond any doubt was his vision of loveliness, the marvellous Samantha. After the show Jim took Samantha for a coffee and they chatted about the show, until the waiter started to clear the tables away and told the pair that they were closing for the night.

That night was the turning point in the relationship. They both realised that they had strong feelings and Jim for the first time invited Samantha back to his house. When they arrived Jim put the car into the garage and had the strangest notion that they were being watched. He walked down his driveway and checked that no-one was loitering. He couldn't see anyone but he felt decidedly uncomfortable. When they entered the house the first thing that Jim did was to check that all the doors and windows were locked and that the curtains and blinds were all drawn. He dismissed Samantha's questions lightly as to what he was doing as he didn't want to alarm her but his feelings of being watched persisted and he found it difficult at first to focus his attention on Samantha. "I'm just checking that everything's locked up and secure for the night, I usually do that before I turn in." He also had the forethought to turn off his mobile phone as he certainly didn't want to be pestered by Flo; not tonight, not tonight of all nights.

For her part Samantha was nervous about her first night with Jim. She'd had boyfriends before but no-one had appealed to her as much as Jim. They talked for an hour over yet another cup of coffee, finding out more about each other. They both admitted to being no longer a virgin but both confessed that they weren't very experienced either. Samantha sat on the end of his bed and decided to be totally honest and to tell him how she felt. She let him know how special she thought he was and Jim, taking his cue from her abandoned his normal reserve and poured out his heart to her. They both confessed to being a little shy but once Jim turned the bedroom light out all nervous anticipation and thoughts of Flo and her antics melted away.

The next day was a Saturday and as neither Jim nor Samantha had to go in to work Jim decided to surprise Samantha with breakfast in bed. She was still asleep as he carefully crept out of bed, not wanting to wake her and let himself out of the back door. He wanted to make the morning special and so picked a bowlful of rose petals and took them into the kitchen. Once he had checked that there were no bugs in the petals he crept silently back into the bedroom and gently scattered the pink rose petals across the bed. He prepared a tray and proceeded to make coffee and toast. He really would have loved to have made scrambled eggs or something exotic but he had no idea how to cook or make anything more complicated than boiled eggs. Once the toast and coffee was ready he gently woke Samantha and presented her with the breakfast. "Oh Jim, what a lovely surprise. Oh, my goodness where did all these rose petals come from? What a lovely idea; you're quite a romantic I think." Jim threw off his clothes and jumped back into bed for their first breakfast together.

The morning was spent chatting and getting to know each other. There was much laughter and an indecent amount of more lovemaking. Eventually Samantha declared it was time to go home, she had work to do and promised to see Jim the following day.

When Jim opened the front door they were both shocked and surprised to see laid out on the doorstep a cat, very dead and showing obvious signs of having been brutalised. Samantha let out a stifled scream and Jim cursed loudly. He instinctively knew who had put the cat there and reassured Samantha that he would deal with it. Jim took Samantha home and once she was safely inside decided to visit the local Police Station to report the incident.

The Police were extremely understanding as Jim reported all that happened since he first met Flo. However, as the senior Police Office explained to Jim there was no proof that Flo had put the cat there or indeed if she had been the one to kill the cat. Jim was sure of it but had to agree that he had no proof. He did however request that a Restraining Order be taken out against Flo. As Jim had no knowledge of Flo's surname or her address he informed the Police Officer that he would obtain that information from his Aunt Bridget or at the very least from the Pilates class. The Police Office assured Jim that once they had served the Order on Flo that the pestering would stop, as it usually did in these sort of cases.

Jim called in on his aunt on the way home and related all that had happened to him since meeting Flo. Bridget was extremely contrite and explained, "I'm really sorry I got you into this Jim, but honestly I had no way of knowing what Flo was like, I really only ever met her at the Pilates class. She seemed such a nice, sweet young thing, how was I to know she was some kind of nutter? Some kind of stalking nuisance?"

"Well it just goes to show that you shouldn't interfere in other people's lives, I know you did it all with the best of intentions but as it turns out you didn't do either Flo or me any favours."

Bridget poured out a cup of tea for herself and Jim, and offered him a piece of fruit cake. At first she didn't like to tell him that it was a cake that had been given to her by Flo and that Flo was actually starting to bother her as well, but once Jim had eaten a large slice of cake she did actually confess that it was a gift from Flo. Jim spluttered and almost choked as he listened to his Aunt confess that it was Flo's cake he had just eaten. "For Goodness sake Aunt Bridget what are you playing at? Why did you accept a cake from the girl?"

"Well I didn't know the extent of her problem when I accepted the cake, I just thought she was being a good friend and it was her way of saying thank you for the dinner. How was I to know she was going to turn out to be a serial pest? If it's any comfort to you you're not the only one who is being bothered by this girl. I'm beginning to get fed up with her visits and phone calls, hardly a day goes by but what she either calls me or turns up, unannounced on my doorstep."

"Oh no, not you as well. Well that clinches it, give me her full name and address and we're going to take out a Restraining Order on her, for both of us. I think she has a screw loose somewhere. Something's got to be done, that's for sure." Bridget looked at Jim with her head to one side and pushing her hair back from her face suggested once again, "You know Jim, as I told you once before, you need a woman in your life. Not a stalking nuisance like Flo, but a real woman, a girl friend, someone you could learn to love." Jim took a deep breath and decided to tell his Aunt what was happening in his life. "Well, this has absolutely nothing to do with Flo, truly, but actually I have met someone; a really nice, beautiful, intelligent girl. We've been seeing each other a few times now and I really think this is the one for me. In fact I did mention her to you a while ago, she's the one with the long red curls."

"Well Hallelujah for that. Actually I do remember you told me you'd seen a girl with red hair. So tell me all about her, and when am I going to meet her?"

"Oh, I guess soon but not yet. She's called Samantha and she has the most beautiful eyes and the most dazzling smile, and for some unknown reason seems to like me too, I can't imagine why."

"Well good luck to you Jim, you deserve some love in your life, it's been tough this last year for you. I truly hope it all works out for you."

Jim left his aunt's house relieved to have told her about Samantha but worried that the situation with Flo was getting out of hand. It was one thing pestering him but absolutely unforgivable that she was now pestering his Aunt. Armed with Flo's name and address Jim called in to the local Police Station and took out a Restraining Order. The Officer there assured Jim that the issuing of such an order in nearly all cases put an end to the problem.

It was only two days after his visit to his Aunt that Jim received a visit from the Police. The Police Officer explained to Jim that he had read the report on Florence Cummings that Jim had lodged previously, and he had noted that a Restraining Order had been taken out on the girl, he now thought it was probably a good idea if they let Jim know the current situation and what had just happened. Apparently Flo was under the care, as an outpatient, of the local hospital psychiatric clinic.

She attended each week for counselling and had a history of disturbing activities. According to the hospital Flo had attended the clinic and her psychiatrist for their weekly session and in the course of the session there had been a terrible argument, a shrieking screaming match and Flo had apparently taken a pair of scissors and stabbed her psychiatrist. She was now being held in custody awaiting charges and decisions were being made as to where she should be incarcerated, either in jail or in a mental institution., probably the psychiatric ward of the hospital. Apparently the psychiatrist was badly hurt but in a stable condition in the hospital and was expected to make a full recovery. Jim was shocked and sorry for the poor psychiatrist who was only doing her job, but nevertheless relieved that Flo was now, hopefully out of his life, and out of his aunt's life.

Jim thought about what his Aunt had said and decided to "kill three birds with one stone." He wanted to let his Aunt know what had happened to Flo and at the same time he wanted to let Samantha know as well. Also he thought it was possibly a good excuse to introduce Samantha to his Aunt. As he knew he couldn't cook anything decent he decided to invite both his Aunt and Samantha out to a city restaurant for an introductory and celebratory dinner. Jim rang both women and booked a table for the following evening. He was unexpectedly quite nervous and fervently hoped that the two people who were now the most important people in his life, would like each other and get on well.

Unbeknown to Jim both women were also acutely worried and nervous at the proposed meeting. Bridget fervently hoped that the girl, this Samantha would be a decent girl, respectable and someone Jim could really love and be proud of. For her part Samantha was also thinking with some trepidation about this meeting with Jim's Aunt. She realised that since his mother had passed away his Aunt was a very important presence in his life and sincerely hoped that Bridget would approve and endorse their relationship.

All their fears were unfounded. The two women put their fears behind them and chatted animatedly all through the meal, finding out about each other and liking what they saw. Jim was circumspect with his alcohol intake as he remembered that he was to be driving his Aunt home later, but the two girls enjoyed the wine which helped them to forget their nervousness at the meeting and to relax in each other's company. The menu was quite extensive and as each ordered something different they laughed as they agreed to taste each other's food choices. Bridget was intrigued with Samantha's work at the Fertility Clinic and neither Jim nor Samantha volunteered the knowledge the Jim had attended the clinic to give a donation. However Bridget did ask Samantha how the two had met and was delighted to hear that they had met when Jim had become a blood donor.

Jim informed the two about his visit from the Police and related the information about Flo and how she had stabbed the poor psychiatrist. The two women were duly shocked with this development but all agreed the demented girl was now, thankfully out of their lives.

The remainder of the meal went pleasantly, with both women drinking maybe a little more alcohol than they would normally, and when Jim took his Aunt home she confessed that she had been apprehensive about meeting Samantha but relieved to discover that she actually liked the girl and highly approved of his choice. She agreed that Samantha was exquisitely beautiful and had a lovely personality. "I can see why you have fallen in love with Samantha, she is a really delightful person, you have great taste in women obviously. You know Jim I realise now I'm useless as a matchmaker. You managed to do a much better job on your own and you were right, you don't need any help finding the right girl for you, not from me or anyone else. I truly hope you can learn to love each other and that you don't stuff it up by doing something stupid."

"Who me? What do you mean, doing something stupid?"

"Well, just make sure you do everything right."

"I will, I will."

14

SOCCER

At the fertility clinic there were twelve young women working in various capacities from receptionist to councillors and pathologists. They were a close knit friendly group and one girl being overweight and had decided to try and get fit in order to lose some weight. There was a park at the back of the clinic and she encouraged the girls to join her each lunchtime in the simple exercise of kicking a ball and running around the park. As the running and kicking became more strenuous the girls took off any jackets or jumpers and left them in two piles. The exercises then became a little more structured and someone suggested they play a modified and simple game of soccer, using the jackets on the ground as goal posts. Although the girls had no soccer skills whatsoever they all enjoyed these games. After a few weeks one of the girls suggested that they form an actual soccer team. There was a women's league and they could have fun at the weekends if they wanted to have a go.

All the girls agreed to sign up and form a team, but they had no real idea or understanding of the basic rules of the game. Jane took the initiative and suggested that before they sign on to the league they should find someone to coach them and teach them the rudiments of the game. Samantha remembered that

Jim played soccer and suggested that if no-one else had anyone in mind she could ask him if he would be prepared to help the girls.

Jim was unprepared for Samantha's request and explained that he was no coach; he only played in an amateur local league and was really not that good. He really didn't think he would be any use as a coach and was really quite nervous at the prospect of trying to lead a group of young women. He knew the rules and how to play soccer of course, but he had never tried to explain things to anyone else. Samantha begged and pleaded; they had no-one else and really needed someone to teach them everything about the game.

Jim did his best to refuse but Samantha was so appealing, so beautiful, she pleaded so pitifully he couldn't find it in his heart to refuse her anything. Eventually he gave in and agreed to meet the girls at Samantha's home the following Sunday to assess the situation and try to get the group organised.

Samantha asked all the girls to meet for coffee at her home on the Sunday morning when she would introduce them to Jim and they would discuss if forming a team was a viable option and how they would proceed. For his part Jim was terrified of meeting so many girls all at once. He had never been a leader of anything and was always happy letting someone else take the lead. Now it seemed, these girls expected him to not only teach and train them but to organise them into a cohesive group.

After introductions Jim realised he could recall absolutely no-one's name and that would have to be the first step. He asked Samantha if she could find him some sticky labels. She ducked into the kitchen and came out with a pack of "stick-its." Jim asked all the girls to print their names clearly and put a "stick-in" on their shirt so that he could learn their names. After asking the girls three or four times to stop chattering and giggling and to settle down he asked if the team had a name. Everyone looked at him blankly. "Well you have to have a name. Anyone got a suggestion?" A barrage of names came at him from all quarters and so Jim held up his hands, "Stop. You can't all talk at once. Now, one at a time, suggestions please."

"How about 'the rabbits?' I like that."

"No, that's poncy."

"How about 'The Gals?' After all we're all girls aren't we?"

"No that's stupid."

"How about 'The Navy Knickers?' We all used to wear navy knickers when we were at school."

"I didn't, my school uniform meant we had to wear green knickers."

Everyone had a suggestion and so Jim asked Samantha if she could get him some pens and some paper.

Once everyone had a piece of paper and a pen Jim asked them to put their suggested team name on the paper. He collected the pieces of paper and slowly read out the suggested names. "Now I want you to vote on the name that you think is best. Put your vote on another piece of paper and we'll see which name has the most votes." Once the girls had written their vote Jim collected the papers and counted the names voted for. "Well that's a bit stupid, it appears we have twelve girls, twelve suggested names and twelve different votes. Are you girls just voting for your own suggestion?" Everyone started giggling and trying to persuade the girls next to her to vote their way. Jim held up his hands, "Girls, quiet! Now vote again and this time you're not allowed to vote for your own suggestion. Try and think of a name that's strong, that would put fear into the opposition, something like sharks, or lions, I know other teams have those names, so don't use those, but think of something original, something that would imply you are a strong team, not a group of rank amateurs."

"But we are amateurs, we don't know what we're doing yet."

Jim crossed is arms and sat down saying, "I know but you will. A good name is just a start, so vote and don't forget, don't vote for your own suggestion. If you can't decide then I'll make the decision for you."

Jim collected the votes and counted them out on the table, "Here we go, twelve girls, twelve votes, twelve different names. Honestly girls, have you all voted for your own suggestions again?" None of the girls, even Samantha looked him in the eye. "Right, you all voted for your own suggestions didn't you? Well I'll give you a name and I don't want any complaints. We'll call this team The Wyverns."

"The what?"

"The Wyverns."

"What's that mean?"

"Well a wyvern is a mythical two legged winged dragon with a barbed tail."

Jane smiled, "Okay, I quite like that, especially the bit about the barbed tail, I guess it might mean we could have a sting in our tail."

"Exactly so, and no arguments. You had your chance and you blew it, so Wyverns it is. Now I'm going to go through the basic rules of the game, so quiet everyone and listen carefully."

Belinda, the overweight initiator of the whole idea piped up with, "But what about our colours, what colours are we going to play in?" Jim drew the back of hand across his forehead and took a deep breath. "We can discuss colours later. Let's get on with learning the rules."

"No, I want to know now, if you're going to make us wear green

I won't play, I hate green, it makes me look pasty." Jim could feel himself getting exasperated, "What's your name? Oh, Belinda, look let's decide on colours later, we can agree not to make you play in green if you like, but honestly let's get to learning the rules, okay?"

"Well if you promise not to make me wear green."

"Okay, okay."

"Oh, and while I think about it I want to play in a nice little pleated skirt, the hockey team at the Rec. centre play in red pleated skirts and they look real dinky" Jane agreed with Belinda but put in her two pennyworth, "I like the idea of a pleated skirt too but the girls in the netball team play in really cute little dresses with sort of circular skirts, and they have matching knickers too. I like that idea." Jim took a deep breath, trying to keep calm. "No, if you're playing soccer you have to play in shorts."

"Who says so?"

"I do. Now can we get on with things?" Belinda's bottom lip started to quiver but she got a stern look from Samantha and decided not to say anything more.

Jim spent the next hour explaining the basic rules of soccer and at the end of the session was exhausted. It was difficult keeping the girl's attention and maintaining the focus of the instructions. The girls kept interrupting with silly questions and objections. Eventually Jim agreed to meet the girls on the following weekend at the local sports field where he knew there were goal posts and no teams playing on Sundays. During the preceding week he organised with Samantha to purchase half a dozen soccer balls and some plastic coaching cones, called witch's hats.

The girls had been asked to assemble at nine o'clock and at nine fifteen only three girls had arrived. Jim was frustrated but remained calm as little by little the other girls dribbled in, the last one at nine thirty five. Once Jim had all the girls there he spoke firmly but seriously to them. "Now listen girls, if you say you'll be here at nine, please be here at nine, not ten past or quarter past. Nine on the dot. If you're going to be a team you have to be disciplined. Got it?"

"Yes coach." They all chorused. Jim looked at the last two girls who had just arrived, "For goodness sake you two, whatever your names are, what have you got on your heads?"

"I've got rollers in my hair, I've got a date tonight and I've got to look my best." Jim rolled his eyes heavenwards, "Well, you can't wear rollers in your hair, it's too dangerous."

"Why is it dangerous?"

"Well if you bump into someone you don't want to poke their eyes out, do you?"

"I suppose not. Anyway if I can't wear my rollers what about Amy, she's got curlers in her hair."

"Amy, I've no idea what the difference is, curlers or rollers, but whatever it is, get them off, out or whatever you do, get rid of them."

"But, coach?"

"No buts, get rid of them, NOW." Amy turned to Samantha and whispered under her breath, "Gosh he's a bossy breaches isn't he?"

"I heard that, and yes, I'm a bossy breaches. Look if you want me to be your coach I have to be bossy, you have to accept it, alright? All of you; alright?" No-one answered and Jim just nodded his head at their acquiescence. "Right let's start with a warm up run around the perimeter of the field."

"What, all the way round?"

"Yes, all the way round."

Five girls took off in one direction and seven girls in the other. Jim could see some of the girls only got half way round the field when they started to walk instead of running. He yelled at them to run but no-one was taking any notice of him. Two of the girls actually sat down on the grass three quarters of the way around puffing and panting, not being used to such exertion. Two others stopped to chat to a couple of young men who just happened to be passing. Jim made a mental note to bring a whistle with him the following week.

Once all the girls were back Jim asked them to pair up and takes one ball between the two. He wanted them just to practise gently kicking the ball to each other. There was much discussion as to who would pair up with whom. Jim shook his head and shouted, "Girls, it doesn't matter who teams up with whom, it's just a simple exercise."

"Yes but Jane's my best friend."

"It doesn't matter!" Jim tried not to shout but was getting quite exasperated.

Some girls separated and tried kicking the ball some twenty metres away from their partner. Jim called them all to order and stated, with much patience, "Girls I want you to just stand about three metres from each other and gently kick the ball. Got it?"

"Yes coach." With each kick the balls went wide and there was much scurrying backwards and forwards picking up the ball and getting back into place. Jim called them to order and showed them how he wanted them to gently kick the ball to their partner.

Tall skinny Kelly had retrieved the ball from a fierce kick and approached Jim moaning and bewailing, "Jim I can't play any more I've broken a nail."

"For God's sake Kelly, its football, you don't need to touch the ball."

"But I've got a date with George Mason tonight; I can't go with a broken nail."

"Put a false nail on. Now get back into line with the others."
Kelly showed two interested girls her broken nail and they all sympathised, giving advice as to how to apply a false nail. Jim looked to Samantha for support and implored, "Can we all get back to the exercise please?"

The next few weeks were a nightmare for Jim, if he hadn't loved Samantha, and if he hadn't wanted to impress her so much he would have given up trying to get these girls into any shape or form that could be called a team. However, slowly the girls did start to improve and learn the rules of the game and how to kick a ball.

At one of the training sessions Kelly stopped and was messing about with her eyes. Jim thought she must have something in her eye and so ran over to assist her. "What's wrong Kelly? Have you got something in your eye?'

"No Jim, it's just one of my false eyelashes has come adrift, it's not sticking properly."

"For crying out loud Kelly, why have you got false eyelashes on? We're trying to play soccer not doing a fashion parade."

"You don't understand Jim, sometimes there are boys watching us, I always like to look my best, I've got such little eyes, I need false eyelashes to make them bigger and better."

Exasperated, Jim called the girls in towards him for a stern talk, "Now look girls, I know you want to look your best, you are females after all, but this is soccer, a sport, you can't be thinking all the time about what you look like. Try and be more professional, more sporting, less girlie, girlie, if you know what I mean. And whilst I'm at it, Belinda, I don't want to single you out but honestly do you think you could wear a sports bra, or something stronger?"

"What do you mean?"

"Well without putting too fine a point on it, you're jiggling around a fair bit, it's not good for you. It's not good for your chest muscles or tendons." Belinda turned to Samantha and asked simply, "Can he say that to us? Isn't that sexual harassment?" Samantha didn't know how to respond and simply looked to Jim for an explanation. Jim strode over to Belinda and addressed her face to face, "No it's not sexual harassment or any other kind of harassment. You, in fact all of you, can you start to wear sports bras or at least strong bras, something that gives you good support, it's for your own good and remember, no false eyelashes, no curlers and no rollers in your hair. Okay."

"Yes coach." They all chorused with little enthusiasm.

Training continued unabated and they were starting to accept Jim's authority and fairly strict rules. The biggest problem the team had was positioning. No-one wanted to play on the wing and no-one wanted to be the goalkeeper. As Jim tried to get each girl to try out for the position of goalie, most refused, and those who didn't actually refuse stood in the goal mouth with their arms crossed and hardly made any attempt to stop a ball from crossing the line. Little Amy who was half Asian, stood in the goal mouth terrified of being hit and let out a blood-curdling scream when a ball actually hit her on her shoulder as she turned to try and avoid it. Jim tried to calm her down and assured her she was not hurt and knew he was going to have a problem getting just one of the girls to stay and be the goalie.

Jim talked over the problem with Samantha and implored her to be brave and help him out by offering to take the position of goal keeper. Samantha, like the rest of the team, really didn't want to play in the goal mouth, but for Jim's sake agreed, but only temporarily. She suggested that once they started playing against other teams that the girls should take it in turns to play goalkeeper. Jim readily agreed and put it to the girls the following week. Everyone looked sulky and muttering under their breath talked it out with each other. They all agreed that it was the fairest thing to do, but still no-one wanted to do it.

Jim put the girls through their paces throughout that winter and even though it wasn't the soccer season, he trained them through the summer too. He had infinite patience and good naturedly yelled at them when they didn't seem to understand his instructions.

"Look girls I want you to put out three sets of two cones, about six feet apart, and have four girls to each cone set. Now one of you take a ball and dribble it around the cone and then pass it back to the next girl. Got it?"

"Yes coach," and so two sets of three cones would be put out and there would be squabbles as to who would play with whom. "No girls, listen; I want three sets of two cones, not two sets of three cones." Some teams would have three girls, and some would have five. Jim's whistle could be heard across the field blasting away every few minutes. He was hoarse barking orders at the girls but never gave up on them. He asked Belinda to kick the ball to Susie who was a frail teenager who always looked as if she was anorexic, but could and would eat as much as the others after each training session. "Belinda, I want you to kick the ball to Susie, and you Susie I want you to turn the ball and then dribble it up the field past two defenders. Okay?"

"Yes Coach"

"And you Jane and Kelly get out there, further up the field and try to take the ball from her."

"How will we do that Coach?"

"You tackle her of course; don't touch her, just move your feet to get the ball from her."

"Right ho Coach." The girls ran up the field and so began twenty minutes of pandemonium. To start with Belinda couldn't kick the ball straight enough for Susie to catch it, and when Susie did eventually catch the ball she would attempt to kick it but invariably kept missing it. "No Susie, I want you to stop the ball and then turn it."

"Well how am I supposed to turn it?"

"With your feet. Stop the ball, then turn around and kick it softly as you run up the field." The minute Susie got near Jane and Kelly she just stopped running and let them take the ball. "No Susie, you've got to try and get the ball past them. Don't stop, just keep manoeuvring the ball so that they can't get it." Susie burst into tears. "I can't do it. I don't know how to do it. I'm just stupid."

"No you're not. Let's try again."

And so the practise session went, like so many others. Jim exasperated, trying to keep calm and not upset the girls. The girls doing their best but never actually looking like soccer players. As the weeks wore on though they did make some progress and what was even more important, they started to enjoy themselves. The girls were all becoming firm friends and they all liked Jim and tried their best to please him. The training sessions were never easy for Jim, if he asked for all the balls to be given to him before starting another exercise the balls would be sent in all directions, very few ever arriving at his feet as he intended. Every week at least one girl complained that her hair was being messed up or her finger nails were just ruined.

Jim learned to take no notice of their complaints and pushed them along as much as he could. Whenever the girls got grumpy and mutinous with Jim, Samantha would step in and calm the waters. They needed Jim and all realised that they couldn't sign on as a proper team without Jim's help and coaching.

Eventually the start of the winter season was looming and Jim signed the team as the Wyvern's into the local novice women's league. They'd had to decide on a team strip and colours. There was much debate and no two girls could agree. Some wanted stripes, some multi coloured shirts, some simply white shorts and shirts. Eventually Jim made the decision, "Honestly girls it's not so difficult, we'll just have everybody in black and that's that. You had your chances to agree, so as you can't agree I've decided. It's black. End of discussion." Everyone pulled a face but no-one was brave enough to actually complain out loud.

The last training session before the start of the season Jim put all the girl's names into a hat and told them that he was going to pull out the first name and that would be the goalkeeper for the first game. Also he would pull out a name and that girl would be the substitute for that game. Everyone was happy except big Belinda who was selected as the goalkeeper. The goalkeeper had to wear green and she complained bitterly. "You promised me I wouldn't have to wear green."

"Yes I know, sorry about that but the rules for this league state that the goalie has to wear green, it's the rules. Next week, and the weeks after you'll just be wearing black like everyone else."

'Well it's not fair, I don't like green, it makes me look pasty." Jim took a deep breath trying his best to remain calm.

The day of the first match approached and Jim watched the television listening for the weather forecast. The forecasters predicted grey skies with a chance of rain. That happened to be the understatement of the year. Once the game started the heavens opened and it just bucketed down. Up to that point the girls had been excited, with nervous anticipation, but once the first few drops of rain fell their enthusiasm disappeared. Four of the girls groaned constantly about how their hair was being "absolutely ruined," The ground became soggy and eventually muddy. They slipped and skidded on the slippery grass. The opposing girls were a more experienced team but they too found it difficult to play a decent game in those conditions. In frustration, as she was being tackled, Jane pulled the hair of the girl who was opposing her. The referee blew his whistle and Jane was given a yellow card. She complained bitterly, "That's not fair Ref. It was an accident. I was slipping in the mud and I only grabbed her hair to stop myself from falling over." The referee was not listening and gave her a stern warning, telling her if she did that again she would be sent off.

At the end of the game the Wyverns lost three nil. Jim was ecstatic, he had expected his team to lose by a much larger margin. He congratulated the girls on a good effort and told them to shower, clean up and then he would treat them all to lunch on the way home. In the small café there was so much laughter and good natured ribbing that Jim realised his girls were now a team. They hadn't been happy playing in the rain but now they were all glowing with good health and enthusiastically looking forward to the next game.

The Wyverns played four league matches before they scored their first goal. Anyone would think they had won an Olympic gold medal. It was almost at the end of the game. All the girls hugged and kissed each other and they made such a fuss of little Amy who was the one who actually put the ball into the net that the opposing team were bewildered, it was as if the Wyverns had won the whole match. The opposition kept asking each other if the match was over, and had the Wyverns won.

The main problem with the Wyverns was not that they couldn't kick goals, which actually they couldn't; they tried very hard but mostly goals were just eluding them. They started to get one or two but not enough to ever win a game. No, the main problem was that they didn't have a goalkeeper. No-one wanted the job and as each week rolled on and the girls had to take it in turns to play goalie, they would make no real attempt to stop the ball. They were all afraid of getting hurt and so stood passively by watching the ball roll into the net, with little or no effort to stop it. Jim was tearing his hair out not knowing what to do. He shouted at whoever was playing goalie, to no avail.

He tried coaching them all into the finer points of goalkeeping but no-one was interested. Each week the match would have a score board that read more like netball than soccer. Eleven nil, twelve one, thirteen nil. It was embarrassing but there was nothing he could do about it. That is until Amina came onto the scene.

Samantha and Jim were still attending the judo class once a week and Samantha was progressing nicely. She had progressed from a novice white belt to a beginner's yellow belt. It was half way through the soccer season and a young lady walked into the judo club asking if she could join. This was no ordinary new member, this was a seasoned player who was already a brown belt. Amina had newly arrived as an immigrant from New Zealand. She was a native Maori, tall, a fraction over six foot and was heavy set, actually built like a ten ton truck. She had short cropped hair and tattoos which stretched from just under her mouth, down her chin, around her neck and across her chest and down her arms. They were thick tattoos covering her arms completely. The whole sight of Amina was overwhelming, overpowering and intimidating. She was a big,

big girl and everyone at the club was overawed by the sight of her. However she proved to be genuinely friendly, quick and agile and incredibly light on her feet. Samantha, being the only other girl in the club struck a friendship with Amina straight away.

Samantha had an idea and talked it over with Jim on the way home after the second week that Amina had come into the club. She wondered if they could persuade Amina to join the soccer group. They desperately needed a goal keeper, someone who was large and fearless. Amina seemed to fit the bill, but would she be willing, would she actually want to play soccer? Samantha chatted to Amina the following week and asked if she had ever played soccer. Amina knew the game but had never actually played, or even thought about playing. "Soccer's not so very popular in New Zealand you know," she explained. "Everyone there's rugby mad, it's almost a religion with us Kiwis."

Amina was new to Australia and so hadn't had time to form any friendships and so readily agreed to join the soccer club, mostly in order to meet other girls and make some new friends. Jim agreed to coach Amina in the finer points of goalkeeping for three or four nights before introducing her to the Wyverns. As he practised with Amina, just the two of them he realised he had a winner. Amina was not the slightest bit afraid of getting hit by the ball and threw herself across the goalmouth with great enthusiasm. She was light on her feet and had quick reactions. She would punch the ball out of the way with her big beefy fists and enjoyed the thrill of making a good save. Jim gave her plenty of encouragement and realised this girl would be the greatest asset to the group.

Jim and Samantha introduced Amina to the girls at the next practise session and everyone crowded round the poor girl asking her all sorts of questions. Where was she from, how long had she been playing soccer, was she going to stay in Australia and every other question they could think of. They were all so grateful that they now had someone willing to play goalie which absolved them all from the one position that they uniformly hated. Amina became popular very quickly and even more so following the next league game. The Wyverns didn't win as they didn't score any goals, but the opposition sent many, many balls towards Amina in the goal mouth. She dived and jumped, saving all but one. It was the best result the team had achieved up to that point. They lost one nil but rejoiced as if it was the English Cup Final.

After the game Jim treated them all to a hamburger and chips at the local fast food outlet. Jane helped bring the food to the table and looking straight at the very thin Kelly pushed a plateful of chips towards the girl declaring, "Get that lot into you Kelly, you're so skinny, we need to get some meat on your bones." Kelly looked around the table and folded her arms defensively across her almost flat chest saying assertively, "listen Jane, I know you think you're giving me some good advice, telling me to eat more but I can't help being thin. Whilst you lot are always on about how you want to lose weight, well I can't help being thin. My mother is thin and so is my father. It's in my genes. And really it's rather rude making personal comments like that, I mean, would you tell Belinda she's fat? No, you wouldn't would you? That would be insulting, so how come it's alright for you to call me skinny?"

"Gosh, sorry, I didn't know you were so sensitive."

"Well I am so cut it out." Jim could see an argument starting and so jumped in to calm the waters. "Quiet girls, now I want you all to raise your glasses; yes, I know it's only orange juice, but let's drink a toast to almost the end of a really good season of soccer. You've all done really well and I'm proud of you all. You've only got one more game, so let's give it all you've got" The girls all toasted the end of the season and peace was restored to the group.

The actual best result that the team had was that very last game of the season. They were playing the Rovers and as the opposition arrived it heartened the Wyverns to see that the opposition were all quite small and timid looking. The game see sawed back and forth with eventually both teams scoring one goal each. Amina saved six attempts at goal and felt a glow of satisfaction as the girls screamed with enthusiasm and joy as she punched the ball away. The game finished with a draw and for the Wyverns this was absolutely wonderful. They'd lost every match up to that point, but this was a draw and they celebrated with whoops of joy. They came off the field patting each other on the back and every one of them gave Jim a big hug with broad grins on their grimy faces.

That first season finished with the Wyverns at the bottom of the ladder in the league but everyone agreed that it had been fun and they all couldn't wait for the next season.

15

FISHING

Jim and Samantha had been dating for just over a year and Jim knew she was the girl for him. The one and only girl he had ever had serious feelings for. As the winter gave way to spring Jim wanted to get back to do some fishing. It had been his hobby for many years and he always enjoyed bringing fish home for his mother to cook for their supper. Since his mother had passed away and since he had met Samantha fishing had been put on the back burner. There were so many other things to do, but with the soccer season over he thought it would be a good idea to get some fishing in.

He asked Samantha if she would like to go fishing at the weekend, not in a boat but from the small town jetty. Samantha confessed she had never been fishing before but knew it was something Jim had really enjoyed in the past and so readily agreed. She warned Jim that she knew nothing about fishing and that he would have to show her how it was done. It was just what Jim wanted; a chance to show Samantha just what a man he was. This was something he could do and he knew he could do it well. He wasn't exactly a show-off but he wanted to show her that he could excel at something and impress her with his manhood.

The weekend was forecast to be cloudy but no rain and no wind, perfect. Jim sorted out his fishing tackle and cleaned up his second best rod for Samantha to use. They set off early in the morning and Jim had bought various packets of bait from the supermarket along with a bag of flour and oil that he had mixed up to make his special brew of burley.

There was only one other person on the jetty, a large well built swarthy man with piercings and tattoos. He had on a bikie leather jacket and looked quite intimidating. Samantha would have been afraid of the man, he did look quite scary but she was with Jim and so had no real worries. The man watched with some amusement as Jim put together the rods and tried explaining how to cast out to Samantha. She had some difficulties getting the hang of the cast. Each time she swung the rod out she kept forgetting to release the line and the whole rig ended up at her feet. It took all Jim's patience and control explaining and showing Samantha how to do it correctly. Over and over he showed her. Eventually she got the hang of it and had a few practise casts before Jim actually baited up her line.

Samantha didn't really like the smelly slimy squid that Jim put on her line but it was infinitely better than the little fish which just disintegrated when she tried to put it on the hook. Jim gave her some river prawns also to use as bait and Samantha was surprised and shocked when she saw the price tag on the packet. 'You know Jim you could have bought ordinary prawns at the supermarket for a fraction of this price." Jim laughed and explained, "You could be right Sam but river prawns are better than ocean prawns, I don't know why, they just are." Both Jim and Samantha eventually got their lines into the water and sat on their foldaway stools waiting for a bite. Jim was able to cast his line out much further than Samantha but she was content to have her line out only a few metres from the jetty. The bikie left them alone and concentrated on his own efforts to catch a fish. After Jim released handfuls of burley Samantha watched the clear water, fascinated by the hundreds of little fish that quickly devoured the burley. Jim explained that those particular fish were blowies and as such a terrible nuisance to fishermen. They had voracious appetites and irritatingly frequently took one's bait. Samantha thought they looked cute and asked, "Why are they a nuisance, they look like sardines, couldn't we catch a load and cook them for tea?"

"Heavens no! They are poisonous. If you do catch one they have big teeth and a terrible bite. They are called blowies because they blow themselves up into a sort of spiky ball. They're horrible and don't try and touch one. If you catch one I'll take it off the hook for you. I use nippers and a large cloth, that's the only way you can get them off the hook."

Just as Jim had predicted they caught one or two blowies and after taking them gingerly off the hook threw them back again. The bikie was also having a problem with the blowies and they could hear him cursing and swearing as he struggled to get the hook out of the mouth of one particularly large one.

After half an hour no-one had caught a proper fish, neither the bikie nor Jim, and Jim was starting to think that they might pack it in and call it a day however suddenly Samantha gave a short yell. "I think I've got something." Her line was tight and her rod was moving ominously up and down.

"Hang on, hold it tight." Jim ran to her side. The rod now started moving sideways, back and forth, and Samantha was struggling to hold onto the rod. "Do you want me to take your rod?" Jim offered.

"No. I can do this." Samantha started to reel her line in with much struggling and laughing. "It's a fish, I can feel it."

Much to the chagrin of both Jim and the bikie Samantha pulled in a beautiful silver tailor fish. It flopped energetically up and down on the wooden jetty before Jim pounced upon it with the towelling cloth that he had brought. Once immobilised he showed Samantha how to extract the hook from its mouth and then put the poor fish into a bucket of water. The fish splashed and thrashed but couldn't escape the bucket. Jim gave Samantha a "high five" and congratulated her on her catch. The bikie looked aggrieved but turned his back to the pair as he renewed his efforts to also catch a fish.

Within five minutes Samantha got another bite and pulled in a large herring. "This is fun. I like fishing, can we keep these and cook them for tea?"

"Absolutely, that's what we're here for."

A further ten minutes passed and again Samantha let out a yell of surprise, "Oh my goodness gracious me, I think I've got another one." Again she pulled in a beautiful large tailor and was jumping up and down with excitement. The bikie in absolute disgust and frustration yelled at the two, "bloody women, beginner's luck. F...... you!" He promptly packed up his gear and stormed off, back down the jetty and left with many bad tempered disgruntled mutterings. Both Jim and Samantha laughed but in his heart Jim felt the same way as the bikie. He had wanted to impress Samantha with his prowess at fishing and instead he had failed to catch anything decent, only one or two blowies. He was glad for Samantha's success but disappointed that he hadn't been able to show off to her. He wanted to be her hero and didn't want her to think he was a failure. For her part Samantha was happy and glowing with success. She kissed Jim and thanked him for bringing her and introducing her to fishing.

"It's great, I love it. I'm getting hungry though, I think we should call it a day and go home."

As they walked along the edge of the beach back to the car park the whole ocean took on a different hue in the fading light of the sunset. A soft shade of pink slowly turned the water into a golden red as the large orb of setting sun slowly sank into the horizon. Samantha stood for a while at the edge of the water fascinated by the mesmerizing spectacle. "I don't think I've ever seen anything so beautiful in my life before." She whispered.

"Oh I have," retorted Jim, "And I'm looking at her now."

Samantha loved fishing even more that evening after Jim had gutted and cleaned the fish. They cooked the three for dinner with lashings of Tartare sauce and chips and Samantha declared it the best meal she'd ever had.

16

OUTBACK AUSTRALIA

J im had owned his old car for many years but with Samantha in his life he decided it was probably time he upgraded. Nothing too flash, but something he could take her out to town in and possibly also take her further out; maybe go camping, show her outback Australia. He advertised his old car and sold it within the week. He knew it wasn't worth too much but enjoyed haggling over the price and eventually settled with the buyer coming up from his first offer and Jim agreeing to lower his first asking price. Both were happy and Jim was paid in cash.

Jim asked the guys at work if anyone knew of a reasonable car that would be safe to take out into the bush. There was much discussion at lunchtime, everyone had a different opinion but they all agreed that Jim should look for a four wheel drive vehicle, and if they wanted to camp out it would be easier if the vehicle was a camper, rather than setting up a tent each night. This seemed reasonable but finding a four wheel drive that was also a camper proved to be quite difficult. There was hardly anything around that fitted the bill, other than brand new vehicles which Jim thought were far too expensive.

Eventually one of the guys brought an advertisement in the

local paper to Jim's attention. It was advertising a Mazda Bravo four wheel drive which had been converted to a camper with a pop up roof. Not too expensive and absolutely ideal. Jim offered five hundred dollars below the asking price and was surprised and elated as his offer was immediately accepted. Both Jim and Samantha agreed to take their annual holiday leave together and go somewhere interesting.

Samantha had never been out of the city and was worried about the stories she had heard of outback Australia. "What about the snakes and spiders? What about the poisonous plants? What about the tics? What about the mosquitoes, the kangaroos, the wasps, the sharks, the flies, the midges, and the toads? What if we get lost, how will anyone know where we are and how will they find us?"

"Oh for Goodness sake woman. We'll be fine. I've lived here all my life and never seen a snake. The kangaroos don't hurt you; if they see you at all they run away, or in their case they hop away."

"Well what about the toads and the mosquitoes? I hear they carry malaria and dengue fever."

"Look Sam we put on insect repellent and you might get the occasional bite from the mozzies but honestly it's nothing. As for the toads, they're over in the east, we don't get them here, not yet anyway. Stop worrying, you'll be just fine, truly. Trust me."

"Well what about the sharks?"

"For goodness sake, if you don't go into the water you won't get eaten, will you? Anyway we'll be driving along the cliff tops and will see the ocean but we'll be camping inland and the sharks won't be bothering you then."

Samantha and Jim went shopping for the many things they

needed to kit out the van. Sheets and blankets, cutlery, crockery, pots and pans. There was a fold down bed in the camper, a fridge, an oven and cook top as well as a sink and water tank. There were two gas bottles and even a solar panel. Jim made sure there were spares of every description as well as a compressor for blowing up the tyres. He purchased tow ropes, snatch straps and recovery tracks in case they got bogged. Samantha packed the cupboards and fridge with food for two weeks as well as clothes, toiletries and towels.

Jim usually asked his Aunt Bridget to care for his dogs, cat and budgie whenever he went away but this time his Aunt Bridget couldn't help him out as she was going on holiday herself. Her bowling club had an annual outing to Bali and she would just not be able to look after Jim's pets. Samantha thought that her parents would probably not mind looking after the animals and once she asked them they readily agreed. The two dogs, the cat and the budgie were taken around to Samantha's house and Jim was introduced to her parents. It was a pleasant visit and Jim seemed acceptable to her parents, especially Samantha's mother Maisie. Her father, Gordon seemed a little hesitant but Jim put that down to a natural reluctance for any father to accept a would-be suitor for his only daughter. The dogs seemed to settle in well once their personal beds were laid out on the laundry room floor and the cat immediately took to Samantha's father, purring noisily on his knee.

Eventually Jim and Samantha packed away all the camping gear and the pair set off in high spirits for all parts north. There was no definite plan as to where they would go, Jim thought they would travel and stay as the fancy took them for one week and then they would just turn around and come home again.

Maisie and Gordon, Samantha's parents had no pets of their

own and quite welcomed the chance to spoil and make a fuss of the pets. Maisie welcomed the excuse for an early morning walk as she felt she needed the exercise. She took the dogs out for their walk and met many new neighbours doing the same thing. She decided it was a great way to get to know people and make some new friends. The cat instantly adopted Gordon and insisted on accompanying him everywhere he went. The cat roamed the house freely and usually sat on Gordon's lap or sometimes walked along the back of the settee and settled around the back of Gordon's neck, always purring loudly like a Boeing Jet revving up for take-off. Gordon was often amused as he sat on the toilet; the cat would jump up and sit on Gordon's lap. He would push the cat off and then have to suffer the loud purring as the cat rubbed itself against Gordon's ankles.

One day the cat followed Gordon into the bathroom as usual and decided to make himself comfortable on the toilet to watch what Gordon was doing in the shower. Obviously the cat's line of vision only reached up to the toilet seat and he wouldn't have known that there was a gaping hole with water in it. He jumped up, presumably expecting the toilet seat to be solid but there he made a big mistake. His front legs skidded on the shiny plastic and the surprised animal made a grab with his incredibly sharp claws for whatever he could. He tried to jump but only his back legs connected with the seat, his front legs collected the toilet cover which was sitting upright.

As the rear end of the cat disappeared into the toilet bowl the lid flipped shut trapping the poor startled animal. There was a banshee like screech followed by much scratching and water thrashing. By the time the naked Gordon was able to exit the shower and go to the cat's rescue the frightened, wet animal had used his extremely long claws to scratch and claw his way up slightly from the slippy S bend. Gordon lifted the lid and rescued the poor demented cat and then had a mad fight with the frightened feline as he tried to clean and shower off the soggy cat in the shower. The cat scratched and clawed at Gordon not really enjoying a morning hot shower but Gordon held him firm until he was sure that the cat was fully clean and only then did he release his hold. The cat thanked Gordon by sinking his claws into the plastic shower curtain and ripping the screen. Once free of Gordon's clutches the cat raced through the house leaving a wet trail and was never seen in the bathroom again.

After three days Gordon started to take an interest in the budgie and decided to see if it would hop onto his finger. Maisie advised him against this, warning, "Careful Gordon, it might bite you. Maybe you should leave it alone."

"Nonsense, we used to have a budgie when I was a boy. They're a lovely pet and you can teach them to talk. What's his name?"

"I think Jim said it was called Bluey, obviously 'cos it's blue." Gordon tried coaxing the bird to talk and hop onto his finger, "Who's a pretty Bluey? Who's a pretty Bluey?" Look Maisie it's a friendly little thing, it's hopped onto my finger."

"Careful Gordon, don't let it out."

"It'll be fine, look he's really friendly." Just then the telephone rang and startled both the bird and Gordon. Gordon retracted his hand from the cage and unfortunately the budgie decided to exit the cage at the same time. "Oh goodness me, catch it quick." Wailed Maisie. "The back door is open." She made a dash for the door leading out to the garden but the budgie got there first and for a moment perched on the edge of the flyscreen. Gordon tried to talk to the bird, "Come on Bluey, come to Gordon. There's a nice Bluey, come on, come back in here. Lots of nice seed for you."

Obviously the bird didn't understand plain English and could see freedom out in the garden. As both Gordon and Maisie made a grab for the bird it took off with much happy chirping. It flew into the peach tree and sat there preening its feathers, having never flown so far before. Gordon started making all sorts of "bird calling" noises. "Cheep, cheep, come on pretty Bluey." He clicked his tongue against his teeth making the kind of noise that he thought would be attractive to a budgie. All to no avail. Each time the worried couple approached the bird it just flew off and landed on either the fence or another tree. Gordon thought if he could get closer he might be able to entice the budgie to perch on his finger again and so brought out of the garage a folding ladder. He climbed the ladder calling to the bird but each time he got close the bird would fly off again.

After a great deal of effort Gordon and Maisie just stood mutely under the Jacaranda tree and waited for the bird to come to them. Maisie had brought out of the house the cage and they hoped that the bird would recognise it and come down from the tree. After half an hour the budgie decided that he was fed up with being in a cage all his life and would like to explore the rest of the world. He flew off into the sunset, never to be seen again.

Maisie and Gordon were distraught, "What are we going to do. Jim's going to be so upset. I told you not to mess about with it. It's all your fault."

"How was I to know the silly thing was going to fly off like that?"

"Well what are you going to do now?"

"How should I know? Well maybe tomorrow I'll go the pet shop, see if I can get a replacement. That's the least we can do."

True to his word the next day Gordon put the cage in the back of his car and went shopping for a new budgie. He found the pet shop on the outside of the main shopping centre and tried to ignore the pathetic whimpering of the cutest puppies in the window. The assistant readily showed him the two aviaries at the back of the shop. One containing finches and the other containing at least twenty budgies of varying colours from green and blue to a beautiful pale grey. Gordon thought the pale grey to white ones were the most beautiful but he was on a mission to find one identical to the one that got away. He told the assistant that he wanted a brilliant blue one, and for it to be an adult, not a baby. He thought it highly unlikely that Jim's budgie had been a young bird. Together they decided upon a bird that was perched high in the aviary. The assistant had a long stick with a net at the end and after chasing the chosen bird around for five minutes eventually cornered the frightened thing and caught it in her net. She instructed Gordon to bring his cage into the shop and once they checked that all the doors on the cage were closed except the main one, she deftly transferred the captured bird from the aviary into the waiting cage. It cost Gordon fifty dollars but he was just relieved that he was able to replace the bird and hoped that Jim wouldn't notice the difference.

Jim and Samantha were having a great time on the road driving through outback Australia. The views were breathtaking, majestic trees in some areas and arid prickly bushes dominating the red sandy plains in others. In some places they drove along the cliff tops marvelling at the turquoise blue sparkling ocean beneath them. They could see dolphins breaking the surface as they rose to breathe and they watched as a flock of seagulls made many dives down to catch small fish close to the surface of the water. It was all a new experience for Samantha who was having a wonderful time seeing all these new things and was determined to remember it all by taking an extraordinarily large number of photographs. She knew her parents would love seeing all her holiday snaps and be as fascinated with it all as she was. They stopped for a lunch break on the top of a high cliff one day and Jim pointed out to Samantha a water spout that was obviously coming from a passing whale. In a short while two or three more spouts appeared showering water meters above the surface. It was a pod of whales and Samantha was thrilled to see how the breaching whales slapped their tails on the surface of the ocean looking as if they were having a great time.

Jim had no intention of staying in caravan parks. If it was possible Jim just wanted to show Samantha the Australian bush and reasoned he could camp for free as they had everything they needed with them. He knew of a camp site that was high on the cliff tops, about a two hour drive from Perth and as the sun started to set he decided they would go there and stay for the night.

As they drove along the coastal road, the setting sun was an incredible sight. At first it started to turn the ocean almost a bright yellow and slowly as the minutes ticked by it changed to a shining golden orb illuminating everything in sight, every ripple on the sea was picked out in twinkling gold. The whole world seemed to be turned to gold; the road, the trees, the ocean. After five minutes the gold turned to pink and eventually to a fiery red. Jim concentrated on his driving, having seen the spectacle many times but Samantha had only seen it a few times and was mesmerised by the wonderful sight. "Look at the golden clouds Jim, look, they're changing to red. Look isn't that amazing?"

"Yes, yes, it's beautiful isn't it?"

"Look the sun is about to go down into the water, it's just sitting on the horizon. It feels like the water should sizzle and hiss. Look it's going down, down, down, Oh it's gone." Samantha leaned back in her seat, a broad smile across her face and shaking her head declared, "Wow, that was incredible."

As they were driving along they could see many kangaroos nibbling grass by the side of the road. Samantha had seen kangaroos in the zoo and on television but had never seen them in their natural habitat. She was all excited and kept calling out as she saw more and more. "Look Jim, there's another one, and another one. Oh look Jim that one has a baby." As Jim explained, "They only really come to the edge of the road as the sun goes down, it's cooler and the grass at the side of the road is more abundant than in the bush.

Jim stopped the car at one point as there was a slow moving large spiky ball in the middle of the road, about the size of a domestic cat, "Whatever's that Jim?"

"Oh, you don't see these very often, it's an echidna."

"What's that, I've never heard of one of those before?"

"Well some people call them spiny anteaters. They're quite unusual, a bit like a large British hedgehog really. They're interesting because they are egg laying mammals." "Look he's got a long nose."

After passing the echidna they found themselves travelling behind a large truck when Jim noticed two large kangaroos hopping out of the bush and into the centre of the road in front of the truck. There was no time to swerve and the truck ran down the first of the kangaroos. Samantha screamed as they both saw what was happening. Jim managed to slow down before he hit the second one. The truck didn't even stop, it continued unaffected on its way. Jim stopped the car and got out to attend to the fallen kangaroo. "The poor thing's dead, there's nothing I can do for it, but it's a female, maybe she has a joey in her pouch." Samantha stood by visibly shaken by the accident but was totally unprepared for what she saw next. Jim reached into the dead mother's pouch and pulled out a tiny joey the size of a kitten. Samantha squealed with delight. "Oh Jim isn't it cute, can we keep it?"

'Well we can try I suppose but they're very difficult to rear and you need a baby's bottle and special formula. We'll have to call in to a vet to get some. I suppose we can try to save it, if you want to. It's too late now though, we'll have to find a vet tomorrow."

"Oh yes, I want to keep it. It's so gorgeous, look at it's big eyes, it's beautiful. What shall we call it?"

"I don't know, whatever you want. Listen though, it takes a lot of work and dedication to keep a joey, are you sure you want to do this?"

"Yes, yes of course."

"Well first of all you need to keep it warm, wrap it in your shirt and we'll see about feeding it when we get to the camp site."

When they arrived at the camp site they found that they were not alone. There were three British girls in tents on the other side of the site. The girls came over and all chatted amiably enough as Jim put the roof of the camper up and prepared the van for the night. The girls all made a big fuss of the baby kangaroo and took turns holding it. Samantha had to change her shirt as the little thing seemed to have a continuous fit of diarrhoea and her shirt was soiled. They all discussed how they were going to feed the little thing and one of the girls produced an eye dropper which she had in her toilet bag, having had a problem with her eyes the week earlier. They all agreed it would be the best thing to try and feed it some milk. As Jim and Samantha only had powdered milk they mixed up a weak solution and tried to feed the baby. The joey accepted the eye dropper and the formula and the girls all discussed what they could call it. After many names were promulgated it was agreed to call the little thing "Skippy," after the television series some twenty or thirty years earlier. Jennie the eldest of the girls stated I know it's not a very original name but it's appropriate don't you think?" The three girls returned to their site about fifty metres away and Samantha started to prepare their evening meal whilst the baby kangaroo just snuggled into one of Samantha's jumpers and went to sleep.

Jim felt nature starting to work and decided to dig himself a bush toilet just out of sight of the camper, behind a bush. He took a toilet roll and a small spade and disappeared from sight. The three girls across the camp site decided to come back to ask Samantha's advice about cooking their supper over a camp fire. Suddenly there was a shout followed by a loud shriek and crude swearing. Jim had been squatting over his home made toilet with his trousers around his ankles. He suddenly felt a sharp pain in his groin and was shocked to see giant bull ants making tracks up his legs and three were already making a meal of his vulnerable soft flesh. In a panic he lost his balance and fell over backwards into a large prickle bush which left him splayed out on his back, his legs askew and his genitals out for all to see. The toilet paper had rolled three feet away and the gaping hole gave evidence of Jim's recent activity.

All four girls rushed to see what the shouting was all about and two collapsed with the giggles whilst Samantha and one of the girls tried to grab Jim and pull him out of the prickle bush. His modesty in tatters and his embarrassment so acute he could have died, all Jim could do was shout "Get out of here. Leave me alone." The three girls retreated giggling back to their tents whilst Samantha tried to soothe Jim's wounded pride and prickled back. Dinner could wait; she spent the next hour, in the dark with a flashlight and tweezers separating Jim from his wounded modesty, and carefully attending his prickled back and bare bum. Not an auspicious start to any camping holiday.

Jim pouted and sulked for the whole of the next day whilst Samantha tried to ease his wounded pride by simply ignoring the whole episode and getting on with life as normally as she could even though she was dying to have a good laugh about the whole thing.

She fed the baby kangaroo and Jim agreed to call into the next town to seek out a vet for some correct formula. The baby kangaroo was so sweet and cute but looking after it was starting to become a problem. Samantha had only a few clothes with her and the baby kept releasing its diarrhoea ruining what few clothes Samantha had with her. The vet in the next town gave Jim some formula and a baby bottle for the joey but advised that it was a full time job and needed much dedication to care for the animal. Samantha was undeterred and determined to do her best for the baby.

The next night found Jim and Samantha further up the coast and camping in a well wooded area. The weather was dry but threatening to be rather chilly and so Jim suggested they light a campfire. Whilst Samantha prepared dinner and fed the joey Jim collected firewood and dry leaves. He arranged a campfire site about two metres from the camper and tried to light the fire with a box of matches. Each match got blown out by the slight breeze and he was becoming quite frustrated with his efforts. His foul cursing and swearing brought Samantha out of the camper to see what the problem was. Although Samantha was no girl guide she could see that first of all he needed to have a wind break and secondly he needed to have some highly combustible material to get the fire started. The more she offered to help the more frustrated Jim became. "I know what I'm doing. I don't need any help. Leave me alone." So Samantha left him alone for a while. After Jim had gone through a whole box of matches Samantha could stand it no longer and asked him to check on the dinner cooking whilst she would have a go at the fire. Jim threw up his arms, and giving in declared, "It's impossible, there's too much wind and this wood must be damp."

Samantha took their two deck chairs and laid them side by side to create a wind break, after which she tore up some newspaper and rolled it into little balls. The first match she struck stayed alight and caught the newspaper. In two minutes flat the fire was roaring into life. Far from complimenting her on a job well done Jim instead spent the evening pouting and nursing his wounded pride. "You just got lucky." He moodily conceded.

"Yes dear, the steak's good isn't it?"

The next morning it rained and so they spent the day travelling further north. Skippy was not well. Samantha was worried as she could sense the poor little thing was not happy. He was not taking his formula and seemed to be in a constant state of weeing and pooing. Her clothes were all soiled and she was down to her last shirt. After lunch she couldn't coax the baby to take any formula and cried as she watched the baby close his enormous eyes and just drift away. He had never made a sound and hardly moved. Jim tried to console Samantha but she was upset and sad. They laid the baby in a shallow grave by the side of the road and Jim, at Samantha's insistence fashioned a tiny cross from two pieces of wood. He thought it was quite ridiculous but had the good sense to keep his thoughts to himself as Samantha cried for half an hour mourning the loss of her little pet.

In the late evening they arrived at the side of a lake and a four wheel only drive track beckoned with a promise of a good camp site. The more they drove along the track the more it became deeply rutted. There were high ridges of earth with muddy ruts in between. Samantha didn't like the look of it at all and expressed her doubts, "I don't think we should go any further, let's turn around and go back, this track is getting too muddy and I can see there are high ridges of earth and they'll be awfully slippy and slimy. Let's go back to where it was smooth ground."

"No, we'll be just fine. I'm going to drive on top of these ridges and you'll see we'll come out of this track further up where it's drier."

"No, I really think you should turn around. I don't like the look of it."

"Don't worry, trust me, we'll be just fine." Famous last words.

The camper drove nicely along the top of the ridges for about fifty metres and then disaster. It was muddy and slippery and the wheels couldn't get a grip. They just simply slipped off the top of the ridges and the camper fell off to one side, into the mud.

Now the water tank in a camper must have a small hole in the top to allow for air to escape to compensate for the suction of the pump. Unfortunately the hole in the tank was on the same side as the camper was now leaning in at a crazy angle. The ruts in the ground were already deep in mud but the water tank now being mostly on its side had the water freely running out and making a really bad situation even worse. Mud mixed with water is an impossible situation for tyres to escape from. Samantha just put her hands over her eyes and moaned. The camper was at such an angle that she couldn't even open her door. Jim took a deep breath and announced, "Well we'd better get out and see what we can do." Samantha tried hard to control her anger and determined that the whole problem was Jim's not hers. "Well if you think I'm getting out of the van and into that mud you must be joking. You got us into this mess and you'll have to get us out of it. I'm climbing into the back of the van and I'll make us a sandwich for dinner, after which I'm going to bed."

"You mean you're not going to help me?"

"No!"

Jim realised there was nothing he could do, it was almost dark and they would have to stay there all night. He would assess the situation in the morning. As Samantha was trying to climb into the forty five degree angled bed she noticed a white liquid coming from the food cupboard. As she opened the cupboard door she gave out a very unladylike swear word and yelled at Jim, "For God's sake Jim, look at what you've done; the toasting fork has pierced a carton of milk. We've got milk all through the cupboard and it's even dripping into the bottom cupboard."

"Oh shit!"

"We'll have to clean it up, we can't leave it until the morning or it'll smell to high heaven."

"Well we don't have much water left in the tank, I think it's all drained out."

"Well we've got a roll of kitchen paper towels, we'll just have to mop up as much as we can." Samantha was angry and frustrated and said almost nothing as she mopped up the spilt milk as best she could. Jim was defensive and frustrated, "It's not my fault, how was I to know the stupid toasting fork would stab the milk in the back."

The cold night was spent fighting over space and blankets. The van was at a crazy angle and as they tried to sleep they both kept rolling downhill, down the bed to arrive in a heap at the bottom, on top of each other. With frayed tempers and freezing limbs they passed the night in misery. No sleep, just bad tempered misery.

The following day saw Jim toiling in the mud for five hours, trying to fix the snatch straps and ropes to the various trees on either side of the rutted road. For her part Samantha was beyond angry. The spilt milk had made a paper packet of sugar break open in the night and now there were millions of ants in the cupboard carrying a grain of sugar each back to their nest, somewhere in the earth outside. She used up their only container of insect spray and was busy with a small hand brush trying to get rid of the dead ants, and kill off those that were still alive and those that were trying to attack her too.

Jim lost the recovery tracks in the mud, they sank in so deeply. He worked hard trying to move the van inch by inch. Every so often he would plaintively ask, "Did you see that? Did we move at all?" Samantha with eyes rolling heavenwards wearily answered each time, "Oh yes! We must have moved half an inch that time. Keep trying, we might just be out by Christmas." Eventually, covered in putrid smelly mud, sweat, slime and fifty thousand flies Jim managed to extricate them from the mire. The large black plastic recovery tracks were nowhere to be seen. The quagmire had devoured them. Jim knew roughly where they were and so started to dig in the mud to get at them.

When he did locate the tracks they were deeply imbedded in the mud and the more Jim tugged at them to get them up the more they seemed determined to suck themselves down into the mud. When Jim was knee deep in the thick, smelly goo he managed to pass a looped rope through the holes in the tracks and once out of the mire himself he was then better able to tie the rope to the van and use the horsepower of the van to pull the tracks out of the mire. As Jim and the plastic tracks were now safe on dry high ground Jim turned off the engine and surveyed their position. "Well thank goodness for that. See, no problem. The way back is easy. The lake is only just over there. I'll carry the tracks and we can both have a good wash and even a swim." Jim tried to look cheerful but Samantha was anything but cheerful. They were both hot and bothered with the flies that the very smelly Jim was attracting. Jim was disgustingly dirty and incredibly weary but stoically carried the heavy plastic tracks to the side of the lake. Neither spoke to the other and tempers were frayed.

After washing the tracks trying to get all the mud off them Jim finally leaned the clean tracks on a convenient tree to dry off, and only then joined Samantha in the cool, clean water for a refreshing swim. Samantha collected all her soiled shirts and jumper and washed them as best she could in the lake. She hung them all out to dry on the closest tree and proceeded to made lunch and although she wasn't really talking to Jim, suggested they go home. Jim was reluctant to admit defeat but realised if he pushed Samantha any further their relationship would be irreparably damaged. It was a quiet drive home interrupted by a necessary stop at a commercial car wash in one of the small towns.

On the way home they passed a familiar small car with its bonnet up. Three girls stood by looking helpless. Samantha piped up with "Hey, aren't those the three girls that were in the tents? Look they've obviously broken down. Stop. We should help them."

Now Jim was a chivalrous young man, always keen to help a damsel in distress but the truth of the matter was that Jim knew absolutely nothing about cars, engines, radiators or anything. His was a world of office procedures, paper work, meetings and conferences. He had lost his father when he was a child and so had never been shown how to do manly things; make stuff, mend stuff, deal with cars and engines. He badly needed to impress Samantha, to show her that he was a capable masculine man and at the same time he desperately needed to patch things up with her. She was obviously still in a bad mood following the muddy episode.

Jim only had the vaguest notion of what could go wrong with a car but pulled off the road willing to do what he could to help the girls. "What's wrong girls? Can we help?"

"Oh hello, it's you again. Yes, could you help us please? How is Skippy can we have a cuddle?" Samantha started to cry as she explained that they had done their best but poor Skippy was no longer with them. Everyone was sad and one of the girls put her arm around Samantha trying to sympathise, "Oh that's too bad, he was a gorgeous little thing." All the girls had something soothing to say to Samantha but eventually the problem with the car needed to be addressed.

The smallest of the girls broke the tension of the moment with, "Well we stopped for some lunch and when we tried to start the car up again it just, well, wouldn't." Jim did at least know that radiators could be a problem and one had to check the water level every so often. He had never done this himself as he'd always taken his car into the local garage for regular servicing. "Well have you checked the radiator? Do you have plenty of water in it?" The girls looked at him blankly. "Radiator, what's that?" Jim did actually know what the radiator looked like and had seen his car mechanic back home occasionally screw the top off to check the water level. There being no other man around and feeling a little like Sir Gallahad he examined the radiator with some fear and trepidation but tried to put an air of confidence in his approach. "Okay let's have a look." He could see the radiator cap and immediately tried to screw the top off. When it wouldn't move he remembered seeing his mechanic push down on the cap before screwing it off. As he did this Jim was shocked as a hissing spray of steam burst up from the open radiator burning his hand, arm, his chest and chin. "Oh shit!" The girls all rushed to his aid but as the steam burns were not too bad he brushed them off bravely. "I'm fine girls, no problem. We'll just let the heat dissipate a bit and then we can top up the radiator, do you have some water? I think that was your problem." The girls produced a small bottle of water and Jim topped up the radiator. Feeling very satisfied with himself he then instructed the girls to start up the engine again. Nothing happened and Jim pulled a face trying desperately to think what could be wrong.

One of the girls advanced a theory and a solution. "Do you think it could be a flat battery? We've got jumper leads in the boot? We could link up your car with ours and try that." Again Jim had no real idea of what to do with the jumper leads but only the vaguest notion that one should attach leads from one car to the other. The girls searched through the camping gear in the boot of their car and eventually found the jumper leads. "Here we are. I think you'll have to back up your camper so that we can get our battery to within distance of your battery."

"Of course."

Jim manoeuvred the camper to get as close as possible to the little car. He lifted the bonnet and could see the battery clearly. Again not having any real knowledge of how to get power from one car to the other he clipped the leads to the girl's car battery and without any surety of what correctly goes where he clipped the other ends of the leads to his car battery. Now in order to get power from one battery to the other it's quite necessary to have the red positive on one battery connected to the red positive on the opposing battery, and conversely the black negative on one battery connected to the black negative on the second battery. Jim didn't know this and as soon as the connections were made it became obvious that he had done it incorrectly; there was an arcing spark followed by an intense creation of heat. Jim and the girls looked on with some consternation. "Is it supposed to do that?" asked one of the girls.

"Err. I'm not too sure."

"Maybe you should take the leads off and try something else."

"You could be right." With that Jim reached out to disconnect the arcing leads. He jumped back quickly as the now, very hot leads burnt his fingers. "Ow! It's too hot to touch."

No-one was game enough to try and disconnect the leads. They just got hotter and hotter. What Jim didn't know was that the incorrect connections were actually draining both batteries, Jim's and the small car. Now neither car would start and Jim and Samantha were marooned just as the girls were. Jim tried to talk to Samantha but she wouldn't talk to him or even look at him. One of the girls kept trying to ring the RAC and her parents back in Perth to no avail. There was no phone reception in that remote area and their mobile phones just couldn't get through at all. One of the girls had an idea that if she climbed the hill close by they might just get reception there. Jim feeling he had to make up for his lack of car maintenance knowledge volunteered to climb the hill. His burnt fingers gave him some grief but he soldiered on bravely. At the top of the hill he did indeed get a clear signal and good reception. He called for Roadside Assistance and the RAC promised to be with them as soon as possible.

Going up a gravelly hill is not a problem however coming down the same hill with only rubber thongs on his feet is definitely not to be encouraged. His rubber thongs just couldn't maintain a grip and Jim found himself slipping and sliding uncontrollably down the steep slope. Eventually gravity took over and the last five metres of the descent were a nightmare. The girls all let out a scream as Jim somersaulted over and over bringing down small rocks and shale. He landed at their feet dazed, dusty and demoralised. His shirt was torn, his knees skinned and his pride in tatters. There was no real, lasting injury but he allowed the girls to nurse and mother him as they all patiently waited to be rescued.

17

FREDDY

Samantha was still angry when they got back to Perth and the pair hardly spoke on the journey back. Jim took her home and collected his pets. He thanked Samantha's parents profusely and presented Maisie with an enormous bunch of flowers and presented Gordon with his favourite brand of whiskey which Samantha had picked out for him at the liquor shop. As they parted Jim mumbled, "I'll give you a call then."

"If you want" was the terse reply. Jim had a shower once he got home and inspected his bruised and burnt body. He was not really seriously hurt but his pride was. He had no idea if he and Samantha were still together or if her coolness on the journey home meant that they were finished. He tried to ring her but there was no answer. He knew she would be at home but she was obviously not wanting to talk to him. He left a message but she didn't return his call. The next day and the next were the same, he kept trying to contact her but she wouldn't pick up her phone. He tried to ring her at work but her colleagues just reported that Samantha was busy and couldn't get to the phone. In desperation he decided to go to the fertility clinic to see if she would talk to him.

In actual fact there was so much happening in Samantha's life.

She was cross with Jim but had no intention of ending their relationship. She just thought it would do them both good to have a few days break from each other and to give her time to get over the unfortunately happenings on their disastrous camping expedition.

The events that were happening to Samantha were actually nothing to do with Jim. Samantha had emigrated with her parents the year before but they had left Samantha's brother in England to finish his University degree. Now he had finished and had emigrated to Australia to be with the rest of his family. Samantha hadn't been able to meet him at the airport as his plane came in at lunchtime and they were short staffed at work, so one of the first things that Freddy, her brother did, when he arrived at his parent's home was to unpack a couple of bags and then make his way to the fertility clinic to meet Samantha as she came out of work. He could have waited until she got home but he was impatient and wanted to see her as soon as possible, he was very fond of his little sister. He thought it would be a nice surprise for her and he would pick her up from work and take her to a restaurant for drinks and then dinner. That way he could have a good chat with her and catch up on all her news.

The two men took little notice of each other as they both waited outside the fertility clinic. Freddy was by the door but Jim was across and further down the road. Jim watched and his heart soared as he saw his beloved emerge from the building. She looked so beautiful and the sun shone on her curls so alluringly. He took a couple of steps forward and then halted in mid step. He saw Samantha throw up her arms in response to the man who had been loitering at the door. He couldn't hear what was being said he only saw his beloved throw herself into the arms of another man. They kissed and laughed as they hugged each other, then arm in arm they proceeded with their backs to him down the road away from where Jim was watching in mute discomfort and distress.

Jim walked the town in abject misery. He didn't want to go home, he needed to walk. He needed to talk and didn't know who to turn to. He didn't want to talk to the guys in the pub or the fellows at work. He decided the only person he could turn to would be his Aunt Bridget. Aunt Bridget had been his surrogate mother since his real mother had passed away. He rang to see if it was convenient for him to pop round for a visit. Aunt Bridget could sense that Jim was troubled and readily agreed to see him.

When he arrived at her house she could see there were tears in his eyes and she put her arms around him and led him to the settee asking carefully, "What's wrong Jim, what's happened?"

"Oh Aunt Bridget, I'm such an idiot. I've lost her, I've lost the only girl I'll ever love. She hates me and she's moved on. She has a new man in her life and I don't know what to do, I don't think I can live without her."

"Now, now young Jim, it's maybe not as bad as you think. Tell me everything. What did you do?" Jim related the whole of the camping trip, his futile efforts at helping the girls and the final indignity of the fall. Aunt Bridget just tut tutted and stroked his back soothingly. "Well Jim, if you really love this girl, maybe you have to fight for her."

"I can't fight Aunt Bridget, this is not the middle ages, men don't actually fight duels any more."

"No Jim, I don't mean literally fight, not fisticuffs, I mean you have to talk to her. Alright so you're not the world's greatest boy scout camper, alright so you're not the world's greatest motor mechanic, but your heart's in the right place. You're a decent person and I'm sure she would know that. You've been seeing

Samantha now for over a year, I'm sure she would know your good qualities and she'll forgive you your imperfections."

"But she's found someone else Aunt Bridget. I saw them together, I saw her kiss him. I know I've lost her forever. What am I to do?"

"Well there's an old saying that goes something like, 'a feint heart never won a fair maiden.' So I really think you have to see her again and tell her how you feel. Did you ever tell her you love her?"

"No, I never did."

"Well you must see her and tell her how you feel. Apologise for the camping trip but remind her of all the good times you have had. See if she'll have dinner with you and spoil her. Be brave Jim. Sitting at home and moping will not get her back. You have to be proactive."

"You really think so?"

"Yes I do, definitely."

"What if she refuses to see me, what if she laughs in my face?"

"Well, you'll be no worse off will you? She'll either come back to you or she won't."

Jim stayed with his Aunt Bridget for dinner and after slowly made his way home thinking carefully what he was going to do. He needed a plan of action. He'd agreed to follow his aunt's advice, but how to go about it? He passed a florist shop and although it was closed he saw the poster in the window which read, "Say it with flowers." He smiled to himself as he resolved to do just that the following day. He would buy an enormous bunch of roses and have it delivered to the fertility clinic. He'd write a note on it saying how sorry he was for the trip and would she see him again.

When Samantha got the flowers she laughed with delight and

pleasure. She felt guilty that she had ignored Jim's phone calls but she'd now got over the trauma of the trip and had never had any intention of ending their relationship, but realised that Jim was hurting and obviously feeling that he had let her down and disappointed her. She had no idea that he had seen her with her brother. She rang him immediately and invited him round to her parent's house for a celebration dinner. Jim thought she was meaning that they were celebrating their reuniting. He thought it a trifle odd but was definitely not going to argue the point with her. Whatever she wanted was just fine by him. He had no idea that what the family was celebrating was the arrival of Freddy.

He dashed home from work, showered and changed and on the way to Samantha's house bought a large box of chocolates for her mother. When he arrived at the house was met at the door by Gordon and Maisie Perkins, Samantha's parents, who ushered him into the lounge telling him that Samantha would be down shortly. Maisie asked politely, "How have you been Jim since we saw you last?"

Well, to tell the truth there's been something of a miracle in my house."

"A miracle, whatever do you mean?"

"Well I've had Bluey, my budgie for about three years now and he's always been a normal male budgie but a few days after I got him home from picking him up here, guess what? He laid an egg!"

"What?"

"Yes, my male budgie who has never been near a female actually laid an egg."

"What do you make of that then? Anything come to mind that you forgot to tell me?"

"Ahhhhhhhh well, actually, well, errrrr, yes I suppose there was something we forgot to tell you."

"I thought so, bit of a surprise really a male bird laying an egg, a miracle wouldn't you say?" Gordon fronted up to Jim and confessed that they'd had an accident and Bluey flew away. "I'm really sorry Jim, we should have told you but we didn't want to upset you." Maisie chipped in with, "Yes Jim, we're really sorry, it was an accident. Are you very angry?"

"No, actually I realised what must have happened. I wasn't that fond of Bluey, he was just a bird, it's not like losing a dog. He wouldn't even talk to me, I tried to teach him to talk, time and time again, but he was a stubborn little thing and wouldn't say a word. Once I saw the egg I tried to protect it and keep it warm and hoped it would hatch out, but it didn't. Anyway no harm done. The new budgie is quite friendly so don't worry about it."

After a few more pleasantries the door to the lounge opened and in walked the strange young man, the same one that Jim had seen kissing Samantha outside her work, Maisie stood up to greet the fellow saying simply, "Jim, this is Freddy, Freddy this is Jim. Samantha will be down shortly, thank you for the chocolates, we'll have them after dinner," and with that short introduction she and Gordon departed to attend to things in the kitchen. Jim was in a quandary. Was he there to meet her new boyfriend? Was she trying to make a fool of him? He just wanted to make a dash for the door, he certainly didn't want to be made to look like some sort of idiot. How could she do this to me? Freddy was all smiles and stepped forward to shake hands. Jim couldn't refuse to shake hands but was confused, the man seemed so friendly. Jim frowned with deep furrows in his troubled brow. He wanted to escape but didn't know how he could extricate himself from this terrible position. He resolved to make a dash for the door, too bad if it was rude, too bad if he upset her mother. Why would Samantha make a monkey out of him like this? He was tongue tied and didn't want to give any explanation, he just made a dash for the front door. Luckily at that moment Samantha descended the staircase and ran to Jim to embrace him with a loving kiss. Jim's body tightened as he held her away from him and asked tersely, "What are you doing? Why are you doing this to me? Haven't I been embarrassed enough without you rubbing my nose in it? How long have you been seeing this man? Is he a better man than I am?"

"Whatever are you talking about?"

"The man, that fellow in the lounge, what did your mother call him, Freddy? Why are you embarrassing me like this? Do you love him?"

"Yes of course." Samantha was about to explain that Freddy was her brother but Jim just ran down the front path slamming the gate behind him. A large semi-trailer truck just happened to be passing at that moment and had a really loud engine. Samantha shouted after Jim, "He's my brother," but Jim didn't hear and ran down the road in confusion, blinded by tears of frustration and anger.

The next week Samantha tried to ring Jim every day but he was refusing to pick up his phone. She wrote to him each day but he just threw her letters away, unopened. He told the guys at work that if she rang he didn't want to speak to her. Jim took his misery out on the bottle. He wallowed in his misery and bored the poor barman at the pub with his constant moaning about the "two timing" Samantha. He would frequently burst into a drunken rendition of various songs about two timing women; *"Jezabel; if ever a pair of eyes promised paradise, deceiving me, leaving me, grieving me too. Jezeebel it was you."* or even "Delilah" which gave him even more solace.

The following week Jim was scheduled to attend an annual Civil Service conference in Albany, a coastal town on the southern coast; a five hour's drive south of Perth. He had forgotten to mention this to Samantha and so she had no idea why he wasn't at work. She waited outside his office each day, hoping to catch him as he was leaving to go home, but for a whole week he simply did not emerge from his office. She tried his home but got no response when she rang his door bell. "Enough is enough," thought Samantha to herself, "if that's what he wants then that's what he'll get. No more tries from me, if he wants me he can come and find me, he knows where I am. I'm not doing this anymore."

With her brother at home life became quite busy for Samantha and so she tried to put Jim out of her mind and get on with her life. Freddy had actually announced that he had been seeing a Swedish girl in England and that she was just organising her affairs and then would be coming to Australia to meet up with him. He confided to his parents and sister that once she arrived he would be asking Agnetha to marry him. They were delighted and held a small family celebration but were nevertheless requested to promise not to say a word to Agnetha. Freddy announced that he would take her somewhere special to do the proposal; they were not to say a word about it, and they all promised.

Freddy met Agnetha at the airport and brought her home to meet the family. She was a beautiful petite blonde with a charming accent and dancing green eyes. Samantha could see why Freddy was so smitten with her; she was a delight and subsequently all the family fell in love with her. A week later Freddy took Agnetha into Perth for a special dinner at the revolving restaurant, high above the city. Once they had ordered Freddy checked no-one was near and then nervously dropped to one knee and proposed to the surprised girl. He had picked out a beautiful diamond ring and when she accepted his proposal he slipped the ring onto her finger. They dined in style taking their time over the sumptuous meal, but Freddy couldn't wait to get home to announce that Agnetha had accepted him.

18

ALBANY

At the conference Jim was distracted and introspective. The keynote speaker could have been an alien from another planet. Jim hadn't heard a word he was talking about. After two days of lectures and workshops Jim still hadn't involved himself at all with the conference. He was put into a discussion group to debate the economics of immigration but he sat at the back of the group refusing to take any part in the debate. When asked for an opinion he just shrugged his shoulders and kept his eyes downcast, refusing to maintain eye contact with anyone. Following that the remainder of the group just ignored him and carried on with their exercise. He was drinking heavily, especially after the evening meal but managed to stay on his feet and not disgrace himself. He poured out his misery to the barmaid who was actually too busy to pay much attention to him. He poured out his heart to an elderly lady delegate who sympathised but she couldn't actually help either.

The conference organisers had hired some private buses and the delegates were all taken on a tour of Albany and the main tourist spots. They visited the blow holes first and climbed down the precarious sloping rocks to be shocked when they saw the unprepossessing small fissure in the rock face which didn't look at all threatening but when the waves below crashed into the rock face there was an extremely frightening loud bang and an astonishing rush of jet propelled wind, as if a Boeing Jet had just taken off down into the bowels of the earth. The tour operator and the other delegates all laughed, especially when one of the men had his hat blown off. Jim didn't laugh though, he was in a world of his own. He couldn't concentrate on anything and couldn't get his mind off Samantha.

Everyone but Jim oooooh'd and aaaarh'd at the incredible banging of the waves at "The Gap," a natural cleft rock formation which sucks in huge waves and creates great clouds of spray covering the spectators at the secure lookout guard rail. Jim just leaned precariously on the rail and watched in fascination as each wave crashed against the enormous rocks. The southern ocean is a dangerous place and the waves can be mountainous, every so often there are also giant waves which have taken many unsuspecting fishermen off the rocks and out to their deaths. He wondered what it would be like to jump over the cliff face and be devoured by the mountainous waves. He was quite a strong swimmer but realised he would perish extremely quickly in the freezing cold water, never mind being sucked out to sea or worse having his body shattered and battered by the powerful waves against the hard granite rocks. He wasn't exactly a coward but he wasn't particularly brave either. He was miserable but not that miserable.

The tour operator took the delegates through the Torndirrup National Park showing them the dramatic peaks, huge granite outcrops and the rugged coast line. He took them to see the Natural Bridge where huge boulders had fallen into the ocean a few million years earlier, forming a natural bridge from one cliff face to the other. One or two of the more adventurous delegates wanted to climb down to the bridge to experience the crashing waves as they rolled under the bridge but the tour operator forbade them from doing so. There were other private individual foolhardy adventurers clambering all over the rock faces but the tour operator was quite strict and explained that he was responsible for the safety of his official party and as such refused to allow any of them to wander from the group.

After seeing the natural wonders of the area the tour operator took the group to a pre-ordered lunch at the old Whaling Station. After lunch a station guide took the group on a tour of the old station and allowed them to clamber all over the only existing, preserved whale chaser ship, the Cheynes IV. He took them around the grounds and through the converted whale oil tanks which had been turned into a museum. The delegates were treated to an extremely informative film show which had actual footage of whales being harpooned. The guide explained that the station had been a working whale station until nineteen seventy eight when whaling off the Australian coast was banned. A young delegate tried to engage Jim in conversation but Jim wasn't interested in talking to anyone. He did however help an elderly female delegate up the narrow iron steps of the old ship. She also wanted to engage Jim in conversation but he just held onto her arm and refused to talk. There's only so much rudeness people can take and eventually the whole group realised that Jim was either too shy to talk, too rude, or simply too ignorant. Whatever, people were learning to leave him alone.

The conference proceedings would have been interesting to Jim had he been in a state of mind to concentrate and participate, but as it was the days flew by with Jim in a stupor, his mind was constantly on Samantha and his ego was bruised. "How could she take up with some other fellow so quickly?" He asked himself over and over. "I know she's beautiful and I know I messed things up on the camping trip, but I thought she really liked me." One of the younger female conference delegates had noticed Jim and thought he looked sad. She took note that he hadn't actually taken any part in the workshops or discussion groups. She was intrigued. He looked intelligent and reasonably good looking so approached him at the bar one night. "Hello, my name's Gillian, I noticed you in the discussion group yesterday. You didn't have much to say. Are you alright?"

"Hi, I'm fine. Just a little distracted."

"Oh, anything I can help with?"

"No. It's a private matter. Oh, do you want a drink?"

"Thanks, I'll have a gin and tonic, Jim."

"How did you know my name?" She laughed, "It's on your identity card round your neck of course." Each delegate had been given a lanyard with an identity badge and they were requested to wear it every day to identify them from the rest of the hotel guests.

The two chatted amiably enough but Jim was loath to explain his malaise to this friendly young thing. Once the bar closed down Gillian suggested they take a walk on the foreshore. They'd both been drinking heavily and Gillian quite liked the look of Jim and thought this evening could lead to other evenings and maybe even the start of a relationship. In his inebriated state Gillian started to look a little like Samantha. He was forgetting for a while why he was so miserable. After their walk along the promenade the two made their way, a little unsteadily but in the right direction to the hotel. Ever the gentleman, Jim chaperoned Gillian to her room and was saying a polite goodnight when she leaned in and surprised him by giving him a passionate kiss. His body reacted as she asked coyly, "Do you want to come in? It's lonely here in this big room all on my own." Jim readily agreed and only when Gillian started to undress him did the full impact of her intentions become clear. He sobered up quite quickly as the memory of Samantha flooded back into his brain. "No, I'm sorry, I can't do this. I love someone else."

"Well she's obviously not here, and if you don't tell, I won't."

"No I can't do this. I'm really sorry." Gillian shook her head and shrugged her shoulders,

"Ah well. That's the story of my life. Someone got to you before me. Off you go then, but if you change your mind you know where to find me." With that Jim let himself out of her room and made his way to his own room. He lay awake for hours pondering on his stupidity at first losing Samantha and secondly at refusing Gillian.

19

THAILAND

When Jim returned to work the fellows in his office reported that Samantha had been trying to get in touch with him but they had followed his instructions and told her nothing about where he was, or how he was. However they were worried about him and one of the guys suggested that they all take a week off and go for a short holiday. He thought it would be good for Jim and they could all share a few laughs and try to pull Jim out of his depression. The manager of that department, Roger Grant was a kindly caring old man who had observed how depressed Jim was and so readily agreed to the three of them all taking a week off for a short holiday.

Bob, one of the guys lost no time and was on the internet straight away, arranging their flights and accommodation in Krabi, Thailand. Jim just allowed himself to be bullied into submission. He kept repeating that he was just fine and didn't need a holiday but the boys were adamant and everything was arranged for a flight at the week end.

Aunt Bridget was once more called in to service and readily agreed to take the dogs, the cat and the budgie. She actually welcomed the company of the pets as she lived alone. The dogs gave her an excuse for taking some much needed exercise each morning. The cat was no trouble at all and sulked around the house. For some reason the cat really didn't like Aunt Bridget and so maintained a haughty disdain from her attempts to cuddle him. The budgie, like its predecessor had nothing to say.

Aunt Bridget was invited to Jim's house to have dinner and agreed to take the pets back home with her. She noticed that Jim was packing his battered old back pack ready for the trip. "My goodness me Jim, don't tell me you're actually taking that old back pack on holiday with you."

"Yes, of course, what's wrong with it?"

"Heaven's above! Well for a start it's old and decidedly grubby. You're not short of a bob or two, go and get yourself a new bag, a case, one with wheels on. Truly you'll thank me, it's so much easier pulling a case than lugging around a heavy back pack."

"Okay, okay. Golly you are a bully. I'll go shopping tomorrow, I guess I could do with a new case."

In preparation for the trip Jim booked himself into the barber for a trim and as promised went shopping for a new suitcase. He'd never had one on wheels before, he'd always managed with a backpack but he decided to splurge out and get himself a really nice, soft sided, bright orange case on wheels with a handle and many side pockets. He checked his passport and once home started to pack his new case ready for the journey.

The boys changed planes from Kuala Lumpur to Bangkok and took the local flight to Krabi. When they filed off the small plane the heat and humidity took their breath away. Immediately they peeled off their shirts and changed their shoes and socks for rubber thongs. The bus ride out to their hotel was an eye opener for Jim. He had never been to Thailand before and was struck by the incredible beauty of the island and the fantastic coast line as they wound their way through the hills and valleys to the small village that was to be their home for the next week. The friendly hotel staff welcomed the boys with bowls of fruit and iced drinks. The pungent smells were intoxicating and they could hear the distant barking of native monkeys in the hillside. Jim thought this was just paradise and couldn't wait to get settled before exploring the beautiful island.

The hotel proved to be a collection of cabins with a main reception and dining area. Jim had his own cabin which overlooked the dark blue lake. He could see hundreds of large carp in the lake and watched fascinated as the indigenous hotel restaurant staff threw bread and lunch leftovers to the fish. He felt his misery drain away and resolved to forget Samantha, at least for a week.

Once the boys had unpacked they met for dinner and Bob suggested they take the local transport, a tuk tuk into the township to have a drink and see what night life there was. As they trundled through the crowded streets they were surrounded on each side by the verdant jungle which had a strange, heady, pungent smell, a mixture of lush undergrowth and spicy local cooking. They passed many souvenir shops with vendors noisily announcing their wares and imploring the tourists to come have a look. They found a bar with a friendly barman and downed a few beers before sauntering along the beach front, enjoying the sight of the long tail boats docked high on the beach and the setting sun, a huge golden orb as it descended into the ocean. The evening weather was perfect with such a gentle refreshing breeze.

Bob spotted a group of beautiful Asian girls and asked if Jim was interested in meeting up with one of them. Jim was not exactly dead drunk, but he'd had enough beer to befuddle his brain. He remembered Gillian and his lost opportunity in Albany.

All he could see now was a beautiful girl with a low cut blouse and a short tight mini skirt. On Bob's suggestion the girl approached Jim and asked candidly, "Would you like come to my room, I very nice room?" Now Jim wasn't exactly born yesterday and realised this was probably a prostitute but he was not thinking straight and the boys were encouraging him. "Go, have some fun Jim. We'll see you back at the hotel."

For some reason the boys seemed to have got a fit of the giggles and he couldn't for the life of him see why, or what was so funny. Bob asked him, "Jim do you have any condoms on you?"

"No, should I have?"

"Jees boy, you should never come to Thailand without your condoms. Here have some of mine. You never know, best to be careful."

"I guess so. Thanks." The boys went off down the beach giggling as the girl took hold of Jim's arm and propelled him to the back of a shop where there were numerous rooms. Jim had never been with a prostitute and started to feel sick with apprehension and worry. The room had a double bed and an on-suite bathroom with toilet and shower. He was changing his mind as his brain started to function and he realised what was about to happen. He was sweating and could hardly breathe. "Look, err, what's your name?"

" Me Carla, what's yours?"

"Jim. Look I'm hot do you think we can have a shower I really don't feel so good."

"We put money on table now, okay?"

"Yes, whatever." Jim checked his wallet and extracted the amount she asked for.

"I help take clothes off you. I nice Carla."

"I can manage thank you." Nevertheless Carla started to

unbutton Jim's shirt and helped him divest himself of his shorts and pants. Jim brushed her off none too gently and stepped into the shower. He watched nervously as Carla started to take off her clothes also. Her slim body was undulating gently as she took off her blouse and was humming an unusual little tune. Jim noticed the very tiny, well rounded breasts and marvelled how they stood up perkily with no need of a bra. She then started to provocatively peel off her tight skirt.

Jim finished his quick shower and grabbed a towel. He watched intently as Carla turned her back on him as she proceeded to peel off her panties. He approached her from behind and put his arm around her waist and turned her towards him. What he saw next took his breath away with shock and revulsion. This was not a woman but a man. A full grown man with the genitals of a man. He pushed Carla away from him and swearing and cursing, grabbed his clothes and started to get dressed. Carla pulled a sad, staged dramatic face and imploringly asked, "No want me? No want Carla?"

"No I bloody well don't. Give me my money back." Carla could get dressed far more quickly than Jim, probably having had more practise. She grabbed the money and was out of the room whilst Jim was still struggling to get into his trousers. As he exited the room he looked vainly for Carla but she was gone and so was his money. He stormed down the beach looking for Bob and Eric. When he found them at the end of the beach they were doubled up with laughing. "You swine, you knew that was a man didn't you?"

"Oh, God that was the funniest thing. You should have known."

"How the hell was I supposed to know, she, or he in this case was really quite beautiful."

"Yes they all are."

The rest of the week was spent sightseeing and enjoying the swimming and boating that the island offered. The boys all took a hired boat out to one of the smaller islands where they drank copious amounts of beer and swam all day in the warm softly lapping waters amongst hundreds of different coloured tropical fish. They dived for oysters and clams and flirted unashamedly with the native girls. Samantha was never far from Jim's mind but he was determined to enjoy the holiday and the boys made sure he did just that.

The tuk tuks were the main means of transport on the island and the boys took a trip into the forest one day to see the monkeys. They took along an esky full of beer and sang at the top of their young energetic lungs causing the locals in the fields to stop work and see what the mad tourists were doing. They stopped at the base of some cliffs and all the boys alighted and started looking for the local monkeys, shouting encouraging invitations to the monkeys, "Come on little critters, come and say hello to some Aussie boys. We'll take your photo and show you how we can monkey about." At that point they all tried to imitate monkey calls to tempt the monkeys to come down from the hills. "Whoop! Whoop!" Shouted Jim, "That's not how you do it. Whooo! Whooo!" Called out Eric. They all had a go at imitating the monkeys and fell about drunkenly laughing at their feeble and failed attempts. Jim started to sing a song he had known years earlier about two monkeys but as he couldn't hold a tune and didn't remember the words they all fell about laughing. Jim tried again to recall the words, "I love you my little monkey, or something. La, la, la, la, bugger, I don't know any more." Again they all collapsed into a laughing drunken heap as they tried to get back on board the tuk tuk. At that point Bob decided their driver had been going too slow and so jumped into the driver's seat to show him how an Aussie can drive. The poor tuk tuk driver tried to stop him but Bob had devoured too much beer to take any notice of his entreaties. "No, no, me drive. You no drive. You no license, you no drive."

Bob had drunk far too much and had no real grasp of the money exchange. He just took out some notes and stuffed them into the hands of the tuk tuk driver. The driver had never seen so much money and ceased his wailing hoping that Bob wouldn't actually kill them all, but happy in the knowledge that he and his family could exist on that much money for many months to come. Bob drove like a drunken maniac and fortunately out in the countryside there were few other vehicles. The boys were all having a great time laughing and singing. Suddenly as they turned a corner they were confronted by a local farmer moving his emaciated cows from one paddock to the other across the rough gravel road. Bob's reactions were too slow to avoid hitting one of the poor animals and the boys, the driver and the tuk tuk all finished up in the ditch. No-one was hurt and the cow made an awful racket at it ran off down the road. Only at that point did the boys notice that at least twenty monkeys had come down from the hills close by to see what the commotion was all about and just sat jabbering on the road and on a neighbouring tree watching the show.

The farmer and the tuk tuk driver had a furious argument which was quickly settled when Bob yet again donated an indecent amount of money to the farmer. The tuk tuk driver took over his vehicle once more and delivered the boys safely back to their hotel. Only the following day did Bob realise just how much money he had wasted on the day. Enough, the other boys told him for the farmer and driver to feed and house their families for probably six months.

As their plane was approaching Perth Jim's thoughts kept returning to Samantha. He hadn't slept on the flight and hadn't been able to concentrate on the film that was showing. He was trying to work out what he was going to do about Samantha. Would he leave her alone or would he try and approach her and find out just how serious she was about this new boy friend, this Freddy whatever his name was.

Once the boys had disembarked from the plane and been through customs and immigration they made their way to the carousel to pick up their suitcases. As the luggage started to come through Jim heard one or two people start to chuckle and wondered what they were laughing about. Amongst the suitcases it became obvious that someone's case had broken open and there on the carousel was a shirt and one sock. As the three boys looked at the shirt and chuckled along with everyone else Jim suddenly realised that he recognised the shirt. He had one just like it. Further down the line a pair of underpants appeared and one shoe. Now he knew exactly whose wayward luggage it was. The shoe was definitely his. Now Jim had a tough decision to make, should he suffer the derision of his fellow passengers and retrieve his scattered clothing, or should he just ignore the stuff and pretend he knew nothing about it, laugh along with everyone else. It was Bob who was the first one to openly recognise Jim's clothing. "Hey Jim, isn't that your underpants and bathers going round and round?" Jim was mortified and in disgust started to collect the items placing them in a heap by his feet. One cheeky young teenager piped up with, "You travelling light mister?" another with, "Couldn't you afford a suitcase?"

His broken case eventually came into view and he could see a large rip down one side. When he collected it off the carousel he read a short note attached which read, "Damaged in transit." No apology, no excuse.

The other boys were helpless with laughter but sympathetic at the same time, however they refused to assist Jim by collecting the remaining one or two items of clothing still on the carousel. The taxi ride home for Jim was taken in stony, moody silence.

20

PLANNING FOR A WEDDING

S amantha and Agnetha became really good friends very quickly. Samantha agreed to help her "soon to be" sister-in-law look for work. Freddy had already been offered a position in the Mining Department, even before he had left England. He had graduated top of his class and so was head hunted by a company sending out their human resources team to various countries to offer employment to the very best in the field of young graduates. Agnetha had family in Sweden but no other relatives in Australia. Samantha's parents took to the girl immediately and she quickly became one of the family. They could see how happy Freddy was and they were delighted for the pair.

Neither Freddy nor Agnetha wanted a long engagement and so started to prepare for a small wedding. It was agreed that they would marry "al fresco" and not in a church as neither were religious. There was a small park not too far from Samantha's home and it was agreed that a celebrant would be booked to officiate at the park wedding. Agnetha asked Samantha first of all if she would be her bridesmaid and secondly if she would help choose a wedding dress.

Samantha was thrilled and excited. She'd never been a

bridesmaid before and was only too pleased to do this for her "about to be" sister-in-law. The two girls set off the next Saturday morning to troll through the various bridal shops looking for suitable dresses, shoes and head dress. It was an exciting time and the girls, arm in arm spent the whole day in and out of every bridal shop in Perth. They tried on so many dresses that they were beginning to get "punch drunk." They laughed as they tried to recall which of all the dresses they had liked the best. They made a short list and decided to return home to enlist the help of Samantha's mother in making final choices. What the girls hadn't noticed was a very startled Jim seeing them go into a bridal shop in the centre of town. He just happened to be shopping for some badly needed new shoes. One of his shoes had been irretrievably lost when his suitcase broke at the airport. He thought it was probably still going round and round the carousel waiting to be claimed.

Jim was shocked to see some way ahead of him, on the other side of the road, the unmistakable red curly hair of Samantha going into a bridal shop. He had no idea who the other girl was and immediately jumped to the conclusion that a visit to the bridal shop must mean that Samantha was getting married. He stood there in utter confusion. He wanted to run but his feet wouldn't move.

Eventually the girls came out of the shop laughing and looking so happy. Jim stood mutely by with tears in his eyes. Samantha spotted him and ran across the road to where he stood. As he saw her approaching he turned on his heel and ran. "Stop Jim." shouted Samantha, but Jim was too utterly devastated to stop. He had wanted to talk to her but he just panicked and ran. Samantha realised what he must be thinking and refusing to following him, decided to go to see him at his house after doing her shopping.

The happy mood was broken and the two girls went home to talk with Samantha's mother about all the dresses they had seen.

That evening Samantha went to Jim's house determined to find out just where she stood. Why hadn't he answered her letters and why had he been outside the bridal shop. When Jim saw Samantha on his doorstep he didn't quite know what to do; invite her in or shut the door in her face. Being ever the gentleman though, he mutely indicated for her to enter. Jim was too tongue tied and anguished to say anything at first but did the English thing and put on the kettle for a cup of tea. Both were loath to start the conversation but Samantha took the initiative and asked cagily, "what's happened to us Jim? We were so happy." Jim couldn't speak, he thought his heart would break. He could only make the tea and place a cup before her. Eventually he found his voice and said really what was on his mind. "So you're getting married. I'm really sorry for us, but I guess I'm glad for you. I really do hope you will be happy with Freddy, he actually looks like a decent guy." Samantha never touched her cup of tea, she just stood up from the table and crossed the room to where Jim was standing. She reached up and put her arms around his neck. "You goose. I'm not getting married, at least not to Freddy. Didn't you read my letters?"

Err, well no actually. So who are you getting married to then?"

"No-one, Freddy is my brother. He's only recently come over from England. He and his fiancé Agnetha are the ones getting married." Jim just looked at her with his mouth open. He didn't know what to think. He tried casting his mind back to the camping trip and the events that followed. "You mean you don't love Freddy?"

"Well of course I love Freddy, as I told you, he's my brother."

"I'm confused. I don't know what to think."

"Well stop thinking. Just know one thing. These last few weeks have been really busy for me with Freddy and Agnetha arriving, but I missed you. I tried to contact you at work and here at your house but no-one would tell me where you were. I know we had some troubles with the camping trip and I was awfully cross with you but the truth is I missed you and I realise now how much I love you. Can we start again and put these last few weeks behind us?"

"Did you say you love me?"

"Yes, you Nellie, I love you."

"Oh Samantha, I love you too. I thought you had found a new man. I saw you kiss him outside your office. I thought the camping trip had put you off and you were finished with me. Oh I love you so much, I was devastated."

21

THE BEST MAN

Freddy had only been in the country a few weeks and so had hardly time to make any close friends. Once Jim and Samantha were back on an even keel and Jim had been to the house a few times the two men became firm friends. They had similar interests in soccer and fishing and the four young people spent a few double dates getting to know each other. As the wedding date was approaching Freddy asked Jim if he would be his best man. "Crumbs Freddy, I don't know the first thing about being a best man. I mean I'm honoured that you would ask me, but isn't there anyone else who would know what to do?"

"No, it's you I want. There's nothing to it really."

"Well if you're sure, but I'll need to read up on what I have to do. I guess I can ask Samantha, she'll know all the ins and outs of it."

"So it's settled then? You'll be my best man?"

"I guess so."

The next few weeks leading up to the wedding were busy for the family. Maisie Perkins, Samantha's mother took control of all the organising; flowers, celebrant, booking the park, reception, and invitations. She booked Freddy, Gordon and Jim in to the formal hire company for a fitting for their evening suits, and ordered her own "mother of the groom" outfit with an overly large picture hat. Agnetha chose her wedding dress and Samantha chose her bridesmaid outfit. Everyone was happy except Jim. He had been told that, as best man he was expected to make a speech at the reception. He'd never made a speech in his life and public speaking was certainly not anything that he felt comfortable contemplating. He enlisted Samantha's help and together they formed the basis of a reasonable speech which included making a toast to the bride and groom. Samantha filled Jim in on a few comments to make about Freddy and some funny incidents in his childhood, as well as a couple of jokes.

When the day of the wedding arrived Jim was in a lather of debilitating nerves. He kept checking his pocket to ensure he still had the rings and checking his folded typed copy of the speech. Freddy was calm and in high spirits and encouraged to Jim to have a couple of whiskies to calm his nerves. When Freddy wasn't looking Jim had another couple of whiskies as the first two didn't seem to calm his nerves at all. Jim usually drank beer and had never had whiskey before and had no experience of what it would do to him.

As the two men drove to the park Jim began to feel quite ill. He had been too nervous to eat any breakfast and now his head was spinning. The car seemed to be going too fast and his stomach was doing somersaults. He barely heard the celebrant going through the ceremony and it wasn't until Freddy dug him in the ribs that he realised the time had come to supply the rings. The celebrant was asking Freddy to place the ring on Samantha's finger and Jim fumbled with the rings in his pocket and came up first with a thick broad band that was obviously meant for Freddy. As he realised his mistake he tried to put the ring back in his pocket and retrieve the correct one. In his nervous state his hands were shaking and sweating and didn't seem to belong to him. He missed his pocket and Freddy's ring fell silently into the grass beneath their feet. Panicking he quickly reached into his pocket for the correct ring and after handing it over bent down to retrieve Freddy's ring. Just as Freddy was placing the ring on Samantha's finger Jim lost his balance and toppled over into the grass. Everyone had a good laugh except Samantha's father who had no sense of humour and complained bitterly to his wife, expressing his doubts about Jim's suitability as a husband for their daughter. "Good grief Maisie, is our girl going to actually marry that clown?"

"Shhh, he's a nice boy, just very nervous."

Freddy had to stop what he was doing to help Jim up. Once the ceremony was over Jim excused himself and dashed behind some bushes and noisily tried to empty the contents of his stomach. Other than whiskey there was nothing actually in Jim's stomach but he retched anyway.

The reception was looming and Jim's apprehension about the speech was crippling his ability to think straight. When a waiter approached him with a glass of champagne Jim just needed a drink. He was thirsty and water would have been preferable but champagne was all that he was offered and so quickly downed two glasses. When the time came for Jim's speech he could barely stand. His words were slurred and he couldn't get his eyes to focus on the typed speech that Samantha had prepared for him. He swayed a little as he tried to steady himself before launching into a maudlin appraisal of how beautiful Agnetha and Samantha were, and all that was wonderful about Freddy. The speech that he delivered bore no resemblance at all to the one that Samantha had prepared. He vaguely remembered a schoolboy joke and delivered that causing some hilarity as he got the punch line mixed up. Only at the end did Jim remember to ask everyone to toast the new bride and groom.

Once his duty was over Jim managed to relax somewhat. Samantha fed him two cups of strong coffee and with some food inside him he started to enjoy the evening. A band playing popular music invited everyone onto the floor for dancing. The bride and groom took to the floor for their first dance and after a couple of circuits round the polished boards everyone else was invited onto the floor. Jim had never been any kind of dancer, and he vaguely remembered the dance class that his Aunt had persuaded him to attend many weeks earlier, but in his current alcohol addled mind he was now an expert.

He asked Samantha if she would like to dance and she readily, in her ignorance acceded. From the first moment it became clear that Jim was no Fred Astaire. He seemed to have little knowledge of the beat or tempo of the music and Samantha struggled to make some sense of what his feet were trying to do. The first piece of music ended and the second piece turned out to be the old hit "Samantha." Jim recognised it immediately and as they smooched, rather than danced, around the floor he started in on a boozy rendition of the song. Like his dancing Jim had no sense of rhythm or timing. He was obviously tone deaf too but nevertheless sang softly, off key into Samantha's tortured ear.

Samantha was somewhat flattered but realised Jim was still quite intoxicated. He had managed to tackle the waltz and a slow fox trot with a certain air of drunken decorum but once the music livened up and started to play some hot jazz Samantha decided that it was safer to sit these dances out. Jim however was on a roll and desperately wanted to dance. When Samantha refused him he looked around for someone else to torment.

Samantha's cousin Jilly was a middle aged overweight spinster who had been sitting alone since arriving at the reception. He made a beeline for Jilly who was only too pleased to be asked to dance. Most couples were dancing facing each other but only jigging around, not actually touching each other. This suited Jilly who just gyrated at her own pace. Jim was fascinated as he watched her rolls of fat undulate up and down, from her many chins to her dimpled knees. Samantha watched in equal fascination as Jim managed to twist his uncoordinated back, arms and legs into every possible weird looking position. His contorted arms and legs didn't appear to belong to him at all, each limb seemed to move to its own rhythm with no actual connection to any of the others, but he wasn't falling over and he actually looked as if he was enjoying himself. Samantha's father, pointing to Jim just muttered to his wife, "Bloody idiot."

22

MOVING IN

Two weeks after Freddy's wedding Samantha agreed to move in with Jim. They were both in love and wanted their relationship to progress to its ultimate end, which they both fervently hoped would be marriage, although the word marriage hadn't been spoken of. Samantha knew her father would be very much against the move, he was extremely protective of his only daughter, but she hoped her mother would be supportive. Samantha and her mother discussed the issue and how they thought Gordon would react. They both agreed that it might be best if Maisie could talk to her husband to try and smooth the way for the pair.

Jim was not a pushy person, he was usually quiet and reserved, even shy, unless inebriated. He realised that Samantha's father might very well refuse to let Samantha move out of his house but he was determined to stand up to the old man and state his case quite plainly. He found his chance when the two were in the dining room alone. "Gordon, I need to talk to you. I know you maybe don't think much of me, and maybe I wasn't on my best behaviour at the wedding, but I sincerely love your daughter and I would like your permission to marry her and I hope you won't stand in our way."

"Are you mad? She's too young."

"She's old enough to make up her own mind. We're wanting Samantha to initially move in with me. We both want this very much. We really don't need your permission but we'd like your blessing."

Samantha's father had seen very little of Jim before Freddy's wedding and hadn't realised how close Samantha and Jim were. He was contemptuous of any man who couldn't hold his liquor and Jim had not impressed him with his antics at the wedding. "Listen young man, I don't want my only daughter hitching up with someone who can't look after her properly. If you want my blessing you're going to have to show me that you are worthy of her, that you can take good care of her and not make an ass of yourself every time you are in company and have a drink or two. So to answer your question, no, you can't marry my daughter and I certainly don't want her moving in with you, not until you can show me that you are a responsible person and can provide for and take care of my daughter."

"Sir, my behaviour at the wedding was an unfortunate occurrence, I admit I'd had too much to drink but I assure you that was not the real me. I was so nervous and when offered a drink I took it without realising what effect it would have on me. Samantha and Freddy have forgiven me. Can't we put it behind us?" Before Samantha's father could answer, her mother Maisie came into the room and asked, "What are we trying to put behind us Jim?"

"Well actually I was asking Gordon if he would give his blessing for Samantha to move in with me. I love her very much and promise to take good care of her."

Maisie Perkins put her arms around Jim and hugged him to her ample bosom. "Oh that's lovely, I know she is very fond of you too." Samantha's father stood with his hands on his hips and addressed the pair sternly. "Listen you two, I didn't give my permission. I'm not happy with Samantha moving in with you, it's not decent, and what if she gets pregnant?" Samantha's mother turned to her husband and wagged her finger at him, "For goodness sake Gordon Perkins we lived together for six months before we were married, don't come the high and mighty. You know very well Freddy was born three months after we were married. Don't be a hypocrite. If the kids are in love then they'll do what they want anyway." With that she turned to Jim smiling, "Of course you have our blessing and permission. You seem like a really nice young man and I know you have a secure job with the government so of course, Samantha can move in with you if that's what you both want." Maisie Perkins took Jim's arm and propelled him from the room leaving her husband frustrated, beaten, impotent and fuming. He knew better than to argue with his wife.

Once Samantha had moved in with Jim they discussed the future in great detail, their hopes, their dreams, their aspirations for work and maybe having a family. They both agreed that Jim's house was central to the city and in good repair. Neither felt that they need to contemplate selling the house or moving into anything else, the house itself was in a good area and was of a good size. It would be entirely suitable if they were to have children and become a real family. The only reservation that Samantha had was that the whole house reflected the lives of Jim's mother and grandmother.

The house was really quite beautiful but the furnishings were all old fashioned, slightly worn and the house needed a good facelift. Jim readily agreed and gave her a free hand. He had no money problems; his grandmother had left him a reasonable inheritance as had his mother. He was happy to let Samantha refurnish and refurbish the old house. She organised for the kitchen to be taken out and a new one ordered. The bathroom also needed upgrading. They were both jobs that needed professionals and all the work was contracted to a well known company in the city. Samantha ordered new tiles for the kitchen and bathroom, and new carpet for the dining room, bedrooms and lounge. It was a busy but exciting time for the young couple. Jim was not emotionally attached to any of the furniture and readily agreed to give everything away to the charity shops and to start again with new and more modern furnishings.

The internal walls of the house needed some attention. Jim could have had the walls repainted professionally but volunteered instead to do the work himself. Being an older house, the walls were no longer smooth and it seemed appropriate to paper the walls rather than just paint them. Jim actually wanted to show Samantha that he wasn't useless and that he could turn his hand to anything if he set his mind to it. Samantha asked tentatively, "Have you ever papered a wall before? I mean have you ever actually done any wallpapering?"

"Well no, but how difficult can it be? I mean it's only a matter of pasting paper to a wall; kid's stuff; no problem."

"No, I think we should get a professional in to do it." Hoping to impress and show Samantha how handy he was Jim was adamant, "No, I can do it, I'll show you; nothing to it."

The following weekend the two young lovers trolled the hardware and furnishings stores looking for suitable wallpaper. They both decided that they wanted something classic which would reflect the age of the house without compromising the modern look. Stripes were out as were polka dots and modern designs. What they both agreed upon was a large pattern of fully blown blue roses. They shopped for paste and brushes as well as a large step ladder.

In the hardware shop Jim wanted to only buy one paste brush but as he looked on the shelves all he could find were packets of three brushes. He approached the young female sales assistant and asked could he buy just one brush. "Sorry sir but they only come in packets of three."

"But I don't want three, I only want one."

"Well I'm sorry sir I don't make the rules, you have to buy all three. If you don't want the extra two just throw them away."

"That's very wasteful and expensive. Why should I have to pay for something I don't want?"

"I'm sorry sir, that's just the way it is." Samantha walked away not wanting to hear any more. She sympathised with Jim but she knew he wouldn't get anywhere arguing with a poor assistant who was only doing her job. Jim wasn't one to give up easily, "This packet says eleven dollars ninety nine. Now that's sheer stupidity for a start, I mean do you really think we don't know that it's really twelve dollars. Why bother with the ninety nine cents bit? It's ridiculous and an insult to our intelligence."

"I'm sorry sir, it's not my fault. I only work here." Jim tried reasoning with the girl,

"Look why don't I give you four dollars and you give me one brush and you keep the other two." The shop assistant excused herself, picked up a phone on her desk and called for the manager. Jim was escorted ignominiously from the shop vowing never to return. Samantha pretended not to know him.

Being an older house the rooms were airy and the ceilings unusually high. Once all the furniture had been covered the old dining room table was brought into service as a work bench. Jim agreed to let Samantha help him on the understanding that he was in charge and she was to act as his helper only. Samantha for her part suspected that Jim probably didn't know the first thing about wallpapering and so was keen to assist if only as an excuse to keep an eye on the proceedings.

Jim decided the first step would be to take a measurement, floor to ceiling, starting at one end, and assumed that all the measurements would be the same. He forgot to take into account that the house was old and the walls were anything but identical, in some places there was a good inch difference in the height, but he didn't know that, well not at the start anyway.

He carefully measured out the length of the wallpaper and cut the first length he wanted, precisely. Meanwhile Samantha was mixing up the paste and trying to take the brush out from the plastic wrapping. The plastic was too strong for her and in desperation she handed it to Jim who wrestled with the unbending container. Eventually in frustration he collected the carving knife from the kitchen and slit one end of the container releasing the brush, but at the same time cutting the end of his index finger. Bleeding profusely he cursed and swore as Samantha ducked into the kitchen and returned with a small sticking plaster. It became obvious quite quickly that the plaster was too small and so two more had to be obtained from the first aid box. Three or four drops of blood splashed onto the newly cut wallpaper and Jim made a hasty attempt to wipe off the blood with his handkerchief. Unfortunately the more he wiped the wider the stain got. Samantha retreated into the kitchen again and came back with a small bowl of water and a sponge. She tried her best to remove the blood stain but the blood had soaked right into the absorbent paper and no amount of rubbing could remove it. "Don't worry Sam. We'll just screw that piece of paper up and start on another one." Jim was a little hampered by the sore finger but soldiered on regardless.

Once a length of wallpaper had been measured and cut to size Jim proceeded to lather it generously with paste. With each stroke of the brush both he and Samantha were being splattered with the paste but undaunted he continued until the full length of the paper was well and truly pasted. Under Jim's instructions Samantha positioned the stepladder in place for him to ascend and make the first positioning. He held the folded paper in front of him and proceeded to mount the ladder. Unfortunately one of the folds decided to give way and dropped to the floor just as Jim took his second step on the ladder. Inevitably, as he couldn't see what was happening beneath him, Jim stepped right through the soggy wallpaper. With much cursing and swearing Jim descended the ladder and again screwed up the damaged piece of wallpaper. Samantha made a funny noise in the back of her throat and turned away. Jim shouted at her immediately, "Don't you dare laugh. It's not funny."

The third piece of paper was eventually placed into position and both Jim and Samantha took a step backwards to admire their handiwork. Only one piece of wallpaper was on the wall but they both agreed it looked lovely, however as they watched the paper slowly, oh so slowly started to slide down towards the floor. With their mouths open they both mutely watched, hardly daring to say a word. "I think the paste was too thin, we need it to be thicker." Samantha just nodded her head not saying anything. A fresh length of paper was cut and hung before they took a well earned break for a cup of tea and started in on the next piece. Jim measured the length precisely and cut the piece with great concentration. He had learnt his lesson about not making the paper too soggy and not making the paste too thin. He was extremely careful not to step onto the paper as he ascended the ladder. When he placed the top of the paper against the wall, butting up to the cornice he carefully smoothed out the fold and guided the paper down to the ground. Only then did both Jim and Samantha realise that one large blue rose on the first piece of wallpaper did not match up to an identical blue rose on the second piece. There was a good five inches difference in the pattern and at the seam no two roses matched up. Jim cursed and called down the wrath of all that was evil. Samantha again made a queer choking sound and quickly disappeared into the kitchen. "Don't you dare laugh. This is not as easy as it looks. You're not helping at all."

Once she had composed herself Samantha returned and saw Jim pulling off the soggy third piece of wallpaper from the wall. Jim took a deep breath and not wanting to be defeated announced, "Look this might be a bit more difficult than I thought, but we're getting there."

"Yes dear."

Jim took stock of the pattern and carefully measured out the length again cutting off the excess five inches from the top in order to get the roses matched up. He pasted the piece and carefully butted it up to the cornice as before. Now with the second piece of paper in place it started to look as if they had got the hang of it and both stood back to admire the effect. Samantha took a step forward and ran her hand up the middle of the paper and asked, "What's that bump in the middle?"

"What bump?"

"It's a thin line, a definite bump."

"Oh for crying out loud, it's the bloody pencil got stuck to the paper." By the time they had manoeuvred the paper backing it up the offending bump the wallpaper was ruined and so the whole sheet had to be pulled off and a fresh one started.

The next four sheets were hung with care and precision. It

was beginning to look like they had mastered the art of hanging wallpaper but the fifth sheet was their undoing. By this time both Samantha and Jim were tired and covered in drying paste. Samantha had paste in her hair and was not contemplating the problem she knew she would be facing when she would try and wash it out. She had a difficult time enough coping with her strong wilful curls, but paste mixed in with the curls was not going to be easy to remove.

The fifth sheet had to be negotiated around a bend in the wall. This was no easy task and the two corners at the top, abutting the cornice just wouldn't stick in place, either one butted up neatly or the other, but not both. Jim in frustration pulled one side too strenuously and it tore off in his hand. He tried in vain to paste it back into place but it just wouldn't fit and so another sheet of wallpaper bit the dust and ended up in the waste bin.

Once round the corner Jim was beginning to feel less confident. It had taken them all day and they had only one wall covered. The next sheet was measured but Jim couldn't understand why it was half an inch short when it reached the bottom. Another sheet had to be demolished and bit the dust. A fresh sheet had to be measured and half an inch added. Jim was only just realising that all the walls were not precisely the same size, and so each length had to be measured again and again. Each time a sheet was destroyed Samantha got a fit of the giggles and had to disappear into the kitchen.

Jim was getting more and more frustrated and angry. He barked orders at Samantha who shouted back at him. These were not the words of two lovers, more like the words of combatants in a divorce court. He called her names and she retaliated with derision of his prowess as a home handyman, or lack thereof. The dogs started barking as their evening meal was late. Samantha disappeared into the kitchen to open a can of dog food for the two animals. She let them in from the back garden and in their exuberance at being allowed into the house and at being fed the two dogs bounded into the living room where Jim was working and one immediately knocked over the bowl of wallpaper paste. Both dogs paddled through the mess on the floor and carried the mess through to the kitchen. The cat not to be outdone followed the dogs and something in the paste obviously attracted him as he started to lap up the offending mess. Jim threw the paste brush at the departing dogs and whacked the cat with a piece of soggy wallpaper.

He sat in the middle of the mess with his hands over his head and gave way to a wave of self pity. Samantha realising how frustrated Jim was thought the only way to save the whole debacle was to make some fun out of it. The carpet was ruined, but was going to be thrown out anyway so she just grabbed a handful of the offending paste and threw it at Jim. He looked up and saw her laughing face and releasing some of the tension he was feeling, retaliated by throwing a handful of the foul paste back at her. They covered each other in paste laughing themselves silly, and finished up rolling, with the two dogs in the mess before taking a hot shower and washing each other's hair.

The next day Samantha telephoned a professional home handyman and arranged for him to buy a new stock of the same wallpaper and to start in on the lounge walls the following weekend.

23

THE CAKE STALL

The winter soccer season was approaching and Belinda called all the girls together and discussed the proposal that they again enter the Wyverns into the Women's Soccer League for another season. All the girls were enthusiastic and Jim was coerced once again into acting as coach. Belinda reported that the Council now required payment for the use of their playing field; the initial season had been a freebie in order to get the girls started, but now they were required to pay a weekly fee. None of the girls had much money and so ideas were put forward to try and do some fundraising.

Various proposals were put forward from door-to-door knocking to organising a raffle. It all seemed like a lot of hard work and most of the girls were young marrieds, with one or two small children and so didn't have an awful lot of spare time. One proposal proved to be very popular and they all agreed on applying to the local Council to see if they could hold a cake stall in the centre of town. Belinda agreed to write to the Council and see what was involved. As she said, "If we all just bake one cake we could sell them one Saturday morning and the income from that would pay for a couple of week's playing field hire. Maybe then we could consider a sausage sizzle or something similar in future weeks. All the girls were willing to bake at least one cake each and it was arranged for the first Saturday the following month.

As it happened almost at the same time Jim received an invitation from his boss, Roger Grant for dinner at the Grant household. Roger Grant was a corpulent gentle giant who was nearing retirement age and Samantha and Jim discussed the invitation and what implications it might have for Jim's future at the Department. They both hoped that it might mean promotion if the Grants approved of Samantha and Jim's social graces. They reasoned that promotion should have nothing to do with socialising with the boss but they were also astute enough to know that sometimes it really did matter. The date for the dinner was set and it turned out to be the night after the cake stall was to be held.

Samantha had meant to bake her cake on the Friday night before the cake stall on the Saturday morning, but two girls were sick at work and she was asked to stay back and do some overtime. Jim had no idea how to bake a cake but volunteered to bake it for her. As he explained, "Look we have two good cookery books that show you how to do it. I mean, how difficult can it be?" Samantha agreed to let him bake the cake on the understanding that he follow the recipe to the letter.

On the way home from work Jim picked up the groceries that Samantha had written on the shopping list and set to with a good heart and much determination. It didn't appear to be too difficult. He mixed the butter and sugar and broke two eggs into the mixture. After a slight mishap he managed to fish out most of the shells and proceeded undaunted. As he was about to put it all into a baking tray Samantha came home and took over. The oven was turned on and the mixture put in to bake.

Half an hour later the beautifully risen golden cake was taken out of the oven and Jim and Samantha praised each other on a job well done. Samantha had written on the shopping list for Jim to buy a packet of pre-mix roll-on icing as she was not too confident about making a good iced topping. She had also included a request for some edible artificial flowers to decorate the top.

The two happy bakers had their supper and watched some television waiting for the cake to cool down and Samantha declared that she would then decorate the cake with the white icing and flowers. There was an interesting programme on the television and so it was nearly bedtime before the two bakers returned into the kitchen to start to decorate the cake. Samantha was the first to see the disaster, "Oh My God, What's happened to the cake? It's sunk." True enough there was a large hole in the centre of the cake. It looked more like a giant donut than a sponge cake. "Oh what are we going to do?"

"Don't worry, we'll just have to make another one tomorrow. We'll have time, we don't have to be at the cake stall until eleven o'clock."

"Oh, do you think we can?"

"Yes, don't worry, I must have done something wrong, but you can help me in the morning and we'll do a new one."

The morning dawned bright and beautiful and the two enthusiastic cooks set about making their second attempt. Samantha took charge and measured out each ingredient with care and precision. The cake went into the oven and both sat like a pair of broody hens waiting for their chick to hatch.

Once the cake had been in the oven for the exact required time Jim brought it out and declared it a winner, "Look Sam, its perfect. It's risen a treat, I'm sure this one will be just fine."

Famous last words.

The two enthusiastic bakers got on with other chores whilst they waited for the cake to cool down. Again Samantha was the first to notice that their baby, the golden cake was looking decidedly sad. "Jim look, I think the cake is sinking again." The two watched disheartened as the cake slowly started to resemble an extinct volcano. The centre of the cake was soggy and the sides were hard. "Oh what are we going to do? I don't know what went wrong, we followed the recipe. We just don't have time to cook another one."

"Don't worry Sam, I know what we'll do, I'll just nip down to the supermarket and buy a commercial cake."

"No, you can't do that. We all promised to bake a cake. It makes a nonsense of the fundraising if we have to go out and buy one."

"Maybe no-one will notice the difference."

"Yes they will, we can't possibly pass off a store-bought cake as our own home-make cake. That wouldn't be right."

"Well what are we going to do?"

"I know. How about this for an idea, we take this Mt. Vesuvious disaster and stuff the hole with tissues and cotton wool. We then roll out the pre-made icing and just cover the cake up, decorate it and no-one will be the wiser."

"Hell's bells you can't do that. What happens when someone cuts into it?"

"No, you don't understand. We'll cover the hole as I said and I'll deliver the cake at eleven. You come along behind me and you buy the cake before any customer can get to it. We bring it home and no-one will know."

"Do you think we could?"

"Yes, but you have to buy it quickly."

"Okay, I guess we just don't have a choice."

So Samantha rolled out the premade icing and laid it over the top of the cotton wool stuffed cake. She decorated the cake with the white icing and the pretty artificial edible bright red roses; she crimped the edges with a fork and it actually looked quite professional.

They drove into the centre of town and Samantha carried the cake to the cake stall leaving Jim to park the car. Jim should have followed Samantha immediately, unfortunately he had parked in a loading zone and an irate parking inspector took him to task and ordered him to move his vehicle and go park somewhere else. It took Jim a further ten minutes to find a legal parking spot and he had to sprint back to the cake stall quickly to buy the cake.

When Jim got to the cake stall all the girls were there except Samantha and Jane. They were a little way off to the side attending to Jane's young child who was throwing a tantrum. Jim scoured the dozen or so cakes looking for their red rose topped offering. He couldn't see it amongst the other cakes and so approached Samantha asking, "Sam where's the cake, I can't see it anywhere?"

"I don't know, I put it at the back, it should be there."

"No it's not."

"Oh, for crying out loud, don't tell me someone actually bought it?"

"I don't know, I guess they must have, it's definitely not there."

"Well where have you been anyway? You should have been here ten minutes ago?"

"I know, I'm sorry, I couldn't help it, an officious parking inspector made me move on. It took me ages to find another parking space."

"Well if the cake's not there, it's just not. Nothing we can do

183

about it, I just hope whoever bought it doesn't cut into it today and come back to complain."

At the end of the day all the cakes had sold and there were "high fives" all round. It was agreed that the fundraising had been a good idea and they had made enough money to cover two week's playing field fees. Belinda suggested they consider holding a sausage sizzle next time and everyone agreed.

The next day Samantha was in a quandary about what to wear for the dinner at Jim's boss's house. "How formal do you think it's going to be Jim?"

"I really don't know."

"Do you think there may be other people, other guests there?"

"I really don't know."

"Well how dressed up should we be do you think?"

"I really don't know. Look Sam, stop worrying; Roger Grant is a really nice old man, just be yourself. Wear something smart but not 'over the top.' You know something like your blue lace dress, that would be suitable, you always look nice in that. Blue suits your red curls."

On the Sunday of the dinner Jim and Samantha drove out to Peppermint Grove to the Grant household and were duly impressed as they drove up the long driveway. At the end of the driveway there appeared a large ornate three storey white stone house with panoramic views looking out over the Swan River. Rita Grant, Roger's wife turned out to be a caricature of Hyacinth Bucket, the main character in the British comedy series "Keeping Up Appearances." Hyacinth is a social climbing snob who puts on all the airs and graces of nobility, with hysterical results. Rita Grant looked like Hyacinth, talked like Hyacinth, and acted like Hyacinth. She obviously wore the trousers in that household and bullied her gentle amiable husband. However he obviously adored her and when Samantha commented on their beautiful home he went into raptures about how Rita was the one with the good taste and how wonderful she was in the kitchen.

Rita had a young woman help her in the kitchen but informed Samantha and Jim that she did all the cooking herself. "Oh yes, Mary is just our helper, you know for cleaning, doing the serving and dishes and things, but I do all the cooking."

Roger was quick to compliment his wife stating, "Oh yes, Rita is a wonderful cook. She studied in London you know."

The meal that Rita served was indeed wonderful. Roger opened a bottle of Krug Champagne, and as he started to explain, "this is a 1998 Clos d'Ambonnay which we..." Rita jumped in talking over the top of her husband and explained, "Oh yes we just love the Clos d'Ambonnay, it has well integrated flavours of raspberry and blackberry along with just a hint of licorice." Roger handed Samantha and Jim their champagne in the most beautiful delicate crystal cut glass flutes which were bright cobalt blue. Samantha took her glass and held it up to the light, "Gosh Mrs. Grant...."

"Oh please call me Rita."

"Well Rita, these are the most beautiful and unusual glasses, such a beautiful colour."

"Well yes, of course, they're Waterford Lismore diamond flutes. Antiques really. We only have the best." Jim's hands started to shake; he was terrified of dropping and breaking a glass. Samantha was indeed impressed with the champagne, it really did taste wonderful. Jim was to be driving home later that night and so it gave him a good excuse not to drink any more and so he drank his first glass but didn't have to worry about dropping or breaking a glass after that.

Rita and her helper, Mary, served their entrée which turned out to be scallops au gratin beautifully served in individual scallop shells. "How was that?" Roger asked Jim.

"It was delicious, thank you."

"There," boasted Roger, "didn't I tell you my wife's a magnificent cook." The main course was served with some flair. It turned out to be Pheasant Vallee d'Auge and was served with its tail feathers still on. Samantha asked Rita, "What is that incredible sauce over the Pheasant, it tastes wonderful?"

"Oh, that my dear is Calvados, it's an apple brandy, from Normandy you know, it's history goes way back."

"Well it's just delicious." After the main course Roger asked his wife, "Rita dear, what do we have for sweet?" Turning to Jim before Rita could answer, "My wife makes the most wonderful sweets, especially her cakes, they're to die for. Honestly."

"Don't go on and on Roger, you're embarrassing me."

"Well its true dear, your cakes are wonderful."

"Well as it happens Roger we do have an iced cake for desert so you'll be happy with that."

"Super!" Roger turned to Samantha and remarked, "You folks are in for a treat, I can assure you."

Now it so happened that Rita, who was usually really well organised had an upsetting day on the Saturday, the day before the dinner. She had prepared all the food for the meal except for the sweet course. She had left that to the last, wanting to take her time and prepare something special, however time got away from her. She was the captain of the local bowling club and they had a scheduled away game in the local league on the Saturday afternoon. She just knew the game, and the journey there and back would take hours. She was really worried that she wouldn't have time to make a sweet course and on the way to the bowling club just happened to pass a cake stall in the centre of town. She saw some beautiful cakes and a wicked idea came to mind. If she were to buy a cake, it would save her an awful lot of worry and she could pass it off as her own making, and no-one would be any the wiser. Without informing her husband at all she bought the most beautiful cake she could see; one that was decorated with icing crimped at the edges and bright red edible roses.

Rita had a conscience about the substitute cake but was really trying to impress Jim and Samantha, and so put her conscience behind her, nevertheless she did have the grace to wince a little as her husband went on and on about what a wonderful cook she was and how brilliant were her cakes. She just hoped whoever had made this cake had done a good job. It looked wonderful and so she hoped that it would taste just as wonderful.

Between courses Roger asked Jim what his aspirations were regarding his work at the Department and the two chatted amiably. Samantha smiled encouragingly to Jim and they both hoped fervently that this meal might be the precursor to some sort of promotion for Jim. After another bottle of the Clos d'Ambonnay was opened Roger was beginning to slur his words a little. Jim was scheduled to drive back home and so refused any further drinks. Samantha and Rita were both in high spirits and with some flamboyance Rita had Mary bring in the cake for sweet. Roger leaned in to Samantha and declared, "There didn't I tell you my wife is a great cook. Look at that cake, magnificent!"

Samantha looked with horror at Jim. Their mouths fell open not knowing what to say as Mary brought in the most beautiful cake, with white icing, crimped at the edges and decorated with bright red edible roses.

Jim was promoted to Assistant Manager two weeks later.

24

CELEBRATIONS

I t took two months for the house to be completed. Jim and Samantha had shopped for new furniture, curtains, bedding; the works. Jim could hardly believe it was the same place, it looked so bright and cheerful. Samantha suggested they invite her mother and father as well as Freddy and Agnetha over for a celebration dinner. It was agreed for the following week and Samantha was really looking forward to cooking a sumptuous meal for them all. She and Jim poured over their only two cookbooks and decided on a three course meal that was laid out quite plainly in the book. Jim confessed not only couldn't he bake a cake but he couldn't cook at all and Samantha admitted that her knowledge of cooking was sparse at best. "You know Jim my cooking comes always comes with two choices, take it or leave it."

"Oh very funny, but honestly Sam, we've got to make a real effort this time, no more failures like the cake at the Grant's. I don't think your Dad likes me at all. Let's try and show him that we are good together and can produce a really good meal."

"Well, we'll give it our best shot, but I'm warning you, I've never been the best cook in the world, and we're not going to attempt a cake again.

Both had relied on their mothers and really never had to do any cooking for themselves. The two made lists of things they would need and went shopping with great enthusiasm. Their menu was to consist of a simple entrée, being fried cheritos with a light sauce served with a mixed green chopped salad tucked into a single leaf of whitlof. Neither of them had any idea what a whitlof was and when they asked the greengrocer he told them "I think you mean a Belgian endive, but actually here In Australia we call them chicory. I've got some newly arrived, here they are nice and fresh." The sauce was easy as they bought one premade from the supermarket delicatessen department.

The main course was to be a fried rainbow trout with a potato pie and baby green peas, and the sweet course was to be individual orange soufflés. Jim decided that they would need wine and even champagne to really celebrate the finishing of the house in style.

The day of the dinner arrived and Samantha spent half an hour dressing the table to look special, with flowers and beautiful woven bamboo table mats. The glasses were polished as was the cutlery. The napkins were new and Samantha tried to fold them into pretty patterns but failed miserably. She didn't swear as a rule but when the napkins wouldn't fold as she wanted she took to calling them one or two unsavoury names. She finished up with just folding them neatly.

The fishmonger had advised the pair how to fry the trout and Jim was put in charge of that as well as the potato pie and the green peas. Samantha agreed to make the orange soufflés. They both enjoyed the challenge of cooking together and all too quickly the doorbell rang and their guests arrived.

Samantha and Jim proudly showed the family around the house explaining all that had been done. They had talked weeks earlier to Samantha's parents about the project and what they would be doing and now felt really good about showing off how it had all come together. Samantha's father remembered that Jim had offered to do the wallpapering and examined the blue rose patterned wall with great deliberation. He really didn't like Jim and wanted to find fault but was denied that pleasure as it was obviously a perfect job. When asked by his wife for his opinion he grudgingly admitted that it was, "Okay I suppose." Neither Jim nor Samantha enlightened him as to the truth of the matter; that it was in the end the work of a professional.

Jim asked everyone to be seated and he would open a bottle of champagne to celebrate the finishing of the house. Samantha made sure everyone was seated and quiet and proceeded to announce their second piece of news. "Actually we have two things to celebrate, the first is the finishing of the house but there's another reason to celebrate, Jim has been promoted to Assistant Manager at the Department." Freddy was the first to shake hands with Jim and Maisie flung her arms around him and planted a loud kiss on his blushing cheek. Samantha's father didn't want to acknowledge Jim's promotion at all and sat silent until his wife dug him in the ribs and glared at him, "Gordon, aren't you going to say anything?"

"Err... yes, well done Jim."

Everyone started talking at once, asking Jim all sorts of questions about his work. "Hang on a minute." Piped up Freddy. "Agnetha and I also have something to tell you all, another reason for celebrating actually." They all looked from Freddy to Agnetha, totally unprepared for what was to be announced. "Well, you see, it's like this. We, that is Agnetha and I are going to be parents. We're expecting."

"Oh my goodness gracious me." Gasped Samantha as she flung

her arms around Agnetha, "that's wonderful." Maisie Perkins kissed her son first and then embraced Agnetha saying, "You clever girl, how marvellous. That means I'm going to be a grandmother. Oh my!" Everyone made a fuss of Freddy and Agnetha and the party was going in full swing with everyone almost talking at once. Unfortunately Jim wasn't paying too much attention to what he was doing as he tried to take the top off the bottle of champagne. He was a beer drinker himself and had never actually opened a bottle of champagne before but had seen it done. He twisted the wires and levered the cork without really thinking about the consequences of his action. The cork shot out of the bottle neck with the force of a cannon and unfortunately hit Gordon, Samantha's father on the bridge of his nose. The nose bleed that followed was not serious but Gordon was hurt, very cross and almost glad to vent some anger on poor humiliated Jim. "You blasted idiot, why didn't you point the bottle away from everyone? You could have hit one of the girls, even worse, you could have taken my eye out with that."

Maisie Perkins tried to calm her husband down as she padded his nose with her napkin. "Now, now Gordon, it's not as bad as all that. Come and sit down and have a drink."

"I don't want a bloody drink now." Jim was all apologies but Gordon wasn't listening, he was angry and embarrassed.

Jim poured everyone except Agnetha, a glass of champagne. He asked Agnetha what she would like to drink as she wasn't drinking any alcohol. "Could I have just some water please?"

"Err, well I haven't got any in the fridge keeping cold but I do have some sparkling mineral water in the pantry. It won't be cold though."

"Oh, that will be just fine. I like mineral water." Jim went to the pantry and brought back a bottle of mineral water and proceeded to take the screw top off. There was a loud hissing and suddenly the whole bottle erupted in a fountain of frothy bubbles and splattered everyone near him. "Sorry, sorry," apologised Jim. "I forgot, if it's not been cooling in the fridge then it just, well sort of explodes, but it's only water."

Samantha's father again verbally lashed out releasing his venom with a scathing, "You bloody idiot, look, you've drenched Maisie and Agnetha. Can't you do anything right?" Samantha's mother tried to calm her husband down again with a soothing, "For goodness sake Gordon, stop making such a fuss, can't you see you're just making the poor boy nervous. No-one's hurt. Let it be."

"What do you mean no-one's hurt, what about my nose?"

"Stop making such a fuss."

"Well he's an idiot. In fact I think Samantha can do better, I really do." Gordon really didn't like Jim and was actually jealous of the fuss that was being made about Jim's promotion. Maisie turned to glare once again at her husband. "Now stop that kind of talk, we're guests here in Jim's house. Behave yourself Gordon Perkins or we're going home."

"Not such a bad idea." muttered Gordon under his breath.

"I heard that. Now shut up." retaliated his wife.

Eventually peace was restored and Freddy stood up from the table asking, "I think it's time for a toast, I'd like to congratulate Jim on his promotion; Agnetha on her wonderful news and also congratulations are in order for Jim and Samantha on completion of their house refurbishing. You've both done a wonderful job, well done. Cheers everyone and here's a toast to Agnetha and Jim and Samantha. Congratulations!" Everyone echoed the congratulations and the meal was started.

The entrée was eaten with many plaudits on the beautiful presentation. Everyone was chatty and amiable except Gordon who was sullen with moody silence. The conversation became quite animated when everyone reflected on Freddy's announcement. Samantha asked, "So have you thought of any names? Have you booked in with a hospital, do you have an obstetrician yet?"

"No it's early days yet, but actually I think I would just prefer a midwife and a home delivery. That's the way my mother had me and it's the way people in my village back home deliver their babies."

There was much discussion on the pros and cons of home delivery and eventually the conversation turned to world affairs. Freddy wanted to know people's opinion on global warming, "Look do you really think it's us humans affecting the temperatures or do you think it's just a cyclic phenomenon as many scientists believe?" Agnetha proffered her opinion, "Well I think it must be said that we humans are affecting the planet, and not in a good way, but I don't know what the solution is." Trying to bring a lighter note to the conversation Jim tried a spot of humour with the answer, "Well actually when I took science at school we were taught that alcohol was a solution." Freddy laughed and raised his glass in answer, "I'll drink to that." Gordon was not impressed and muttered under his breath to his wife, "Bloody smart arse!"

Samantha collected the dirty dishes and disappeared into the kitchen to plate up the main course. The trout was presented with much flamboyance, and with a top up of champagne they commenced the meal. After devouring half the trout suddenly Samantha's father started gagging. Immediately Jim jumped into action thinking that Gordon was choking.

He thumped the poor man hard on the back twice before Gordon held up his hand telling Jim to stop. Now Jim had no idea that Gordon actually had false teeth; a full set, both bottom and top. The violent thumping forced the teeth from Gordon's mouth and they shot out of his mouth onto his half eaten trout. Making strange rasping noises Gordon managed to convey to all that he wasn't choking but that he had a bone lodged in his throat. Freddy went to his father's assistance directing him firmly with, "Open your mouth Dad, wider I need to look and see if I can get at it."

"Aghhhh!" was the only sound emerging from the poor man. Freddy looked to Samantha, "Do you have any tweezers, if I can locate the bone maybe I can get at it with tweezers." Samantha disappeared into the bathroom and returned with a very small pair of ladies eyebrow tweezers. "Will these do?" Freddy had his father's mouth open as wide as it would go and was peering down his throat. "It's no good I can't see a thing." Gordon couldn't speak properly and was only making strange gagging sounds. Freddy took charge and announced, "Well we'll have to take him to the hospital, they get this sort of thing all the time. They'll get it out soon enough. I mean it's not too bad, you can at least breathe alright Dad."

It was agreed that Freddy, Agnetha, and Maisie would all go to the Emergency Department of the local hospital to get the bone removed, and then go home from there. In all the panic and upset no-one remembered to pick up Gordon's false teeth. They just lay there on the plate looking abandoned and disgusting. Samantha very nearly cleared them into the rubbish bin along with the left over trout, but at the last minute rescued them. She felt quite squeamish and didn't want to touch them and so picked them up with a plastic bag and put the package to one side. The party was over and she felt worried for her father and quite dejected. The celebrations had not been exactly what she had hoped they would be. The orange souffles had sunk and were abandoned.

At the Emergency Department of the hospital Freddy explained to the triage nurse what the problem was. The nurse ascertained that Gordon could breathe alright and so asked the group to take a seat in the waiting room. It was two hours later that Gordon was eventually seen by a doctor. By this time he was in a lather of frustration, and bad temper. He had been complaining bitterly for all the two hours to Maisie and Freddy making ridiculous noises in the back of his throat but couldn't actually formulate any understandable words. Maisie and Freddy tried to calm him down and repeatedly asked the triage nurse if he could be seen more quickly. The triage nurse again asked Freddy, "Is you father having difficulty breathing?"

"Well actually no."

"Is he bleeding profusely?"

'Well actually no."

"Is his injury actually life threatening?"

"Well I guess not, but he's in a great deal of discomfort."

"Do you think I should put him ahead of that man over there who has a nail through his hand?"

"Errr probably not."

"Do you think I should put him ahead of that child who has burnt his leg and foot?"

"Errr probably not."

"Do you think I should put him ahead of that little girl there who has fallen off her horse and probably has a dislocated and broken arm?"

"Err, well I guess not."

"Right sir, as I said before, and the time before that, please take a seat and the doctors will get to your father as quickly as they can."

When the doctor did finally examine Gordon it only took five minutes to locate the bone and extract it with a special instrument. The doctor made Gordon gargle with an antiseptic mouth wash and at last declaring Gordon fit, hale and hearty sent them all on their way. By this time it was too late to return to Jim and Samantha's house to retrieve the false teeth. Gordon was acutely embarrassed and repeatedly demanded that they return to pick up the teeth but Maisie put her foot down declaring, "No Gordon. We're not going back to Samantha's place, they'll be in bed by now. We'll pick up your teeth tomorrow."

"But I want them now."

"I said tomorrow. Now shut up, you've said enough for one night." Gordon sulked for the next five minutes of the journey but as they were approaching their home couldn't help himself, ignoring his wife's directions to be quiet came out with a new accusation.

"It's all his fault, If Jim hadn't served fish and if he hadn't hit me so hard everything would be alright. He's a.... he's a...." Gordon was struggling to find a description bad enough to suit his wrath. "Blast and dam, I can't express what I feel about him. You know Maisie, honestly, the supply of available swear words is simply insufficient to meet my needs."

"For the last time Gordon Perkins, shut up!"

Unfortunately Samantha forgot to tell Jim that she had put Gordon's false teeth into a plastic bag and Jim unwittingly just thought the rumpled bag was rubbish needing to be thrown out. In helping Samantha to clear everything away he just put the plastic bag into the rubbish bin along with all the waste food and other rubbish.

When Maisie and Gordon arrived the next morning to collect

Gordon's false teeth they were no-where to be found. Only then did Samantha remember putting them into a plastic bag. Jim eventually realised that the plastic bag had probably been thrown out with all the other rubbish and would be in the large wheelie bin on the front verge waiting to be collected by the council workers. The local council workers were scheduled to empty all the bins in their area that afternoon so time was of the essence before all was lost. Although he wasn't relishing the job Jim volunteered to go through the rubbish to rescue the lost teeth. There were many plastic bags in the large outside rubbish bin and they all looked alike to Jim. It took half an hour to go through the many bags but in the end the teeth were located, washed and returned to their owner. Gordon was embarrassed, humiliated and extremely angry. He released a torrid vitriolic description of what he thought of Jim as his wife bundled him out of the house and back into their car.

25

SAMANTHA'S BIRTHDAY TREAT

Samantha's birthday was approaching and Jim was at a loss as to what to get her. She seemed to have everything she needed and he really wanted to get her something special or do something special. He turned to his Aunt Bridget as usual for help and advice. She suggested, "Well young Jim, why don't you simply ask Samantha if there's anything that she would like, or is there anywhere she would like to go. If you don't ask you might be spending a lot of money on something that she really is not all that bothered about. You've known her long enough now to be honest with her."

"Right, yes, you're right as usual, thanks Aunt Bridget I'll do just that."

The following evening after dinner Jim managed to bring the conversation round to Samantha's impending birthday. "Listen Sam, it's your birthday coming up, is there anything you'd particularly like or is there anywhere you'd particularly like to go? I'd like it to be special, I mean I know we could just go out to dinner, but if there's anywhere you'd like to go that you haven't been to already we could think about it. What do you say?"

"Oh, I don't know. There's nothing really that I need, and

there's nowhere that I can readily think of that I want to go but there is one thing I've always wanted to do."

"Yes, what?"

"Well, promise you won't laugh."

"No, I won't laugh, what would you like to do?"

"Well I've always wanted to jump out of a plane. You know, do a parachute jump."

"Good God, are you serious?"

"Yes, it's just something that I've always fancied doing, and never had the chance."

"Why on earth would you want to jump out of a perfectly good aeroplane? I mean if it's on fire I could understand it, but why would you put your life in danger for no good reason?"

"For the thrill of it, no other reason. Something different, something exciting, and there's no danger, they make you have a tandem jump, you know, with an instructor strapped to your back, he does all the work you just have to enjoy it."

"Well if that's what you want I can easily arrange that for you. I think it's crazy but no problem."

"Oh thank you darling, that would be marvellous, something really special for my birthday."

"Okay I'll organise it straight away."

"Oh and you'll love it too, just think of it free falling and then floating down gently, you'll love it."

"Not likely, this is for you not for me. I'm not doing it."

"Yes you have to. I can't do it on my own."

"You'll not be on your own, you said yourself you have an instructor on your back, you do it as a tandem jump."

"Yes I know but I'd want you to do it too, I'm not doing it if you don't do it with me."

"No, I really don't want to."

"Please, please, for me, it's my birthday wish. It's something I want us both to do, together. You know if we start a family we're not going to be able to do that sort of thing. We can only do that sort of thing whilst we're young. Please, please just agree to do it with me, please."

Jim could never say no to Samantha, she looked so beautiful, her large expressive eyes pleading with him. He answered limply, "I really don't want to."

"Please?"

"Oh, alright but I'm not too happy, and I don't say I'm going to enjoy it."

"Oh, thank you, thank you. You will enjoy it. You'll see. It will be a great experience, and I know they take a movie mini film of you doing it, so we can watch it later, even years later. You'll see it will be fun."

The day of the birthday flight came around too quickly and Jim was not looking forward to the jump. It was all organised and he drove them both out to the airfield some fifty kilometres out from Perth. He was nervous and fearful, completely the opposite to Samantha who was high spirited and excited. They had packed a picnic lunch which they proposed to have after the flight. "Assuming," Jim stated soberly, "that we land safely and are alive and kicking and able to enjoy it."

"Stop being a nervous Nellie, you'll see, it will be a real thrill, we'll have a great time."

They could see four or five small aeroplanes on the tarmac as they approached the tiny airfield. There was a large hangar and three smaller ones with many advertising boards attesting to the wonderful services offered by the sponsors of the sport. Once they checked in with the staff they were given bright orange flight suits and goggles to wear and the senior officer took thirty minutes instructing them on what to do and how to land correctly. The instructors would have movie cameras attached to their helmets and a small movie film would be taken of each individual jump. The DVD's would then be available for them to take home at the end of the afternoon. Samantha's face was flush with excitement but Jim's was pale with beads of sweat already forming on his upper lip. He was scared, in fact terrified but refused to let Samantha down and resolved to go through with it, just for her sake. He felt a bit like an early Christian about to face a pack of hungry lions in the Colosseum. He just knew he was going to die, but he had to go through with it, he couldn't let the love of his life think he was a coward.

Once they were in the aeroplane they were strapped to the front of their respective tandem instructors and all was checked. It was agreed that Samantha would go first, followed immediately by Jim. It had been explained that they would free fall for about thirty seconds and then the instructors would deploy the parachutes which would bring them down gently. They were to lift their feet and legs up just before landing, tucking their knees into their chests as best they could which would give the instructors the room and manoeuvrability to run a few steps before coming to a halt at the end of the jump.

The plane revved up noisily and before they could collect themselves they were taking off into the blue yonder. Up and up they went, round and round ascending higher and higher, like eagles soaring on the warm thermals. Jim started feeling the same way he had on the ferry going across to Rottnest. He could feel his stomach churning and bile ascending into his throat. He was sweating profusely and started retching. He desperately wanted to get out of the plane, he didn't want to jump but he didn't want to throw up in the aeroplane either. He shouted to his instructor, "I have to go.... now; I have to get out, I'm going to be sick!" The instructor indicated to the pilot that they were going to jump and let Samantha's instructor know that Jim was going first. Jim was panicking, "I have to get out; let me out NOW!"

The free fall was a disaster for poor Jim and his instructor. Jim's stomach started to empty of its contents as soon as the instructor let go of his rail and commenced the fall. The vomit was lighter than Jim and his instructor and so as it exited Jim's mouth it splattered itself across Jim's face, his goggles, the instructor's face and goggles too. Jim continued vomiting all the way down. He was helpless to stop it and was being covered as they floated gently to earth. He was so sick and appalled at his own weakness that he completely forgot to tuck his legs up as they hit the ground. His legs got tangled with the instructor's legs and they both collapsed in a tangled vomit covered smelly heap. Jim screamed with pain as he felt his left ankle twist and as he put out an arm to cushion his fall he felt a crack that he was sure would be a broken wrist. His chest hit the ground quite hard and completely knocked the wind out of him. He lay on the ground helpless gasping for air.

The instructor was incredibly angry as he collected the parachute and left Jim on the ground whilst he went for help. Jim was in agony and simply couldn't walk or talk. He watched with immense relief as Samantha landed safely and gently but he was unable to get up and greet her. The airfield staff put Jim on a stretcher and took him into the small bathroom to shower him off before allowing Samantha to take him to the hospital.

Once he got his breath back Jim was all apologetic and embarrassed but the damage was done and there was nothing he could do to make it all better. His instructor was nowhere to be seen and Jim couldn't wait to get away from the field. After Jim was cleaned up the Senior Officer gave Samantha a copy of the DVD films for them both and helped to get Jim into the car. She drove Jim to the local hospital where he was taken in for X-rays on his ankle and wrist. It was confirmed that he had sustained both a broken ankle and a broken wrist. They kept him in for observation and Samantha drove back to Perth alone. Jim was being kept in hospital as a precaution but the doctors thought he would probably be well enough to return home the following day.

Instead of going home Samantha went to see her parents and to report on the jump. She had enjoyed it so much but was sorry that Jim had not had the same experience that she'd had. Maisie and Gordon had been anxious about the flight but once they saw Samantha at their door they were much relieved and happy to see her. They were perplexed as to why Jim was not with her and Samantha related how he been airsick and was now in hospital following his disastrous landing. After a pleasant dinner relating all that had happened Maisie decided to put the DVD into their player to watch how the jumps went. Jim's film came up first and they watched horrified and yet fascinated as they saw how sick the poor man was and what happened to the vomit as the fall progressed. Both Maisie and Samantha were so sorry for Jim and so sympathetic but Gordon was in his element. He really didn't like Jim and was actually enjoying seeing the spectacle of poor Jim's distress. He laughed and made rude jokes about Jim's masculinity calling him one or two unsavoury names. "He's just a big girl's blouse, honestly Samantha I don't know what you see in him. He's as dumb as a brick."

"No he's not Dad, he's a good man and he's intelligent, he just has a weak stomach."

"Alright he's not as dumb as a brick, but he's no smarter either."

"Dad don't say such things, I love him. Mum tell Dad not to be so awful, Jim's a decent man, he loves me and he's good to me."

"Gordon stop it. Stop making fun of Jim, he can't help it if he has a delicate stomach."

"Delicate? Delicate? The man's an idiot, honestly Maisie, some famous person once said 'some people seem to have descended from the apes much later than most,' and you know what? I think he was talking about Jim."

"Now that's quite enough Gordon Perkins. I don't want to hear another word out of you."

"Oh for heaven's sake, can't a man make a joke?"

'I said that's enough, now just shut up."

"But I only said...."

"Shut up!"

26

PARIS

Some months passed in relative peace and calm. Jim's injuries healed and he had settled into his new position at the Department. He was earning more money and all was well with him and Samantha. Gordon Perkins refused to attend any family birthday celebrations at Jim's house and Maisie was the peacekeeper who regularly met up with her two children and their partners. Both Jim and Samantha had annual leave accumulated at their respective work places and so started to plan a special overseas holiday. Samantha was adamant that they had to be back in time for the birth of Agnetha's baby so timing was very important. Jim had it in his mind to propose marriage to Samantha and wanted to do it somewhere out of the ordinary. He had never been to France and had heard so many times how romantic Paris was. Samantha had been there on a school trip when she was a teenager but could remember almost nothing about it, and so it was agreed that they would spend a week in Paris followed by a week in England looking up some of Samantha's old friends and one or two relations who still lived there. Samantha had studied French at school but was by no means fluent. Jim had absolutely no knowledge of French and so left the organising of the accommodation to Samantha whilst he agreed to book the flights and a hire car for their use once in England.

Not wanting to make the same mistake as he did in Thailand Jim bought a sturdy large case with wheels and handle. He needed some new clothes and with some excitement the two went shopping. As they passed a window display in a jeweller's shop Jim tried to sound matter of fact as he asked, "What sort of jewellery do you like Sam, I mean in rings and things." Samantha looked up at Jim with a big grin on her face, "Why are you suddenly interested in jewellery?"

"Oh, no particular reason, but what kind of jewellery do you like, large, small, round, square; you know, that kind of thing." Samantha had a good idea of why he was suddenly so interested in jewellery, but pretended to be matter of fact about the whole thing. "Well, as you know I don't wear a lot of jewellery, especially costume jewellery, but I guess if I had to make a choice, well, I would go for something not too flash, but small and good. Only diamonds, maybe square cut but no other stones." Jim just nodded his head taking it all in and they moved off in the direction of the clothing shops.

Jim hated shopping for clothes but Samantha took him in hand and made all the decisions for him. New shoes, shorts, trousers and shirts. He really didn't mind what he wore but Samantha was quite choosey for him picking out the colours that she liked and styles that would be appropriate for their holiday.

The next day Jim went shopping, alone in his lunch hour and bought a beautiful princess cut solitaire diamond ring. The assistant in the jeweller's shop tried to talk him into clusters and sapphires with diamonds but Jim was adamant, he remembered what Samantha had told him and he was quite deliberate with his choice. He had thought about the where and when to do the deed and decided that at the top of the Eifel Tower would be the place to pop the question. His only problem was going to be keeping the ring away from Samantha as she seemed to be taking charge of all their packing. He decided to take the ring out of the box and tuck it into the back flap of his wallet; he would keep it there until the time came to pop the question.

Samantha booked their accommodation for a week in Paris at the hotel "Le Croquignole." When she told Jim the name of the hotel she laughed as he tried to pronounce it and he finally gave up telling her, "Couldn't you just have booked us into The Grand Hotel it would have been much easier to pronounce."

The day of departure arrived and Freddy drove Samantha and Jim to the airport. They were both so excited. Jim had managed to get them window seats and although it was an overcast day it was warm with only a slight breeze. On the ground it was dull and grey but once their aeroplane had gone through the cloud cover there was the most beautiful spectacle to be seen. Huge cumulous clouds, looking like large cauliflowers loomed up before them. Samantha watched in fascination as the plane went through each seemingly dense cloud only to come out of each bank into a wonderland of valleys and clear sky. She watched for an hour oooohing and aaaahing at every new formation. "Look Jim, isn't that just so beautiful?" Jim knew that the journey would be incredibly long and boring and had thought it was a good idea to have a stopover. He was over six feet tall and found plane travel extremely uncomfortable, and so the happy couple agreed to break the journey and have an overnight stop in Singapore. By the time they had disembarked and passed through customs and immigration is was quite late in the evening. They booked into their hotel and although quite tired decided to go out into the town to have a look around. They were due to catch their connecting flight the next morning but agreed that a few hours looking around Singapore would be fun.

It was incredibly hot and humid in Singapore but there was a small market close by and the smell from the street vendors cooking Asian food was intoxicating. They both sampled something on a stick and nibbled it as they wandered around. They had no idea what it was but both agreed it was simply delicious. They next sampled some chopped vegetables with a hot sauce wrapped in a banana leaf. Again they had no idea what it was but both agreed that it was amazingly good. Samantha chose one or two items to buy as souvenirs to take home for her family. She bought a silk scarf for her mother and a silk top for Agnetha. She pointed out to Jim that neither would not take up much room in her luggage. She bought a small bronze ornament for Freddy and a silk tie for her father. Both agreed that buying gifts early on in the holiday would relieve them from worrying about it later on. Jim bought a small wooden figurine and a parchment painting for his Aunt Bridget; he knew she would like the figurine as it was a delicate carving of a bird, and he knew she loved birds, not caged ones, but free flying natural birds, also it was not too heavy so no encumbrance for his luggage.

They changed planes once more on the way to Paris and eventually disembarked at the Charles de Gaulle airport and after going through customs and immigration made their way to the taxi ramp. There was an enormous queue for taxis and so Samantha decided it would be faster and cheaper to travel by the Metro underground railway system. As Samantha was the only one who knew any French she guided Jim to the ticket machines where she purchased two Paris Visite ticket passes. In order to reach their hotel Samantha worked out which line they would need to take and which stop to disembark to be closest to the hotel. Jim was happy to let Samantha do all the organising as he was hot and tired and the case he was pulling along was not behaving itself. One of the wheels must have been damaged in transit and was wobbling ominously. Samantha had a much smaller case, also on wheels but hers seemed to be working perfectly.

The Paris Metro is an incredible multi facetted series of entry and exit points, different lines and many levels. There were many lines passing through the airport station and each line was on a different level, all connected by escalators; sometimes these escalators were side by side going up one level or two or three. It was complicated and Jim was happy to let Samantha negotiate their way towards the first escalator. Samantha had worked out that they were to take the RERB city train which was on the blue line going towards central Paris. She tried to indicate to Jim on a large map on the wall the stations they would change lines at. "See here we are at Terminal 1 and we take this city train stopping at Gare du North and then on to Chatelet Les Halles. That goes down to Denfort and Rochereau. We change at Rochereau; are you listening?" Jim was miles away. His thoughts were on the proposal that he was planning. He couldn't interpret anything on the complicated Metro map, his mind was elsewhere. He just kept nodding his head, not taking in anything Samantha was saying. She showed him the places they would need to change trains and told him the stations but he couldn't concentrate on what she was telling him and he was happy to let her do all the planning of the journey on the underground system.

They took their first escalator down three levels and caught the first train to the next station where they were to change lines for the next part of their journey. When they approached the escalators to go up they found that there were three banks of escalators going up, side by side, and further on three more coming down. Samantha was careful and again scrutinised a large map on the wall to ensure they caught the right escalator going to the right level. Unfortunately their journey coincided with the Paris rush hour and so it was incredibly busy. People were rushing hither and thither, and all pushing and jostling each other. They all seemed to know exactly where they were going but Samantha was circumspect and took her time before deciding which escalator was the right one for them. She checked that Jim was right behind her as she joined the queue for the escalator that would be going three levels up.

Just as Jim was about step onto the escalator the wheel finally came off his suitcase. It shot off to one side and Jim stepped out of the line to retrieve it. At that moment he was bumped and jostled and actually fell over. He hung onto his suitcase handle but twisted his ankle as he tried to right himself. Two kindly strangers moved out of the line and physically pulled Jim to his feet. They talked to him in French but he didn't understand a word of what they were saying. He did however remember to say merci, the only French word he knew, as they left him and went on their way

When Jim looked around him he couldn't see Samantha anywhere and so just joined the queue for the escalator presuming to meet her at the top. Unfortunately Jim had joined the wrong queue for the wrong escalator and found himself going up only two levels.

Samantha saw Jim on the wrong escalator and shouted as best she could to him. Even though it was extremely noisy Jim did manage to hear her and realised his mistake. He had no idea where his escalator was going and so tried to back track going down. With a heavy large suitcase and the rush hour traffic no-one was allowing him to retreat back down the up escalator. As he tried to push past people they jostled him and shouted at him, in French of course. He presumed they were swearing, obviously not wishing him a happy welcome to Paris. It was obviously impossible to descend on a very busy ascending set of stairs and so Jim had to be content with going all the way up his two levels. Once at the top Jim had no idea how to reconnect with Samantha. He had no idea if he should sit tight and wait for her to come looking for him, or vice versa. He had a look at his suitcase and screwed the wheel back in place. His ankle was hurting but there was nothing he could about that. After five minutes of sitting idly on his case he decided it might be the chivalrous thing for him to go looking for her.

The different levels of the Metro are connected by many tunnels and diverting pathways. Jim regretted that he hadn't taken more notice of Samantha when she had tried to show him which station they would have been headed for and how to get there. He had left that to Samantha and now hadn't the faintest idea how to find her or how to find his way around, and didn't even know where they were headed. For the next two hours Jim pulled along his much too large suitcase, limping on a twisted ankle wishing he had never left Australia. The suitcase seemed to get larger and larger the more he pulled it along.

He went up escalators, and down others, he traversed different levels with an increasing sense of doom. Along some of the tunnels there were buskers and he noticed that he had passed three times an old man playing a violin. He passed an accordionist twice, once going one way and half an hour later when he was going the other way. Exhausted, hungry and demoralised he decided that he would try and get out of the Metro and see if Samantha was waiting at the top, on the street level. He stopped for a moment to get his breath and took his baseball cap off as he rested. Two French old ladies dropped coins into his hat thinking he was a beggar. Jim was too tired and dispirited to chase after them to give them their money back and anyway he reasoned he couldn't speak the language and wouldn't know what to say. He dropped the money into the hat of the next busker he passed, a child of about fourteen who was playing a mouth organ.

As he tried to exit the Metro guards stopped him and demanded his ticket. He tried to explain that his partner, Samantha had his Paris Visite pass. He didn't speak a word of French and it was apparent that the guards didn't speak English either. When he couldn't produce a ticket he was escorted to a side office where an officer was waiting and who demanded money to pay for the ticket.

Jim realised what was being asked and reached into his jacket for his wallet. "Oh dear God no! What new hell is this?" He ran his fingers nervously through his hair, his heart pounding. He turned to the senior officer and tried to tell him that his wallet had gone. He presumed been pick pocketed. Jim was given a ride in a Police Car and taken to a local station where a young officer was called in who could translate for them. Jim managed to convey to the young officer why he had no ticket. The officer asked him to tell them which hotel he was booked into. Jim was exhausted and just shrugged his shoulders. He was too weary to try and remember and he knew anyway he couldn't even pronounce the name of the hotel. After a while a terrible thought came to Jim. Not only was his wallet missing with his money and credit cards but at the back of his wallet was the ring he had bought for Samantha. He groaned and tears were in his eyes as he reported the theft to the young officer. Notes were taken with a description of the ring and Jim had to sign some form of declaration. As he couldn't read French he just signed it, trusting that it was the correct thing to do. The young English speaking officer took note of the description of the ring that Jim was reporting missing. He sympathised but could do nothing to help.

The police allowed Jim to sit in the police station until they could locate Samantha. He fell asleep across his suitcase and they left him whilst they attended to other matters. It was midnight before news came through that a young woman answering Jim's description was looking for her lost partner. It appeared that once Samantha had lost Jim on the Metro she had gone to the hotel to wait for him there. She had wandered up and down the tunnels and escalators at the Metro, as Jim had done, but after only half an hour had given it up and gone on to the hotel. She knew she had told Jim the name of the hotel and hoped he could remember it. Eventually the two were reunited. The Police drove the couple back to Le Croquignole and wished them well.

As soon as Samantha had Jim in the hotel room she started to question and harass him. He just held up his hand and stopped her mid sentence. "Sam, I really can't talk, I'm so exhausted, please can we discuss it all tomorrow morning. Let me sleep, please."

Jim slept until nine the next morning and as soon as he was conscious he fell into a deep depression. Samantha questioned him about the events of the day before and she was able to contact his bank and cancel his credit cards. He was depressed mainly because he had lost the ring and knew he just couldn't afford another one whilst they were on holiday; his credit cards had a limit. He had so desperately wanted to have a ring when he proposed now his plans were shattered, he couldn't propose without a ring. He knew he could get another one when they returned to Australia but he wanted one now, to do the deed at the Eifel Tower. It just wouldn't be the same once they got back to Australia.

The bank organised new credit cards and within three days Jim had funds, but not the ring. He was still extremely upset by the whole episode and depressed at losing the ring. Samantha found it difficult to understand why Jim was taking the loss of his wallet so badly, especially in view of the fact that new credit cards were now available at the central bank in Paris. He hadn't told Samantha about the ring and tried to put the whole episode behind him and enjoy the sights of Paris, but found it was just too difficult and painful to forget.

Their days were spent sightseeing by day and dining out by night. It was a wonderful holiday for Samantha but she was puzzled by Jim's quiet depression, he seemed to have something on his mind but each time she asked him he would just reply, "No, nothing wrong, just angry with my stupidity for letting myself get mugged."

"Well you weren't exactly mugged were you?"

"Well pick pocketed, it amounts to the same thing. You know Sam, I've been thinking I think it was the two fellows that helped me to my feet when I stumbled at the bottom of the escalator, that must have been when they took my wallet."

"Yes probably, but try and put it behind you. Relax; try and enjoy the rest of the holiday. You have your new cards and the bank has stopped any unauthorised transaction, so no great problem really.

The sightseeing was a nightmare for Jim; his ankle was swollen and quite painful. He didn't want to spoil Samantha's holiday and so told her nothing of his discomfort but stoically carried on in silence. They walked around the Louvre Museum after waiting two hours to get in. When they got to the gallery that housed the Mona Lisa there was another hour's wait. Jim was impatient and just wanted to sit down. When they did eventually get in to see the world's most famous painting he couldn't believe his eyes. "My God Samantha! Is that it? It's tiny. What's all the fuss about, it's just a painting, yes, I know it's supposed to be all that's wonderful, but come on; it's not much to look at is it? I mean there's millions of other pictures here, just as good, and much bigger."

"For Goodness sake Jim it's not about the size, its about the artistic perfection, the brush strokes, or in this case the lack of visible brushstrokes; the history; the great man Leonardo da Vinci. You know it's over five hundred years old and has never been restored, that's because it's painted onto a cotton wood panel as its surface, and so hasn't deteriorated as many older paintings have done. Look at her face Jim, she's so enigmatic."

"Yes, yes I suppose so."

"You know Jim; Leonardo was not just a painter but he was a scientist, an inventor and a doctor, really quite brilliant when you think about all that."

"Yes, yes I suppose so."

Samantha was having a wonderful time dragging Jim around the various sights of Paris. They walked the length and breadth of the Champs-Elysees and Jim was absolutely disgusted as he inadvertently stepped into one of the hundreds of piles of dog poop. It took him twenty minutes to find a public bathroom to get rid of the offending mess and smell. Even when he found the bathroom there was no toilet paper or hand towels, he had to resort to washing his shoe in the hand basin.

He felt quite sick as they drank a cup of exquisite coffee which was ruined by the awful thick cigarette smoke from the many patrons both in the café and those just outside.

They did a tour of the Notre Dame Cathedral and were jostled rudely by the busy crowds of tourists and residents alike. Jim tried not to complain too much but couldn't help himself as he voiced his annoyance to Samantha, "Honestly Sam, there are just too many people here, they just don't seem to have any sense of personal space. It's not like Australia is it?"

"No it's not Jim, its different and really that's one of the reasons we're here; to see things that are different." Jim just sighed and resolved to try and be more positive, he realised Samantha was in her element, having a wonderful time and he didn't want to spoil it for her, but for himself he was uncomfortable. Being an Australian he simply wasn't used to so many people; so much rush and crush; he much preferred the open spaces and endless vistas that were Australian.

They strolled along many cobbled streets and discovered old passageways. Samantha was enthralled and loved every moment. They decided to leave the Eiffel Tower until their last day. It was to be the highlight of their stay. Samantha was excited and didn't mind the two hour wait to go up in the lift; Jim on the other hand was in pain with his ankle and just wanted to go back to the hotel, but he managed to keep his woes to himself. The ascent in the lift was slow and claustrophobic for Jim and when they did finally reach the top he was actually glad that he wasn't going to propose to Samantha there. It was far too crowded and noisy, it would have been a disaster, not what he had imagined at all. For Jim Paris was a let-down and he couldn't wait to get on the plane to go to England. He knew they had booked a hire car and he wouldn't be expected to walk all over the place. Samantha for her part had loved Paris. She didn't actually feel that it was a romantic holiday, Jim seemed so introspective and depressed. She put it down to him losing his wallet and hoped that their time in England would lift him out of his depression.

27

ENGLAND

Samantha and Jim took the flight across the English Channel to London's Gatwick Airport and hired a car there to take them around England. They both quickly realised that a week was definitely not going to be long enough to see everything that they wanted to see and to visit as many friends and relatives as Samantha wanted but they booked into a hotel and sat down to decide exactly what they would do first, and list their priorities.

Jim wanted to see the Houses of Parliament and Buckingham Palace, especially the Changing of the Guards. Samantha wanted to visit the British Museum and the National Art Gallery. They agreed that they would spend a day doing what the other wanted and after three days booked for a river cruise to take them up the Thames to Hampton Court Palace. It was all too much to take in, the size, the grandeur, the history. Their tour guide had their brains spinning there was so much, of everything, but they loved it and had a wonderful day. Jim was so glad that he wasn't expected to walk for miles and miles. The best tour of all though was their visit to the Tower of London. They marvelled at the crown jewels, they gasped at the armoury and listened intently as the guide told them all about the various nobility that had been imprisoned and even executed there. The highlight of the sightseeing was a glimpse of the Queen as she drove by following the Changing of the Guards. Neither had ever seen Her Majesty in the flesh, only in pictures and on the television. To see her live was a thrill neither would ever forget.

The days flew by far too quickly. Samantha managed to organise for those of her relatives who lived in north London to meet at one house and a party was organised for the Friday night. Jim was introduced to Samantha's relatives who all made a big fuss of the pair. There was music, dancing and a large amount of free flowing beer and spirits. Jim promised Samantha that he would be circumspect and only drink in moderation. They both knew he was not at his best with a large amount of alcohol in his system. Unfortunately Samantha's cousins kept filling his glass and insisting on drinking toasts.

One of Samantha's cousins played the piano and the party turned into a competition between cousins singing British songs and Jim keeping up with them singing Australian songs. They started by singing a loud and proud chorus of *"Rule Britannia"* and Jim took up the challenge with a drunken rendition of *"Waltzing Matilda."* The cousins countered with *"Maybe It's Because I'm a Londoner,"* and Jim not to be outdone followed with *"On the Road to Gundergai."* One elderly cousin actually wept as the English party gustily sang out *"Land of Hope and Glory"* and asked for encore after encore. This went on for a solid hour before Jim found himself running out of songs. Those that he knew he couldn't remember all the words and so there was much la, la, la,ing. Everyone was laughing and having a great time. Jim started to get maudlin and cross with himself for not knowing all the words, especially when he started in on *"Click go the Shears."* He started to sing the song three times and each time couldn't get past the first line. "Bugger that's not right. Start again."

"Not likely. We've heard enough of that one. Don't you know any more?"

"No, let me try *Click go the Shears* again." Jim had definitely had too much to drink and slumped down heavily on the settee next to Samantha's elderly aunt. In his drunken mood Jim suddenly started serenading the old lady. He held her calloused hand and gazed into her rheumy eyes: "*Give me a kiss lady, you are so beautiful.*" In acute embarrassment Samantha cut the song short and announced that really it was time they were getting back to their hotel.

She drove back to the hotel with Jim singing a very much out of tune "*Waltzing Matilda*" loudly through the open window of the car, much to the amusement of the other road users that they passed.

Jim had heard so much about Cornwall that they both agreed to spend their last two days touring the south west point of England. Samantha had seen it before but for Jim it was a revelation. The roads were so narrow and winding and the coastal villages so quaint. He saw many thatched cottages and tiny harbours. They wandered the tiny lanes at Falmouth, Mullion Cove, Mousehole and Porthcurno. At Porthcurno an idea came to Jim. He let Samantha have a lie in that next morning and left their hotel early saying he was just going for a quick walk. He called in to a small jeweller's shop and purchased a sweet small plain band with a tiny heart in the centre that was an eternity ring. He wanted to give her a proper engagement ring but that would have to wait until they returned home, however an eternity ring might just serve as a substitute and Land's End was where he decided he wanted to do the deed.

The drive out to Land's End was as scenic a drive as one could wish for and Jim was so nervous he couldn't drive. He let Samantha do the driving as he was preparing in his mind what he was going to say. When they arrived at Land's End, the most southerly and westerly part of England they stopped for photos under the sign that shows all the different directions to all the major points on the globe, New York, Moscow, and about twenty other places. Jim asked Samantha to go with him to the furthest point away from the other tourists and made sure they were completely alone before dropping to one knee and with a nervous wobble to his voice stated with incredible sincerity:

"Samantha I love you so much, I'd go to the ends of the earth for you, and so here at the Land's End I think it's appropriate that I ask you; no I beg you; will you please marry me?"

"Oh Jim, I thought you'd never ask. Of course I'll marry you. I love you too." With that Jim produced the small gold band that was the eternity ring. Samantha looked at it with surprise. She knew Jim was not short of money and had really expected something a little better for an engagement ring. Jim immediately saw her look of disappointment and quickly followed on from her answer with an explanation. "Look I know this is not what you might have been expecting but this is an eternity ring. You remember when I lost my wallet in Paris, well unfortunately I had a beautiful diamond ring for you and it was in my wallet. Once we get back to Perth I'll get you another one, I promise. However this is an eternity ring and it's fitting that I promise to love you for an eternity."

"Oh thank you, it's just beautiful, and a wonderful sentiment." The happy pair returned to London the next day and started to prepare for their journey home. They had their bags packed and were due to leave the hotel for the airport at two in the morning.

Jim thought it would be fitting to have a last meal in a really good restaurant before leaving and so arranged for a table at a famous west end restaurant which he had heard was reputed to have gained a Michelin three star rating and two Gold Plate awards.

They had an entrée that had an unpronounceable name but was supposed to be liver pate infused with truffles. Samantha declared it the best pate she had ever tasted but Jim was not too sure, it tasted sort of off to him but was overruled by Samantha who raved about how gorgeous it was. Their main course was a large steak with prawns stuffed inside. This was more to Jim's liking and, being a typical Australian he tucked into the meat with relish. They finished the meal with a Bombe Alaska brought to their table with flames emanating from a brandy sauce and all washed down with a large bottle of Nicolas Feuillatte champagne.

28

THE RETURN FLIGHT

It took Samantha and Jim four hours from leaving their hotel to actually boarding the plane. They had to go through the checking in process before passing through immigration and finally to the transit lounge. About half an hour before they were due to board the plane Jim started to feel a disturbance in his stomach. He knew it couldn't be hunger but felt quite uncomfortable. Once on the plane his stomach started to rumble quite alarmingly and a sweat appeared on his upper lip. He turned to Samantha shaking his head, "Oh, what hell is this? I think my stomach is about to explode."

As the plane was taxiing on the runway the flight crew were preparing all the passengers for takeoff and Jim was taking no notice of the safety demonstration, he was concentrating on his stomach which seemed to be doing acrobatics. He realised he would have to get to the bathroom before there was a terrible accident. As he made a bee line for the toilet the stewardess barred his way and asked him to take his seat again as they were about to take off. "Listen lady, I have to get to the bathroom or my bowels will take off, and I think you will be really, really sorry. It's an emergency I have to go, now." And with that he pushed past the poor girl and entered the toilet slamming the door behind him. After five minutes the stewardess was insistent on Jim coming out of the bathroom and taking his seat. She knocked on the door politely, "Sir, you have to take your seat. We are about to take off." There was no response and so she tried again, banging on the door this time, "Sir, you have to take your seat, we're about to take off."

Many passengers turned to look at the very green looking Jim as he gingerly exited the bathroom and made his way to his seat. He was sweating profusely and Samantha took one look at him and realised what his problem was. There was nothing she could do to help him except assist with the tightening of his seat belt. Jim's breathing was coming in short gasps and his mouth was wide open trying to gain every bit of oxygen that he could. As soon as the plane left the ground Jim unclipped his seatbelt and made a dash for the bathroom once again.

The stewardess who was still in her seat took hold of his arm as he tried to get past her, "Sir you have to take your seat, the seat belt sign is still on, it's not safe, you should return to your seat until the sign goes out." Jim took no notice of the girl, he was on a desperate mission. He brushed off her hand and proceeded to the bathroom. As it was he was too late and had an accident in his pants.

For the next hour Jim stayed in the bathroom. He had a terrible case of vomiting and diarrhoea. He was too sick to stand and simply lay down in the foetal position on the none too clean bathroom floor gasping for breath. His six foot frame simply folded up like a sea side deck chair. He would dearly have loved to stretch out on the floor, even though it was quite grubby, but there was just no room.

Once he was able to stand he had the job of washing his trousers and underpants. The sink was tiny and the tap was a hold-down contraption, not the usual turning tap. That meant he had to hold down the tap with one hand and try to wash his trousers and underpants with the other. He managed as best he could and with the aid of many paper towels, all the toilet paper, and the whole box of tissues tried to dry them out. Eventually he came out of the bathroom, white and shivering and within three minutes had to make a dash back to the bathroom. There was nothing anyone could do to help and eventually the nausea passed and Jim, uncomfortable with very damp trousers and pants tried to sleep.

Jim's six foot frame and long legs were always an encumbrance on aeroplanes, he could never find a way to be actually comfortable enough to sleep. In his boredom he picked up the Safety Manual from the seat pocket in front of him and started to read aloud. Samantha hushed him but Jim was determined to read every morsel of what to do if the plane should go down. "I've heard it all before Jim, can't you read it to yourself and why do you want to read it anyway, the stewardess gave us the stage performance at the start of the trip?"

"Well if you remember I was somewhat distracted and certainly not listening to all she was saying. I have to read this now, all the airlines are different, this one may be telling me something that I don't know, it might be different from all the others. It might be the one piece of information that saves our lives."

"Well do it quietly."

"I learn better if I read it aloud."

"Oh, do whatever you want." with that Samantha returned to her book and left him alone.

Jim couldn't face any food at mealtimes. By the time they got to Dubai for the change in flights Jim was feeling much better. He was hungry but extremely careful with what he ate for the remainder of their journey back to Perth. He swore he would never eat pate again, not even if it was the last morsel of food on the planet.

Their last meal on the plane home was a welcome break from the monotony of the long flight. The stewardess came down each aisle offering pre lunch drinks to all the passengers. Jim took the proffered red wine for himself and Samantha and as he was passing hers to her the plane suddenly took a slight lurch. It was only mild turbulence but unfortunately the red wine spilt onto Jim's already none too clean shirt. Samantha did her best to dab him down with some water but it only made the stain travel further. Jim was not in a good mood and after downing a small bottle of wine called for another.

The lunch that was being served on the last leg of the journey turned out to be a choice between spaghetti bolognaise or lamb pilaff. Samantha and Jim were sitting at the rear of the plane and the stewardess had been taking orders from the front of the plane first.

When she got to Jim she asked politely, "spaghetti or lamb sir?"

"Oh, I think I'll take the lamb, how about you Sam?"

"Yes I think lamb would be good for me too."

"Sorry sir but we've run out of the lamb, I can recommend the spaghetti bolognaise though."

"Good grief woman, if the lamb is not available why on earth did you offer it to us?"

"I'm sorry sir, I was just hoping you'd pick the spaghetti."

"Well in view of the wide choice I think we'll take the spaghetti."

"An excellent choice sir!"

The bolognaise, as the girl had said, turned out to be really good. There was plenty of the rich red sauce but the tiny plastic forks proved to be totally inadequate for the job of conveying spaghetti to Jim's mouth. Another slight lurch of the plane and a forkful of spaghetti covered in the red sauce went down Jim's poor suffering shirt. Samantha tried to clean Jim up but his usual good placid nature was starting to show cracks. Samantha could see he was beginning to get quite angry, not necessarily with the stewardess, but more frustrated with himself. They disembarked from the plane and made their way to immigration and finally to customs.

During the flight the passengers had been asked to complete a customs declaration form. Jim had completed his and the only item he had declared was a small jar of Cornish honey that was another gift for his Aunt Bridget.

"Do you have anything to declare sir?" asked the smart young customs officer as he looked at the grubby stained front shirt of poor Jim and made a mental note to check all of Jim's luggage. He was not supposed to prejudge any passenger but he didn't like the look of a man who was quite messy and actually had a funny smell about him. A sort of combination of sick, sweat and spaghetti.

"Well officer, I ticked one item on the food list but that's all."

"And what is it that you have sir?"

"Oh, just a small jar of honey, a present for my aunt."

'Oh, I'm sorry sir, you can't bring honey into Australia."

"Why ever not?"

"It's on the prohibited list sir."

"What's wrong with honey? Don't you know it's one of the purest forms of food you can have, and anyway it's in a jar; sealed."

"I'm sorry sir, but we have to confiscate it. Do you have anything else to declare?"

"I think it's a scandal, stealing my honey and no, I don't have anything else to declare."

"Okay, so could you empty the contents of your luggage on the table for me please?"

"Oh, for crying out loud, everything?"

"Yes, everything." The customs officer helped Jim to take absolutely everything out of his suitcase. At the very bottom of the case they came to the small wooden ornament, a carving of a bird, and the parchment painting that Jim had purchased as a souvenir gift for his Aunt Bridget. "I'm sorry sir but these two items cannot be brought into Australia. I did ask you if you had any other items to declare, why didn't you declare these?"

"Well they're not food are they?"

"No sir, but on the form that you signed it asks if you have any items made of wood. You ticked the 'no' box and this bird is definitely wood and I think the parchment picture is originally made from a bamboo of some sort and so would be classed as wood."

"Well I made a mistake, sorry. Is that it? Can we go now?"

"Oh no sir, we will be confiscating the honey and the carving and the picture too. You didn't declare the wooden carving and so you will be facing a fine."

"What? Are you mad? That's ridiculous, I made a mistake, so what? I declared the honey. How much of a fine are we talking about?"

"I'm not sure I have to bring in my superior officer. You can begin packing your suitcase and then take a seat we'll be with you shortly."

Samantha waited patiently by the exit door. She knew Jim was in a terrible mood, frustrated and tired and decided that discretion was the better part of valour, leave him alone to sort his problems out, she knew instinctively that any offer of help from her would be met with a barrage of further vitriolic complaints.

Eventually Jim wrote a cheque for the fine and together with Samantha departed the terminal to be met by Freddy who had arrived to pick them up and take them home. Samantha was excited to see Freddy and all the way home related to him all the highlights of the holiday. She carefully left out the not so good bits. Jim was morose and silent at first but when Freddy asked what was wrong Jim gave vent to an outburst of the most deprecating reference to airline procedure, from bathrooms that were far too small, to lack of choice of food and finally to his mind, stupidly unnecessary customs rules and officiously pedantic customs officials. Samantha intercepted with a placating, "Now, now Jim, it wasn't so bad and the customs guys were only doing their job. Take no notice of him Freddy, he's had a bad journey and he's tired out."

29

A FAMILY HOLIDAY

The next day Jim and Samantha were to meet up with the family for dinner and to tell them all about their holiday. Samantha was so excited and looking forward to announcing the she and Jim were now engaged. They hadn't told Freddy on the journey back from the airport, they wanted to make an announcement to everyone at the same time. As soon as they were settled round the table and holiday souvenirs handed out, Samantha stood up and made the announcement, "Mum, Dad, Freddy, Agnetha: Jim and I are really happy to tell you all that we are engaged, we're going to be married. Jim asked me in England and I said yes."

"Oh that's wonderful." Gushed Maisie as she rose from the table to kiss the happy couple. Freddy and Agnetha congratulated her and there were hugs all round.

Gordon was none too happy and was the first to take hold of Samantha's hand to have a look at the ring. "Good Lord Maisie, look at this." Holding Samantha's hand up for all to see and looking straight at Jim he asked bluntly, "My God man, is this the best you could do? What the bloody hell is that? That's the most pathetic effort at an engagement ring that I've ever seen. You should be ashamed of yourself." Samantha tried to appease her father and started to explain that it was only an eternity ring. "No, you don't understand Dad," but the stubborn old man wouldn't listen. He was full of his own importance and anger and stormed out of the room and upstairs to his bedroom, not listening to Samantha at all.

Maisie looked embarrassed and turned to Jim for an explanation. Samantha and Jim both started talking at once and Maisie had to hold up her hand to stop them as she looked to Jim for clarification. When all was explained Maisie decided to punish her husband for his stupidity and leave him in his room whilst they got on with the dinner without him.

Once everyone had departed Maisie went up to her bedroom to confront her husband. "What a stupid thing to do. Do you realise what an idiot you made of yourself? You really don't like Jim do you?"

"No I bloody well don't. If that's the best he can do for an engagement ring then it's just not good enough. My daughter deserves better than that. By the way, I'm thinking of taking up photography, that way I can shoot him and cut his head off without being done for murder."

"Oh, very funny."

"I'm hungry, did you save me any dinner?"

"If you want anything you can jolly well go and get it yourself. Gordon Perkins you are one stupid stubborn cantankerous old man. Jim Emery is a good man and Samantha loves him. He has a good job, a nice house and loves our daughter very much. He's going places in the Department of Immigration and I think Samantha will have a good life with him."

"So that's how he shows his love is it? Buying her a crappy little ring; not even a stone of any kind in it. Shabby I call it. Honestly Maisie our girl can do better, she's beautiful and intelligent, why does she saddle herself with that loser?"

"He's not a loser. If you had only listened to her, Samantha was trying to tell you that what he gave her was an eternity ring and they are going shopping tomorrow for a proper engagement ring."

"Oh, well why didn't she tell me that?"

"Good Lord she tried to but you weren't listening. You stormed off upstairs before she could tell you the whole story. You're a stubborn old man and I really don't know why I bother."

"So I suppose I have to call her and apologise?"

"I should flamin'well hope so, but it's not her you have to apologise to, it's Jim."

Following that incident peace reigned in the family for a short time. Jim took Samantha shopping and bought her the most beautiful Argyle diamond solitaire ring which set him back three month's wages. Agnetha had five weeks to go with her pregnancy. She'd had a difficult time with morning sickness and Maisie thought it might do them all good to get away for a week for a short holiday. She discussed it with them all and it was agreed they would rent a holiday cottage in Exmouth, some one and a half thousand kilometres north of Perth.

The day before they were due to leave a small parcel arrived from France for Jim. Wondering what on earth it could be he opened the package with a great deal of curiosity. There was a letter, in English from the French Police accompanying his old wallet. "*Dear Mr. Emery, Following your statement made to the French Police we are happy to inform you that a gang of pick pocketers was arrested and their premises searched. The description and most of the contents of your wallet tallied with the information you gave us and we have pleasure in returning your wallet to you. We realise that some items are missing but we are unable to assist any further with your loss. We most humbly apologise for this unfortunate incident and truly hope that the French reputation for trust, integrity and honesty has not been tarnished. We wish you well and it is our hope that you feel safe enough to visit our fair country some other time. Yours sincerely,* Michelle *Totnes Chief of Police."*

Jim turned out the contents of the wallet and noted that whilst all his credit cards were there all his money was missing. His main concern was for the ring and he heaved a sigh of relief as he delved into the deeper recesses of the folds of the wallet and realised that neither the thieves nor the police had suspected that a valuable ring lay in the recess of the folds.

Samantha was delighted to see what Jim had chosen originally for her but agreed that it should go back to the jewellers. Two expensive rings were a little "over the top" and she was more than happy with the ring that she now wore.

It was a three hour flight to Exmouth from Perth and Jim couldn't help reflecting on the disaster that had been the last flight that he and Samantha had been on. He was careful to the point of stubborn stupidity for the five or six hours before take off. He refused to eat any lunch and only had milk, just to be absolutely certain that his stomach would behave itself.

Exmouth is on the eastern side of a large peninsula, the North West Cape, with the sheltered Exmouth Gulf on one side and the open Indian Ocean on the other. As they flew over the flat red plains it brought home to them just how vast a country Australia is. Small townships are hundreds of kilometres from the next and looking through the small windows of the aeroplane they could see there were hardly any rivers, or mountains or any significant landscape feature. It was all miles and miles of red sandy dried out flood plains and only the occasional thin straight ribbon of a line that indicated an isolated road.

The cottage turned out to be a medium sized three bedroom house with a swimming pool overlooking the bay. The weather was warm without being too hot and whilst most of them went for a daily swim in the tropical waters Agnetha was content to sit by the swimming pool under a cooling umbrella sipping fruit juices.

Samantha was reading a small brochure put out by the tourist department and noted that they were advertising water skiing lessons in the adjacent bay. She looked to Jim and asked "Hey Jim darling, I've never done any water skiing, have you?"

"No, why do you ask?"

"Well, apparently there's a sort of ski school in the next bay. I'd love to learn how to water ski. Can we go and have a look?"

"I guess so, that might be fun. Let's go have a look at it tomorrow morning."

The next day Jim and Samantha walked over the dunes to the next bay with their bathers, towels and such to have a look at the advertised ski school. It turned out to be a small operation with a tin shed housing much equipment and two instructors attending to a ski boat tethered up to jetty. Jim paid the instructors and agreed to the terms and conditions which they were asked to sign. Jim and Samantha were the only customers and so, after changing into their bathers, were given their lesson straight away.

The two instructors, called Mark and Dean were competent and quite professional with their handling of two absolute beginners. Attached to the shed wall were two ski ropes about three metres long with a wooden bar at the end. They demonstrated to Jim and Samantha how they wanted the pair to hold the bars and pull themselves up from a sitting position to a standing position. It looked quite simple on dry land and

234

Samantha was keen to get into the water, Jim on the other hand was a little more reserved and hoped he would be able to master the art of skiing. He realised, like most things, it might just not be as easy as it looked, and as usual he wanted to show off in front of Samantha and hoped he might impress her with his skiing.

Once the pair were capable of pulling themselves up from a sitting position to a standing position Mark declared it was time to try out the theory in the water. "Ladies first." He declared as he led Samantha to the end of the jetty. "By the way" explained Mark, "the water around the jetty is about two metres deep but be aware just to the right beyond the jetty the water is quite shallow and it is quite muddy as it's the mouth of a small river. There are reeds growing and it's not always obvious that the water is shallow, so avoid that area and stick to the open sea from the jetty outwards. When you come in from the "pull" come in to the beach where its clean or to the jetty. Dean was in the boat and Mark showed Samantha how to put the skis onto her feet. The jetty was about 55 cm. above the water and Samantha was able to sit on the edge of the jetty with her feet in the skis beneath her, in the water. Mark joined Dean in the boat and handed the wooden bar to Samantha whilst explaining that they would take up the slack of the rope and when she felt the rope become taut she was to let the boat pull her forward and whilst keeping her body in a sitting position on the jetty she was then to trust the skis to hold her weight and simply stand up. It sounded simply enough but not as easy as she first thought.

The boat started out quite slowly as it took up the slack of the rope and as Samantha felt the rope become taut she allowed the tension to help her stand up on the skis. She actually skied about three metres before she overbalanced and fell head first into the water. Mark shouted for her to collect her skies which had come off her feet and for her to swim back to the jetty. Jim helped her out of the water with a worried look on his face. "Are you alright?"

"Yes I'm fine, I think I know where I went wrong, I leaned too far forward. I'll do it better next time." True to her word Samantha learned from her first mistake and on the second attempt actually stood up on her skis. The boat towed Samantha around in a large circle with no problem. Samantha was skiing on the flat water that was the wake of the boat, however as soon as she tried to cross the wake her feet were at different levels and this completely disrupted her balance. Once again she fell over but this time she was exhilarated and couldn't wait to have another go. On Samantha's third "pull" she stood up quite confidently on her skis and enjoyed the thrill of being towed in a large circle round and round. At last Mark and Dean brought Samantha in close to the shore and shouted for her to let go of the bar as she glided smoothly to the beach without falling over at all.

Now it was Jim's turn and he was quite apprehensive, realising that he may not be as competent as he would like to be. Dean stayed in the boat whilst Mark jumped out to instruct Jim, as he had done with Samantha. Jim forced his feet into the rubber tight fitting ski shoes and sat on the edge of the jetty hanging onto the bar waiting for the rope tension to be taken up. When he felt the rope go taut he allowed himself to be pulled forward, but forgot to stand up and so was pulled through the water, still in a sitting position. Dean towed Jim about ten metres until it became obvious that Jim wasn't able to stand up. The boat stopped and Jim had to collect his skis and swim back to the jetty. He clambered out and sat down at the end ready to have another go.

Mark shouted from the boat, "Okay Jim, this time try standing up straight away." Jim gave the thumbs up sign and Dean started the boat up once again. As instructed as soon as the rope tension was taken up Jim allowed himself to be pulled forward and stood up on his skis, only to be pulled off balance forward and to land in the water, face down. Undaunted Jim swam back to the jetty with his skis being pushed in front of him in the water. His next attempt was no better than his first. On his thumbs up sign Dean drove the boat which pulled Jim forward, but Jim forgot to stand up and was pulled through the water for about fifteen metres with Jim still in the sitting position. Mark kept shouting, "Stand up Jim, stand up." But Jim found it impossible, the water was heavy on his chest and much of it was going into his mouth making it difficult to even catch his breath. On Jim's fourth "pull" he fell forward from the jetty without even moving a metre.

In exasperation Mark got out of the boat and went over the basic teaching principles once again with Jim. "Okay I've got it," Jim assured the frustrated instructor. On the fifth, sixth and seventh "pull" Jim never progressed beyond three metres, and that was still in a sitting position with water filling his mouth, threatening to drown him. On the eighth "pull" Jim actually managed to stand up and progressed about ten metre in a straight line. He was overjoyed as Mark, Dean and Samantha back on the jetty were all shouting encouragements, however in his excitement at actually getting to his feet he forgot the warning about the shallow water just beyond the jetty where the reeds were growing and as he felt himself heading towards them he just let go of the bar and inevitably came to a slow stop. He felt himself slowly sink into the mud and could do nothing to save himself. Dean turned the boat around and Mark shouted for Jim to return to the jetty. 'I've lost the skis, they've sunk into the mud." Shouted Jim,

"Well you have to retrieve them and get them back to the jetty." Shouted Mark.

'They're in the mud."

"Yes I heard you the first time. Get them out. You can't leave them there."

Jim had to reach down into the mud to pull the skis from the sticky, smelly goo. The more he pulled at the skis the more they seemed to suck themselves into the slime. Eventually he managed to extricate the skis from the mud and, exhausted pushed the skis in front of himself, getting back to the jetty.

After giving Jim a few minutes to get his breath back Mark decided to try a different approach. "Look Jim, not everyone can master a start from the jetty, I think we should try you starting in the water."

'How will that be any different?"

"Well, it's just a different method and it may be more suited to your body weight."

"Okay, let's give it a try." Mark showed Jim how to sit in the shallows of the beach with the skis on his feet and the tips of the skis just poking out of the water. "Now Jim, I'm going to hand you the bar and again, when you feel the tension on the rope you allow the boat to pull you up into a sitting position on top of the water and then immediately try to stand up. Keep your arms straight out in front of you, got it?"

"Yes, got it. Lets go." Mark scrambled back into the boat and Dean drove straight forward at an even pace. Jim felt the rope go taut and hung onto the bar, determined to stand up. He felt himself being pulled through the water and the strain on his arms was quite severe. He desperately wanted to succeed and so for quite a while refused to let go of the bar. Unfortunately he was being pulled through the water, still in a sitting position. The water was waving into his face and he just couldn't catch his breath. He hung on for as long as he could but in the end had to let go of the bar. Dean turned the boat around and Mark shouted instructions to Jim. "Okay Jim, we'll have another go but this time keep the tips of your skis out of the water and try standing up immediately, don't wait to get your balance." On the next "pull" Jim did actually manage to stand up for three seconds only to overbalance and fall forward.

Mark was getting exasperated but remained calm. "Okay Jim, that was much better, you very nearly had it. We'll try again, I think you're getting the hang of it now." Dean and Mark were extremely patient but after six more unsuccessful "pulls," some with Jim not being able to stand up at all and some with him standing up but then overbalancing and falling forward, face down in the water, they eventually had to acknowledge that Jim was probably just not going to get the hang of skiing. They drove the boat back to the jetty as Jim retrieved his skis and swam dejected back to the shore. Mark asked him if he wanted to sign on for more lessons but that was enough for Jim. Once again he was depressed at his own overwhelming failure to achieve success in front of Samantha. For her part Samantha was sympathetic to Jim's under achievements but ecstatic at her own efforts and success at waterskiing. She had loved every moment of it.

The next day was again a beautiful calm sunny day with a temperature just under thirty degrees. Jim and Samantha decided to go for a swim in the warm tropical water and sauntered slowly down the boardwalk to the beach. They passed a young family also making their way down to the beach. There was a mother, father and two children. One of the boys was obviously disabled, being in a wheel chair and was being pushed by his father. As Samantha and Jim were preparing to go into the water Jim noticed that the father was having some difficulty getting the wheelchair through the sand. Jim ran back to where the father was struggling and offered to help lift the chair onto the beach. Once the family were settled with a sun umbrella up and towels laid out the youngest child ran down to the water and commenced playing in the shallows. The disabled child looked longingly at the water and his father decided to pick up the boy, who was about twelve years old, and take him into the water. The boy was overweight and the father was having a difficult time carrying the child through the soft sand. Jim offered to help and the two men ferried the boy easily into the shallows.

Once in the water the boy squealed with delight as each small wave lapped his legs. He apparently couldn't stand on his own and so Jim and the father just supported the child in a sitting position getting slightly deeper with each step. The father thanked Jim for his help and assured him that he could manage on his own. Jim and Samantha stood back to one side watching the two children having a great time, one running around splashing everyone near to him and the other happy to be in his father's reassuring arms enjoying the warm water covering his torso.

After about five minutes Samantha noticed an ominous black shape appear in the water just ahead of the group and screamed as she saw a fin appear and just as quickly disappear. She clung to Jim as she shouted, "Oh my God I think it's a shark!" Jim laughed and held Samantha back from scrambling, panic stricken back to the shore. "No, it's not a shark it's a dolphin, in fact look further out there's another one."

Samantha was reassured and stood in the waist high water watching fascinated as the two dolphins swam around the group, sometimes breaking the waves coming in and then diving down again to disappear for a while. The disabled child had an enormous grin on his chubby face as he splashed the water with his free hand. Eventually the dolphins seemed to understand that this child was special and slowly swam close to the group and even closer to the handicapped child. The father remained still and calm as the dolphin nudged the boy, encouraging him to reach out and touch. The child put out his hand and the first dolphin surprisingly allowed himself to be touch and stroked. Samantha, Jim and the youngest child all stood by mutely watching the gentle giants of the ocean giving so much pleasure to the boy in his father's arms. The dolphins made funny squeaking noises and blew air noisily from their blow holes. The boy was in seventh heaven with tears of happiness running down his salty face.

Eventually the dolphins turned tail and slowly made their way back out to sea. "Wow!" Was all Samantha could say, over and over again. The two boys waved childish "goodbyes" as they watched the dolphins slowly swim away, diving up and down. Jim helped the father back up the beach carrying the boy. Everyone was affected by the encounter and the two children excitedly related the happenings to their surprised mother who had been reading a magazine and hadn't seen the remarkable event. The father thanked Jim for his help and Samantha and Jim made their way back down to the water for their intended swim. Jim had heard of such things happening in Australia but Samantha had been totally unprepared for such an experience. She couldn't wait to get back to the cottage to tell all the others all about what had happened.

On the fourth evening that the family were at the bay they were visited by the owner of the house who told them that if they were lucky they might just see a fabulous phenomenon that evening or the next. He explained that it was the season for the baby turtles to emerge from their underground eggs that their mothers had laid some six weeks earlier.

Apparently the breeding turtles mate out at sea and the females drag themselves ashore during a nocturnal spectacle to dig out a nest and lay their eggs. The house owner explained that only a few baby turtles actually survive. They emerge from their eggs and make a hasty dash down to the sea but there are predators; sea gulls and crabs waiting to grab them and only a small percentage actually make it to the open waters. Jim thought it would be a good idea if they all helped the tiny turtles and put it to the group to see if they could save as many from the predators as they could.

They all agreed to sit up to watch in the sand dunes for any sign of baby turtles hatching. Jim thought that if they could scare off any seagulls and crabs they might be able to save a good many babies. Gordon was his usual scathing self and declared the idea preposterous. "Listen you idiot, it's mother nature at work. The seagulls have to eat and so do the crabs. You can't save all the babies, if you did maybe there'd be a glut of turtles. No, you should let nature take its course. It's a futile and stupid idea." Samantha stepped in to support and defend her fiancé, "Well I think it's a brilliant idea, I'm sure turtles are far more valuable to the world than seagulls or crabs. They can find their dinner elsewhere, they don't have to eat baby turtles." Maisie cut in with, "I agree, let's do what we can, let's save the baby turtles."

They all took deck chairs into the sand dunes to watch for the hatching but Gordon declared the whole exercise futile and ridiculous and so remained back at the house.

It was ten o'clock at night when the first sign of a hatching began. There was a rustling in the sand and the seagulls obviously knew what was about to happen as there were twenty or more just stood waiting to pounce. Maisie, Freddy, Samantha and Jim, even Agnetha all got to their feet and started to chase off the seagulls. The seagulls flew off in fright but only a little way away and then calmly walked back looking for their quick easy supper. One by one the baby turtles cleared their way through the sand and started the long journey down to the safety of the water. Their little flippers acted as legs as they flopped and flapped trying to outrun the predators. Everyone started to shout at the seagulls and they all had to be careful in running around that they not only scared off the seagulls but that they didn't actually tread on any of the babies.

Everyone was laughing and shouting as they flailed their arms at the seagulls.

Agnetha picked up one of the flapping baby turtles and examined it carefully, "Oh aren't they the cutest little things?" Samantha decided she could save quite a few by picking them up and carrying them in the folds of her skirt. She collected six and giggled as they wriggled and squirmed over each other in the confines of her skirt, however she did manage to deposit them safely into the sea. Maisie followed Samantha's example and collected five or six in her skirt and managed also to transport them safely to the sea.

In no time at all there were hundreds of other babies all hatching from other nests along the coast line. It was impossible to save them all and the family spent an exhausting three hours trying to save as many as they could. Gordon just watched from the confines of the cottage and snorted with derision at their efforts. When they returned exhausted but triumphant to the cottage he turned on his heel declaring them all "stupid idiots" and went to bed. Everyone else was flushed with health and happiness and congratulated each other on a job well done. It was "high fives" all round. They knew the seagulls and crabs had got a lot of the babies but they also knew that they had managed to save an awful lot more.

The next day Gordon announced that he would like to hire a four wheel drive vehicle to take them all across the peninsula to the ocean side to do some surfing and maybe fishing. Everyone agreed it would be a fun day's outing but Jim, being the only Australian had his doubts. He knew that coast was the open Indian Ocean and as such could be wild and dangerous. Gordon quite rudely dismissed Jim's concerns stating, "Look, you wimp, it's a beautiful calm day, hardly a breath of wind. We'll be fine, you'll see, I've always wanted to do some surfing." Jim tried to point out to Gordon that surfing was not all that easy, "Listen Gordon, surfing looks quite easy but in actual fact it can be quite difficult and you have to have a good sense of balance Really you should take some lessons before heading out into the surf."

"Rubbish, I've seen it done hundreds of times in the films and on the tele. You just wait for a big wave and it pushes you along, simple."

"No Gordon, it's not that simple, really; in fact if you like I can give you a lesson and a few pointers before you go out deep, I've done a bit of surfing before over the years." Gordon was not going to acknowledge that Jim knew more about anything that he did. He felt confident that it was a simple matter of laying on a board and then standing up on it. "No thanks, I can manage on my own, I don't need you to show me how to do anything."

Gordon collected a couple of surf boards and some fishing

tackle from the local hire store and the group set off with much anticipation and enthusiasm. Samantha remembered how she had enjoyed fishing from the jetty back home in Perth and was looking forward to the possibility of catching some really big fish. They left the township in high spirits passing palm trees laden with screeching cockatoos. Gordon insisted on driving and pushed the Landcruiser more than was necessary showing off to his family. Jim cautioned the old man "steady Gordon, be aware that kangaroos can jump across the road at any time. They usually come out in the evening but really they can cross the road any time of the day."

"Don't worry Jim, I can see the road clear ahead and if any kangaroos jump out on the road I'll just go round them."

"Well it's not only kangaroos but there are goats, cattle and even camels. They can all give the car a nasty bump."

"Yes, yes, I heard you. God Samantha, is he always such a wimp, such a worry wart?" Maisie cut her husband off with the stern admonishment, "Gordon Perkins will you cut it out. Jim is only telling you for your own good. You're going too fast, now slow down."

The road was really only a rough track and the ruts rumbled the car annoyingly and bounced the passengers numbing their rear ends. Agnetha was distinctly uncomfortable but managed to keep it to herself. She was quite heavy with her advanced pregnancy but didn't want to complain. When Freddy asked if she was alright she stoically smiled and assured him that all was well. They were the only ones on the road and passed no other cars, only a large racehorse goanna and a million or so large termite mounds. Just as Gordon predicted, when they got to the ocean there was hardly any wind and the sea was crystal clear. They were the only people on the beach and they had been the only people on the rough rutted road leading to the beach.

Jim tried to explain to the group the dangers of the open ocean. "Listen guys, I know it all looks calm and gentle but the seas on this western coast can be deceptive. I've lived here all my life and I can tell you it can be treacherous. Generally on a beach the surf life savers put up flags indicating where it's safe to swim, and they keep a watch on all the swimmers. Here it's too isolated, we're the only ones on the beach, in fact we're the only people for miles around, so be very careful. Also I've brought a large bottle of good sun tan cream, so you should all put plenty of cream on your exposed parts. You're all English with fair skin, you can get burnt very easily." Samantha's father wasn't even listening as he started to pick up one of the surfboards. Jim tried again to warn Gordon, "Listen Gordon, it's not only the sun but quite often there's a mild wave on top of the water and unseen below is a really strong undertow. It can take you by surprise and suck you out to sea. It's called a rip and can be very dangerous."

"Yeh, yeh, yeh." Ignoring Jim, Gordon took the board down to the water's edge. Jim tried again to warn Gordon and showed the old man how to attach the rubber ankle safety leash. Gordon dismissed Jim's warnings and refused to attach the safety leash to his ankle. "I don't need that: leave me alone."

Leaving Jim shaking his head in the shallows Gordon paddled out safely to where the waves were starting to build up. Jim watched, worried that the old man hadn't taken his warning seriously enough. Gordon allowed a few waves to pass and when a large one presented itself he kicked and paddled furiously trying to catch the wave. The large wave tipped Gordon off the surfboard and the old man lost his hold on the board. Jim watched with some consternation as Gordon seemed to struggle in the water. Instead of swimming towards the shore Gordon seemed to be moving perpendicular back out to sea. He had his arms above his head and was waving frantically. He was shouting something but the noise from the surf made it impossible to hear what he was shouting.

Jim immediately realised that Gordon was being taken out to sea by a strong undertow. It was common on that coast and many people had lost their lives not being able to swim against the strong current. Jim turned to Freddy and barked the order, "You stay and look after the girls, I'm going out to get Gordon." Without a thought for his own safety Jim took the remaining surfboard and paddled furiously out to where Gordon had been. Jim couldn't actually see Gordon any longer and it wasn't until he was much further out that he stopped paddling to look for the old man. Fortunately the water was crystal clear and so Jim spotted Gordon's body just below the surface. He abandoned the surfboard and dived down to pull Gordon up. Freddy and the girls were watching from the shore and Maisie was near hysterical with anguish and worry.

Samantha put an arm around her mother and tried her best to calm and reassure her that Jim would get her husband back safely. "Jim's a strong swimmer Mum, he'll get Dad back you'll see." Once he had Gordon on the surface Jim made a grab for the surfboard and heaved Gordon's lifeless body across the board. There wasn't room for both of them on the board and so Jim pushed and kicked to get the board back to the shore as quickly as he could.

On approaching the shore Freddy waded out, narrowly missing stepping on a small sleepy manta ray which as it was disturbed darted off into deeper water. Freddy helped Jim to pull the old man onto the beach. Immediately Jim felt for a pulse and any sign of breathing but Gordon was unconscious and seemingly dead. Jim had been trained as a teenager to practise first aid and CPR. His instincts clicked in straight away. He tilted the old man's head backwards, scaped his hands across the old man's mouth with a scooping action pulling out his false teeth which fell unnoticed into the sand. Once Gordon's mouth was empty Jim started compressions to the inert chest, followed by mouth to mouth resuscitation. The women were all distraught and crying hysterically. Freddy had never been trained to do first aid and could only stand by helplessly watching and willing his father to respond. After five minutes or so Gordon's body suddenly convulsed and a stream of frothy water gurgled up and out of his mouth. Jim turned Gordon onto his side and more water dribbled out. Gordon still wasn't conscious but he started breathing and Jim announced that they must get him back to Exmouth as quickly as possible.

Freddy and Jim lifted the old man onto a surfboard and carried him to the car. They laid him across the back seat and they all squashed into the car as best they could. The journey back to Exmouth was a bumpy rough ride with Maisie trying to coax some life into her unconscious husband. She patted his hands and stroked the side of his face, "Gordon wake up, Gordon talk to me." Suddenly, above Maisie's entreaties to her husband Agnetha let out a yell, "Oh my God, my waters have broken." Freddy held onto his frightened wife and entreated Jim who was driving, "Can't you go any faster?" Jim was going as fast as he was able in the circumstances and was trying to be as careful as he could on the dusty, deep rutted rough track. As they neared the town they all began scouring the side roads for signs of the local hospital. Samantha spotted the hospital sign first and directed Jim down a side road to the Emergency Department. Jim parked the car and ran in to request two gurneys and to inform the staff that he had two emergencies, first a near drowning and second a baby about to be born.

The staff took Gordon one way and Agnetha a different way. The family split up with Freddy accompanying Agnetha and the rest going along with Gordon. The doctors assessed Gordon who had regained consciousness and admitted him to the hospital for observation. They praised Jim on his quick thinking and saving Gordon's life. Maisie stayed by Gordon's side whilst Jim and Samantha went to the labour ward to see how Agnetha and Freddy were getting on. Once Gordon felt able to talk he started to ask Maisie what had happened and where his teeth. "Well Jim took your teeth out to stop you choking on them and I have no idea where they are, probably in the sand back on the beach, that was the least of our worries."

"What you lost my teeth again? Are you trying to condemn me to an old age of only being able to eat porridge and custard? You have to go back and get my teeth."

"Are you mad?"

" What an idiot that man is, honestly Maisie I don't know what Samantha sees in him, he's just a no good idiot. Words fail me." Maisie took a deep breath and prodding her finger to his chest she almost shouted, "Now listen here Gordon Perkins. I've just about had enough of your stupid denigrating poor Jim. Who do you think went into the surf to rescue you? Without a thought to his own safety it was Jim who dived down and fished you out of the water. You didn't take any notice of his warnings, Oh, no not you. You think you know it all, well you don't! You were dead, you'd stopped breathing and it was Jim who knew what to do. He gave you mouth to mouth resuscitation, he saved your life and drove us back here at breakneck speed to make sure you were alright. You owe him big time and I don't want to ever, and I mean ever, to hear you put him down again. Do you understand?"

At that moment Jim and Samantha came into the room with a very happy Freddy. "Guess what Mum, I'm a father. Agnetha just gave birth to a small but gorgeous baby boy. Mother and child are doing well and you're a grandmother." We don't know if the rough track bouncing us up and down did it or the trauma of Dad nearly drowning but whatever it was we now have a marvellous little baby. We've agreed to call him Jim Junior in honour of Jim who saved Dad's life. There were kisses all round and Freddy went back to be beside his wife who slept for the next seven hours.

Gordon was kept in hospital for observation but was released three days later no worse for his ordeal. He had complained bitterly to the hospital doctors that he felt just fine and wanted to go home but the doctors were adamant, explaining, "Look Gordon, you had a near death experience and we need to keep you in the intensive care unit to monitor your recovery. We have to be aware of any neurological and ongoing circulatory problems. We need to monitor your blood sugar levels and make sure you are maintaining your normal body temperature. You see in near drowning, and especially in sea water near drowning, there is obviously a lack of oxygen which is hypoxia and that can affect your fluid and electrolyte balance, but there is a different reaction in your lungs with sea water. We need to be aware of higher acidity, that is lowered PH of your body fluids and make sure you don't have any seizures. At your age we do need to be really careful and there is no way I would agree to releasing you from our care for a while yet."

Agnetha and the baby were released a week later and all the family eventually gathered back in Perth to celebrate the birth of Jim Junior. Gordon had to eat a very large slice of humble pie but at Maisie's insistence made peace with Jim. He invited Jim out to the back garden and confessed he had been wrong, "I misjudged you Jim and I gave you a hard time. I'm truly sorry, I should have had more faith in Samantha and her judge of a good man. You see, it's very hard for a father to stand aside and let some other man take his only daughter away from him. I have struggled with that concept for some time now but I realise now how stupid that is, or was. Samantha is a grown woman and can make up her own mind about who she is going to love. I hope you can forgive me and that we can make a fresh start." Gordon held out his hand and Jim shook his hand and patted him on the back at the same time. "Of course."

Three months later a very proud Gordon escorted Samantha, the most beautiful bride there ever was down the aisle to her waiting groom. He handed her over to Jim with a bear hug and a very unmanly kiss. "I'm truly sorry I was such a pain in the rear end, I give you my daughter with my heartfelt thanks and blessing." He took Samantha's hand and placed it in Jim's hand and with tears in his eyes choked out the words, "I love you both and wish you every happiness."